A Demon's Deception

∘Book One∘

H. M. Huntress

Please be advised this book contains explicit content and darker themes. It is not intended for readers under the age of 18.

This one is for my husband who helped create the outline of this story and who always cheers me on when I need a little extra push.
<3

Here is a Spotify playlist of songs
which remind me of *A Demon's Deception*!
*Please note this playlist is subject
to change at any time*

Scan the QR code with the camera
on your phone to listen now!

Prologue

I peered through the railing overlooking the entryway to our home. Pain radiated up my arms from how tightly I gripped the rungs, but I couldn't ease my grip, and I couldn't look away.

For the first time in my short life, I looked at the king of Hell himself: Lucifer. His wings were furled against his back, and he had giant curving horns that were bigger than any other demon's I'd seen. His skin was a dark shade of red that matched the blood that had flowed over our doorstep the night my parents were murdered.

Most demons went their entire lives without seeing Lucifer in the flesh. Now, because my brother and I had survived the single worst moment of our lives, we were granted the *privilege* of a visit from him. Lucifer usually only punished humans sent to Hell, not its inhabitants. High rank demons like my parents dealt with that, but this was a rare incident.

Tears dripped from my chin onto my fleece pajama pants. I was supposed to be asleep in bed. Instead, I watched Lucifer deliver the two demons responsible for my parent's deaths to my brother.

Those demons knelt in the center of the foyer on the blue medallion rug that Mother had picked out only a few weeks prior. They couldn't look more smug despite staring straight at the Devil.

Lucifer paced in front of the pair with his hands clasped behind his back. "As everyone in Hell is aware, I have *one* simple rule for all to live by. And yet, here we are."

I'd learned that rule as early as I could remember: no killing upper rank demons.

Killing my parents had broken Lucifer's rule. I'd overheard my brother saying it was worth the risk to the Eastside drug lord. He lost two of his runners, and Southside lost both of its drug lords.

None of that made too much sense to me, all I knew was the two people I loved most in Hell were gone.

A piece of a streamer fluttered under my breath on the railing. It was left over from my seventh birthday party we'd had the week before. It had been me, Mother, Father, Dominic, and the house staff. They were the only ones who knew I existed, for reasons similar to what had happened to my parents.

It didn't matter if the people below saw me, two of them would be dead soon, and Lucifer knew of every demon in Hell, regardless of if he ever met them.

I swiped away my tears as my brother replaced Lucifer in front of the demons.

"In order to even the score and restore balance, Dominic Russo will end both of your miserable lives. After that, I shall deliver your corpses to Viktor's doorstep along with a message that there shall be no retaliation, and this feud is *done.*" Lucifer pulled a gun from what seemed to be thin air and pressed it into my brother's hands.

2

Dominic's newly full-grown wings flexed on his back.

"Thank you." His voice was so quiet I almost didn't hear him.

I knew I should look away. I should run and hide in my room until Dominic came to find me and console me. But my body refused to move.

Dominic stepped forward, pointing the gun at the female demon first. There was no tremor in his grip, no sign of distress or unease. If I didn't know any better, I'd say he'd done this before.

The gun cocked and I clenched my eyes shut as it fired. I waited for the sounds again, and only after hearing the second shot did I open my eyes. The sight of the demons lying in pools of their own blood on Mother's rug would be burned into my brain from that point on.

Crawling away from the railing, I retreated to my room and curled up under the bed, sobbing and praying to a god who had never turned his favor to the underworld, that he would bring back my parents and undo what could not be undone.

Chapter 1

Ember

Blue, green, red, and yellow lights swirled above me and around me, disorienting me as I danced to the club music. A steady but upbeat rhythm kept me moving around the dance floor, sticky from the spilled drinks, as I bounced between my friends and strangers. Here, it didn't matter who I was, or who I was related to. No one knew, and it would stay that way.

Sweat slicked my back, suctioning my already tight top and leather pants to my body. It wasn't the best choice of attire, but I chose fashion over comfort.

A large hand wrapped around my upper arm, pulling me out of my haze. I often lost myself in the music when I was dancing, like it took over and I was along for the ride. It was a surreal feeling, and I loved it.

I turned to see a handsome demon clutching my arm, his eyes widening and mouth pulling up into a cocky smirk as he looked me over. Before I could even pretend to have any interest in him, Mazie slapped his hand away from me and inserted herself between us.

"Back off, sleazeball," she hissed, her spade tipped tail lashing. "She's with me."

Rolling my eyes, I twirled my way back over to Penny who watched it all from the sidelines. She leaned against a half-wall that separated the dance floor from the tables and bar. Her glass was almost empty, and she drained the last of it as I approached her.

"Mazie always ruins my fun," I said, leaning my elbows on the wall to support myself as I stood beside her. "For once I want to dance with someone other than the two of you."

Penny scoffed, flipping her long, dark purple bangs out of her face, but they caught on one of her small spiral horns and swung back into her face. The purple, though not natural, complimented her blue skin well. "Neither Mazie nor I will ever let that happen. If your brother found out, he would *literally* kill us. Don't forget, we're only here because he pays us to be." Her jet-black eyes twinkled, and she gave me a saccharine sweet smile.

I swatted her arm and kicked her combat boot with my own heeled boot. "You haven't cared about the money since the week we started hanging out. You know you love me." I made a kissy face at her, and she laughed.

Running a hand over the shaved side of her head, she ducked closer to me. "Let Mazie keep the men at bay, it makes her happy to think she's doing her job."

The music changed to a faster, techno-style song and the crowd jumped to the beat. Mazie squeezed her way through them to join us.

"He was kind of cute!" she yelled over the music, throwing her thumb over her shoulder to indicate the guy she'd effectively scared off. If only his cuteness had saved him from her duty.

"Come here," I said, taking Mazie's hand and pulling her closer. One of her fun buns, as she called them, had come undone at the back of her head. Turning her around, I twisted her long-ass white hair up and pinned it back in place. Her two little horns poked out at the top. Sometimes she liked to wrap her hair around them and use them as a part of her styling.

I'd kept my pink hair shoulder-length because I hated dealing with figuring out hairstyles. It was so much easier to deal with when it was short, though Mazie insisted on trying out her different styles on me.

Mazie turned and hugged me. "Thanks, Emmy," she said. She was the only one, other than Dominic on occasion, who called me Emmy. Everyone else didn't feel the need to shorten my already short name, Ember. I think she secretly did it so all three of our names would rhyme. *Mazie, Penny, and Emmy.* "Can we go now, though? I have some *serious* work to catch up on and my feet are killing me."

I glanced down at the five-inch stiletto heels she wore and raised a brow.

"I wonder why," I chided. Mazie always wore heels. No matter if we were headed to a club or a diner, she had on her heels, and she paid for it. I couldn't say too much, since I almost always wore heels along with her.

Pushing away from the half-wall, Penny led the way out of the club. She was the best at clearing a path for us, since she gave off the perfect *don't fuck with me* vibes.

The air outside was hotter than it had been inside creating a heat shimmer in the red sky above us which had darkened to a deep maroon.

Nighttime was a more active time for us all and the streets were filled with demons. It was slightly cooler at night, so it made it more comfortable to be out and about.

My brother, being one of the most lucrative drug dealers in Hell, did almost all his work at night, so I'd formed my schedule around his. Not that it mattered much, he didn't let me anywhere near his operations. None of his friends or employees even knew I existed. Mazie and Penny kept me company and kept me out of trouble.

Something loud crashed in an alley to our left and we all jumped. Penny had her pistol out of its holster and aimed before I could even calm my heart enough to take a normal breath.

When no one emerged from the alley, we kept walking, Penny in front and Mazie at my side. I had Mazie's hand in mine, and she swung our hands between us. It was a little comical how opposite she and Penny were. I was like the happy medium between them, and we made the perfect trio.

"Have you heard of The Mausoleum?" Mazie asked, cocking her head to look at me. "They just opened, and I heard they have the *best* drinks. To kill for."

"If you haven't told me about a place, then assume I've never heard of it," I said, laughing half-heartedly. It was the sad truth. When I was younger, I wasn't allowed to leave the house, my only friend being Dominic and the staff who worked in the mansion. Once our parents died and Dominic took over their drug business, I hardly saw him. Which is why he hired Mazie and Penny to keep me company once I turned sixteen. They'd been eighteen at the time.

Now, I was twenty-one and they were still my only friends. When they both decided to stop taking his money because we'd become real friends, I insisted they keep taking it as long as they could. My brother deserved a little payback for keeping me the family secret.

"Well, we're taking you there next time we go out!" Mazie chirped. "Penny, put it on your calendar, Thursday is The Mausoleum with me and Emmy!"

"It's locked away in the vault," Penny said, glancing over her shoulder at us. She had a crazy good memory. I, on the other hand, had to write everything down or else it was gone from my brain in the next moment.

The street we were on was lined with apartment buildings, and light filtered out from the windows, creating an eerie glow.

"This is me," Mazie said, kissing my cheek, as if I didn't know exactly where she lived because I stayed there at least once a week. "I'll see you Thursday!" She waved and ascended the steps to the front door of her apartment building. Her room was one of the better rooms available on the top floor. The extra cash she had coming in from my brother helped her acquire that spot.

Quickening my steps, I caught up to Penny. She would stay with me until I was safe inside the mansion, doors locked behind me. We still had about half a mile to go before we reached it.

"Thanks for coming out tonight, Pen. I know you wanted to stay in, but I'm glad we changed your mind," I said, nudging her arm with my elbow.

"Your brother would have never let you leave the house if only Mazie had shown up," she said, keeping her gaze straight ahead. Every so often she scanned our surroundings, but she didn't look at me.

I twisted my ring around my index finger trying to come up with a response to that. Sometimes I couldn't tell if Penny resented me for having to watch over me.

My prolonged silence seemed to have been answer enough, because Penny sighed and nudged me back with her elbow.

"I wanted to come out tonight, truly. Mondays are the best nights for Primetime. I've just been strapped for time these days," she explained.

Primetime was our favorite club, and she wasn't wrong about Mondays being the best night to go there. It was strange to hear her say it though, because she never danced or seemed to enjoy the club.

"If you ever don't want to go out, tell me, okay? I don't mind staying in with you and Mazie, or if you're busy, just Mazie." I shrugged. "And if you don't want to go to The Mausoleum on Thursday—"

"Oh, don't worry, I'll be there. I've been wanting to check it out," she said.

"How new is it?" I couldn't imagine there being a place in Hell that Penny hadn't been. She always seemed to know about all the noteworthy places in or out of town.

"It opened a month ago, but there isn't much known about it. Other than the fact that, like Mazie said, they have great drinks. It's super exclusive and cloaked in mystery. My kind of place." She winked. "I'll be surprised if Mazie can get us in, but I won't put it past her."

I nodded. "She has her ways."

We stopped outside of a wrought iron gate set into a stone wall. The fence was too high to see over and perfect to keep out any unwanted guests. Penny buzzed us in with her code, and we strolled down the rocky driveway. The mansion was far too large for the demons it housed. My brother and I were the only ones living in it, yet it had six bedrooms, three sitting rooms, a dining room with an attached kitchen, and a meeting room Dominic used for all his business meetings. From the drawn curtains and the light peeking out, I could tell he was still in there with all his employees.

I called them 'employees,' but really, they were drug runners and dealers. A few helped him with the logistics side of things, but mostly they were his mules.

Penny and I walked around back to the servant's entrance. I wasn't allowed in the front door in case anyone was watching the house. That way they'd assume I was working for my brother, rather than living there. Penny, Mazie, and the few staff who took care of the house and cooked for us were the only ones who knew who I was. To them I was Ember Russo, sister to Dominic, who was leader of the Russo drug syndicate, but to the rest of Hell, I was just Ember.

And if the rest of Hell found out what my friends knew, I'd become a prime target for all of Dominic's rivals. I was lucky Dominic let me out of the house at all.

"After you," Penny said, holding open the back door that led into the kitchen.

Maurice, our chef, was cleaning up and smiled at us as we entered. He had flour in his long beard, and on his bright purple nose. Purple wasn't a rare color for demons, but it was one I envied. Being *red* was common, Mazie was red, too, and I

10

wished I could be a little different. But it was what my brother and I inherited from our parents. To be fair, my skin was more pink than red, but it was still common.

"Welcome home, Ember," he said, dipping his head. "Penny, good to see you as always." Lifting a platter cover, he waved his hand at a fresh loaf of cheesy bread. "Help yourselves."

I skipped over and snatched a slice, taking a big bite and moaning in delight. "So good," I said, my voice muffled.

"Don't talk with your mouth full, you'll choke," Penny said, taking a piece for herself. "I'll be back Thursday around eight to pick you up, okay?" She pointed at me, waiting for my response.

Finishing my bite, I swallowed and gave her a thumbs up, saying, "Perfect."

She backed out the door, waving to Maurice.

"Any fun tidbits from tonight's meeting?" I asked Maurice.

Maurice's eyes flicked to the swinging door that led into the dining room. No one else was in earshot, but we could never be too careful. Maurice had worked in the Russo household since my parents acquired the mansion, long before they'd ever decided to have me or Dominic. He was my intel on all things related to the Russo drug business.

"I overheard there's been a dip in sales this month. Nothing to be alarmed by, but a notable difference." Grabbing a dish towel, Maurice started drying the dishes he'd finished washing. "I'd bet there's another boss trying to encroach on Southside territory again."

"Again?" I asked. I hated being so ignorant about my own family's business, but Maurice never judged me for it. He knew my brother's rules and that I wasn't allowed anywhere near the meeting hall when he was in there. Thankfully Maurice was on my side and thought I had a right to know at least *some* of the goings on with the family business.

A slow nod was Maurice's response. Shuffling and muffled voices filtered into the room, which meant the meeting had adjourned and everyone was leaving.

"Shit," I mumbled, sneaking to the far wall next to the swinging door and peeking out through the crack between it and the trim. "Dom would kill me if he knew I was down here right now."

Maurice chuckled.

"But might as well take advantage of this moment." Lightly pushing on the door, I opened it enough to slip through and eased it back into place behind me. The dining room was dark, besides the light coming in from the foyer through the arched entryway.

Keeping along the wall, I eased toward the archway and peered around it. Directly across from me was the side of the grand carpeted staircase that everyone had to pass to exit the mansion. It led upstairs, where all the bedrooms were. Leaning a little out of the dining room, I could see to the end of the stairs, and it seemed like almost everyone was gone, but a few demons lingered.

My gut twisted with anticipation as I looked for any familiar face. If I was caught, I'd be locked away in my room forever, I assumed.

Heavy footsteps announced my brother exiting his meeting room, which was the room next to where I hid, nearer the end of the staircase. I ducked back into the dining room and held my breath.

"I wouldn't worry too much about it," he said. "It happens every so often."

Peeking around the doorway, I caught sight of who my brother spoke with and inhaled sharply. I'd seen the demon before; he was my brother's closest friend, but I didn't know his name. Dominic had refused to talk to me about his world, even back when our parents were alive.

Much like my brother, he was well-muscled and fit, someone who made an intimidating drug runner for sure. His dark blue hair was wavy, almost concealing his curling black horns and looked soft enough that I yearned to run my hands through it. He wore the leather vest that marked him as a part of my brother's crew better than anyone else.

What made me whip back into place against the dining room wall though, was when I looked at him, his bright blue eyes were looking back at me.

Chapter 2

Jayce

I could have sworn I saw someone peeking around the corner of the dining room, but they were there and gone so quickly it could have been a trick of the light. Or it could have been one of Dominic's house staff.

Either way, I had more important things to deal with. Like the fact that one of the other drug lords was encroaching on Dom's territory, whether he thought so or not. So, after leaving his mansion, I decided to head out on the streets.

I caught up with Dom's other enforcer, Oliver, who'd been with Dominic almost as long as I had. He was propped on his Harley, smoking a cigarette. Everyone else had gone.

"Want to join me for a few quick stops?" I asked. There were some of Dominic's regular customers who I frequented for any information on strange activity in the streets. They'd know if there were any dealers who weren't usually selling around.

"Who needs sleep?" Oliver joked, dropping his cigarette and crushing it under his boot. He smoothed his hand over his

14

short, black hair and straddled his bike. "Dom seems confident this whole drop in sales will blow over."

I nodded, climbing onto my own bike, but I could see Oliver watching me out of the corner of my eye. "He does," I said. Dominic was my best friend, and the boss, so I'd trust him. But I'd also have his back and make sure there was nothing shady happening.

"But you don't agree," Oliver said. "And I don't either. We should be putting whoever it is back in their place."

I revved my Harley and pulled down the driveway. It wasn't that I didn't agree with Oliver, but sometimes it was harder for him to understand Dominic's motivations. I'd known Dominic much longer and never questioned him about anything. I trusted him with my life, and he felt the same.

The streets were still lively as people went about their debauchery. If Oliver or I saw anyone causing too much trouble, as Dom's enforcers, we had the authority to take care of it. So, I didn't look too closely at anyone I passed. I wasn't up for policing anyone that night.

Turning right onto a street lined with an assortment of bars and clubs, I pulled around to the back lot of one called Fever Dream.

I killed my engine and turned to Oliver. "You know as well as I do that Dom has to be one hundred percent sure before we make any moves against any of the other bosses. Otherwise, he could stir up a feud and end up with his own head on a platter."

"I know," Oliver said as he hopped off his bike. I followed suit. "Doesn't mean I think we should sit by and do nothing." He readjusted his pants, revealing his glock in his waistband. I kept mine in the same place for easy access.

15

I patted his back. "That's the spirit. Come on. Let's see if Sheila's heard anything about any new dealers in town."

Sheila, the owner of Fever Dream and one of my customers from before I'd become an enforcer, hadn't heard anything from her people or anyone else about new dealers. She did, however, hear that the new club, The Mausoleum, was serving cocktails that were giving people more than a little buzz. According to her source, they were using different drugs to boost the effects of the drinks. You could order whatever mix you wanted for whatever mood you were in. And I knew for a fact those drugs weren't coming from Dom.

It wasn't mandatory for anyone on Southside to buy from Southside dealers, but it was an unspoken custom.

"Maybe we should check out The Mausoleum," Oliver suggested, punctuating his statement with a yawn.

The sky was brightening, and the air grew more stifling by the minute.

I shook my head. "Nah. The clubs are winding down now. Let's head home and get some sleep." I'd add The Mausoleum to my rounds the next time I was out. No point in heading there when most of the crowd would be on their way out.

After saying goodbye to Oliver, I headed to my usual coffee shop down the street from my apartment. As much as I needed sleep, Victoria had texted saying she was waiting for me in my bed, and I'd need a boost of caffeine to keep up with her.

She'd made it clear she didn't want anything more than sex from me, which I was absolutely fine with. We were both too busy to try at a real relationship, and we didn't really have enough in common to make one work anyway.

The Devil's Brew had the best coffee in Hell, and the best beer. When I walked in, Grace waved animatedly from behind the coffee counter opposite the front door, her face lighting up. She was the only demon who ever looked excited to see me. Everyone else seemed to understand I wasn't to be messed with and avoided eye contact.

"Usual?" she asked, grabbing a to-go cup from the counter and writing my name on it.

"Yeah, thanks." Leaning against the counter I scanned the room. The bar for beer and other coffee-flavored liqueurs was to the right, and a few demons were there, probably from the night before. There were also a couple demons at the tables to my left, drinking coffee and eating baked goods. Grace made the best chocolate croissants.

"Rough night?" Grace asked, scooping ice into my cup.

I lifted a shoulder. "Not bad. How about here?"

Chuckling, Grace moved to the coffee maker. "More interesting than anything. I had a brawl start outside over a parking spot."

"They didn't cause you any trouble, did they?" I asked, looking out the door as if the culprits might still be lurking around. I hadn't had a good reason to kill anyone in the past few weeks, and my trigger finger was getting antsy.

"No, they went on their way. But it made quite the show for our patrons." She snapped a lid onto my cup and passed it over the counter. "I'll put it on your tab," she said, winking.

"Thanks, Grace." I took a sip, relishing the bitterness of the coffee, with the splash of cream. It perked me up. "I'll see you tomorrow."

Grace had been the owner of The Devil's Brew for as long as I'd been around, and probably long before that. I had no idea how old she was, but she didn't look a day over a hundred. Most powerless demons started to decline around then. She always had her black hair pulled back in a tight bun, and she *always* had a smile on her face.

"Sure you will," she said, waving to me as I walked out the door.

I paid my tab at the shop once a month, and Grace knew I was good for it. Besides, I always overpaid so she couldn't really complain.

Sipping my iced coffee, I rode the last half mile to my apartment building and parked in the garage. The elevator took me up to the top floor and opened into my apartment.

"Vic, you here?" I dropped my keys on the kitchen counter and walked past it to the entryway of my room. Shrugging off my leather cut, I dropped it onto the end of my bed and found a note by the pillows.

I rolled my eyes. She could have texted me, but for some reason, she liked to leave notes as if we were secret lovers trying to hide our relationship from anyone who might snoop on our phones.

Sorry! Boss needs me. See you tonight!

Honestly, I was relieved. It had been a long night and morning, and the initial boost of energy the caffeine had given me was already wearing off.

I shot a quick text to Dominic, letting him know I'd be checking out The Mausoleum sometime that week, and then went to bed.

When I woke later that day, I couldn't remember any of my dreams, except for a pair of light purple eyes, watching me.

Chapter 3

Ember

Shit. Shit. Shit. I practically wheezed as I tried to catch my breath. *One, two, three ...* I counted the seconds as they passed, expecting my brother to march down the hall and into the dining room at any moment and lose his mind.

Ten, eleven, twelve. The voices faded and my brother's footsteps echoed as he went up the stairs.

A chime made me jump nearly three feet in the air as my cell phone went off, alerting me to a new text.

"Fuck," I breathed.

Taking my phone from my pocket, Mazie's name flashed on the screen along with her message.

Mazie: *Got us on the list for*
The Mausoleum on Thursday!
Can't wait! <3 <3

"Ember!" Dominic called. His steps returned to the stairs, and I slipped around the corner into the hall, meeting him in the foyer.

"Miss me?" I teased, skipping to his side. "Penny, Mazie and I hit up Primetime tonight, it was so much fun! You should come some time."

Dominic sighed and shook his head, his black curls shifting across his forehead. We were the opposite in almost every way. He had black hair and black eyes; I had pink hair and light purple eyes. He was serious and grumpy all the time, and though I wasn't quite as cheery and upbeat as Mazie, I was *much* closer to it than Dominic would ever be.

"What are you doing down here? My meeting ended minutes ago. You could have been seen." He reached his hand out and cupped my elbow, leading me to the stairs. It wasn't like there was any chance of me being seen *now,* but it was habit I guess to get me out of view.

Seen? You mean like by Mr. Sexy? Yeah, that happened, I thought. Mazie was the one who had deemed Dominic's friend as *Mr. Sexy.* I'd told her about him the first time I saw him, and she'd been hounding me for information on him ever since.

"Well, I missed them. So, no harm done," I said instead, forcing a smile.

Huffing, Dominic released my elbow and let me finish walking up the stairs by myself.

"No more going out on nights I have my meetings," he said. "You'll stay in your room until they're done, and everyone's gone."

I whirled around, almost losing my footing. "No! That's not fair! You have meetings like every night!"

"Two times a week, Ember. I think you can survive staying in *two* nights a week."

I curled my lip and stuck my tongue out at him. "It's not so much the number of meetings as the *days*. Primetime is the best on Monday nights, and you have meetings on Mondays. I won't miss out on Primetime Mondays!"

Dominic passed me and turned to the right, heading for his bedroom. "You're starting to sound like a spoiled brat, Ember."

I jogged up the last few steps. "And whose fault is that? I'd *love* to work all day or night like you. But since I have literally nothing else to do but go out with my friends, cutting me off from certain experiences isn't all that fair!"

Daylight filtered in through the giant round window above the front door, filling the stairway and upper hall with a reddish morning glow.

"We can talk about this later, right now I need sleep," Dominic said, rubbing his temples.

"Fine," I huffed. "You know, if you let me help with the family business you might not be so tired all the time."

He didn't deign to answer, and I didn't press him as he turned his back on me and walked away. My room was at the opposite end of the mansion, and when I reached it, sleep was the furthest thing from my mind.

Pulling out my phone, I texted Mazie.

> **Me:** *I saw Dominic's sexy friend.*
> *Still sexy.*

I smirked as I hit send. Almost immediately my phone rang, and I answered it.

"Stop it. I'm going to need a picture of this demon ASAP. Next time he's there, sneak a few would ya?" Mazie said.

I laughed. "Dom would kill me, and I'm already possibly in trouble. He saw me tonight." I bit my lip, anxious.

"Wait, who? Dom or Mr. Sexy?" Mazie asked.

"Mr. Sexy. I looked around the corner and I think he saw me." *I know he saw me.* But for some reason I was too scared to admit that out loud.

Gasping, Mazie said, "Shit, Emmy. Did he say anything to Dom? Scratch that. I'm assuming *not* since you're not on lockdown."

She was right. If Dominic had found out, he would have locked me away somewhere he deemed 'safe' and taken my phone.

"I don't think he did. That's weird, right? You see a random demon in your boss's house, and you don't say anything? Would *you* have said something?" It was almost more nerve wracking that he *hadn't* told Dominic.

"I don't know," Mazie said. "Your brother is kind of scary, so who knows what his friends feel comfortable talking to him about. Mr. Sexy might have thought you were your brother's lover or something." She made a gagging sound.

"EW. Don't ever say that again." I made a similar gagging sound.

"I'm saying that's what *he* thought! Like, who else could you be? None of them know he has a sister."

"You're probably right, but still, ew." I shuddered.

Mazie chuckled. "Don't tell Penny about this, she'll flip."

I sighed. It was hard keeping things from Penny, but Mazie was right. "I know. She's been acting a little weird lately, have you noticed?"

There was a brief pause, and then Mazie said, "Mmm, nope! Same old grumpy pants to me!"

She was probably right. Penny went through phases where she'd seem a little down for a while, but then she'd bounce back.

"Maybe you're right. Maybe I'm being paranoid." It was hard not to be paranoid when my brother was always so worried about my safety.

"Get some sleep, Emmy. You need it."

"Fine." I couldn't argue with that. My recurring nightmare had come back recently, and while I didn't have it every night, it had stolen a few nights of sleep from me, and I needed to catch up on it.

We hung up and I flopped onto my king size bed. It was a little ridiculous how big my bed was, but it meant I could roll around all I wanted. It wasn't like I ever had anyone *in* it with me, other than Mazie or Penny when they slept over.

Thanks to my brother's excessive overprotectiveness, I'd never even come close to having a boyfriend.

Sprawling out on the bed, I lay on my stomach and let my wings furl out fully. They weren't nearly as large as my brother's, but they suited me. The leathery bat-like quality of them made them sensitive to the touch, so I kept them furled most of the time. Unfurled, they stretched about a foot to either side of my shoulders and were about a foot long. I was able to hide them under baggy shirts if I wanted to.

My wings would have grown if I'd inherited my mother's power. *But* if I was ever going to inherit it, I would have already. Which meant her wings had been taken from her *before* she'd been killed. Demons with horns or wings were higher ranks, and other demons could steal their power by stealing those. It was horrific, but we were in Hell, so most things were.

When I was little, Dominic explained demon ranks to me in terms of video games.

"What are you doing, Emmy?" Dominic huffed.

I stood in front of his TV, blocking his view.

"Why are my wings smaller than yours?" I asked, pouting.

He craned his neck to try and look around me but ended up pausing his game with a long sigh.

"Your wings are smaller because you're smaller," he stated and waved his hand to try and get me to move.

Shaking my head, I stomped a foot and said, "How come yours grew a lot and mine didn't grow at all."

"You mean after ..." His gaze dropped to the floor. "Last year, when our parents died, Father's power passed on to me, which is why my wings started growing."

"Power?" I'd heard it mentioned in the past, but I wasn't entirely sure what it was, or why it was important. I didn't have any superpowers like the people in the books Maurice read to me when I snuck in the kitchen while I was supposed to be sleeping.

Dominic patted the cushion beside him on the couch, and I hopped onto it, bouncing a little.

"You know in the video games you watch me play, how every character has a different level?" he asked, and I nodded eagerly. "It tells you how strong they are and how powerful. You can have them complete tasks to get stronger, and level up. But for us, there is no leveling up. We are born in our levels. Unless

we have parents who are stronger and pass their power on to us."

I scrunched my nose and bit my lower lip, trying to fully understand what he was saying. "What level are we?"

"I'm a level five, because our father was a level five and his power passed on to me. It's the highest level, other than Lucifer," Dominic explained.

"How?" I asked.

He rubbed a hand over his forehead, sighing. "You might be a little too young to understand all of this."

I shook my head. I wanted bigger wings like Dominic, so I wanted to understand how to get them. "Tell me, Dommy!"

"Fine," he groaned. "When two demons have a child, a piece of them is given to the first born that marks them to inherit the stronger parent's power. If they have another child, another piece is passed on from the less-strong parent to mark them, so power is passed to the second child when that parent dies. Demons don't usually have more children than that because they'll only be powerful if they're born with it at that point."

Something clicked and I blurted, "So I have Mother's power?"

His gaze flicked to the ceiling. "Not yet. When you're older, you'll get her power. Right now, your body is too small to handle it."

"I can handle it," I argued, crossing my arms.

Dominic chuckled. "I'm sure you can, but I don't get to decide. You have to be patient."

"Am I level one?" I scrunched my nose.

"No. Level one demons have no more strength than a human. You're level three." He poked my wing closest to him. "Level three and up have either wings or horns."

"Will I grow horns?" I asked excitedly.

Laughing again, Dominic shook his head. "No, sorry Emmy. You'd have been born with them."

I pouted a while longer, wishing I'd been born with horns, and Dominic returned to playing his game.

Thinking back, I was pretty sure that was the last time I saw Dominic playing video games. He never had time for it anymore. I certainly didn't envy the amount of responsibility he had, but I wished he'd let me help out.

I grabbed a book from my side table, propping it on the pillow in front of me. Just because I wasn't allowed to date, didn't mean I couldn't fall in love with fictional men, and I had plenty of toys in the drawer of my side table to keep me company.

At some point, I dozed off, sleeping through most of the day. My phone alarm woke me at five P.M.

Groaning, I rolled over and grabbed my phone, checking my messages. There was a whole series from Mazie.

Mazie: *I couldn't sleep so I did some digging*

Mazie: *You're going to kill me*

Mazie: *I FOUND HIM*

Mazie: *MR. SEXY HAS A HELLBOOK ACCOUNT*

Mazie: *Surprise surprise, he's friends*

with your brother so he wasn't hard
to find I should have done this ages ago

She sent a screenshot of an image that *did* look a lot like the demon I'd locked eyes with the night before. But it was a blurry picture. His name was Jayce Orion.

Mazie: *Jayce? STOP. That's a sexy name*
Okay. I'll leave you alone now <3

I laughed. Mazie was out of control, but I loved her for it. I wasn't allowed to have a Hellbook account, for obvious reasons, so Mazie kept me up to date on all things social media worthy.

> **Me:** *I'm never vaguely describing*
> *someone to you again*
> *You're too good at sleuthing*

She didn't respond, unsurprisingly. She was probably finally sleeping.

Thursday came around and I called Mazie in a panic.

"What's the dress code for this place?" I asked, the screeching of the hangers echoed in my oversized closet as I slid them from side to side, searching for something to wear.

Mazie hummed and said, "Not too fancy, but maybe a little dressier than Primetime? I've never been, so I can't say for sure. But you always look good, so I wouldn't worry."

"Super unhelpful," I grumbled. A brown corseted leather dress I'd borrowed from Mazie ages ago jumped out at me and I grabbed it. "I think I have something. I'll send you a picture when I'm ready!"

Hanging up my phone, I threw it onto my bed. I squeezed into the dress, a little unsure if it would be long enough to cover my butt, but it did.

Huzzah! I thought, shimmying in front of my mirror.

My makeup was already done, simple with sleek cat-eye wings. I recruited our maid, Serena, to help with that. She always had perfect eye makeup looks.

One loud knock on my door made me jump. Dominic's signature knock always caught me off guard.

Opening the door, I did a twirl for him. "Ta-da! I'm going to The Mausoleum with the girls tonight."

He furrowed his brow and shook his head. "It's Thursday. I'll have the Lieutenants over tonight."

I cocked my eyebrow. "And?"

"And that means you're staying in. We talked about this." He ran a hand over his hair, making it stick up in places. "Please, Ember, I can't deal with this right now."

"I made these plans before your stupid new rule! I promise I won't come back until after the sun rises so there's no chance they'll still be here." Even if I had to sneak out, I was going.

He groaned. "Fine. But this is the *last* time."

I let out a breath of relief. He wasn't always accommodating, and it surprised me he gave in so easily. Whatever was weighing on him that week must be serious. But if he wanted to keep it to himself, I wasn't going to pry. I'd tried to be a part of the family business, so if he chose to suffer alone, that was *his* decision.

The stairs creaked, meaning someone had hit the fifth step.

"Must be Penny," I said. Turning back into my room, I grabbed my black heeled boots and purse.

"Nice to see you again, Penny," Dominic greeted her as she slipped past him into my room. "Keep her out until daybreak, please." He shot me a look before turning and disappearing down the hall.

Chapter 4

Ember

The Mausoleum looked like an *actual* mausoleum on the outside. It was the size of one too. Penny and I hung back at first, but Mazie pushed us inside. A spiral staircase took us down into a dimly lit room with an iron door at the back of it. There was a small line waiting to get in, but Mazie skipped past it, knocking on the door.

"Name," a disembodied voice demanded.

"Mazie Steinham," she chirped.

A few seconds passed and the door swung open, letting out smoke and the smell of something burning. I pinched my nose, trying to stop the stinging.

"This isn't creepy," Penny said, but she couldn't hide the glint in her eyes. She was almost as excited as Mazie.

The door slammed behind us, and we walked down a dark corridor. Upbeat club music grew louder as we neared the end and another door.

"Welcome, Mazie and friends." A demon with green skin, curling horns, and wearing a long-tail coat jacket swept his arm out toward Mazie. "It's an honor to entertain you tonight. Right this way." He opened the door, and the music poured out. It was a familiar pop song, but it had been remixed.

Inside, a dance floor three times the size of Primetime's was at the center, with a long bar stretching across the entirety of the back wall. I leaned my head back and gaped at the cages hanging from the ceiling with all kinds of demons dancing in them. I wondered what it would take to be able to dance up there.

"Come on!" Mazie grabbed my hand and pulled me toward the bar.

Columns like the ones at the entrance of the club stood in each corner of the dance floor, separating it from the tables. To the right, there was a stage and a small catwalk, but there was no one on it.

There were a couple doors labelled different things around the room. The only one I could see from where we were was labelled *Ice Room.* I had no idea what that meant. It could have ice in it, but for some reason I doubted that.

In the left-hand corner, beside the bar, there was a roped off area with curtains all around it, concealing whatever or whoever was inside.

Mazie towed me up to the bar and sat in the first empty seat we came to. Penny stood behind her, facing the rest of the room. I took the seat beside Mazie.

As always, the bartender gravitated to Mazie, even though there were other demons who had been there before us waiting to order.

"What can I get you?" the demon asked. She had chin length bright pink hair and matching bright pink eyes that almost glowed under the dim lights.

"Three of whatever those are!" Mazie said, pointing to a drink that the demon beside her had. It was a purple drink with glitter and a whole stick of fruit on top. Mazie leaned over to me. "I'll eat the fruit if you don't want it, I skipped dinner tonight." She laughed.

The drinks were in front of us shortly and we each grabbed a glass, clinking them together before any of us took a sip.

It was tart and sweet at the same time and left a tingling in my mouth.

"I hate it," Penny said, but she took another long sip, grabbing her stick of fruit and dropping it into Mazie's drink.

"I love it!" Mazie ate her fruit and swiped mine next. "Mmm," she hummed, dancing in her seat.

Turning on my stool, I looked out at the rest of the demons in the place. The dance floor was full, and most of the tables, too. A demon with wings larger than my own flew up to one of the cages and helped one of the demons down.

"Look!" Mazie pointed to the winged demon. "Could you imagine if your brother came here? I can't even picture him in a place like this."

"He'd never be caught dead any place I frequent or else someone might guess our relation," I pointed out, sadness gripping my chest. It had been so long since Dominic and I had done anything together outside of the mansion and I missed spending time with him.

"Come on." Mazie finished her drink, so I did the same, and she tugged me out onto the dance floor. Penny remained by the bar.

As the drink settled in, a strange sensation washed over me. Every time I blinked, my eyes strained to stay open, while the rest of my body felt lighter than a feather. The sounds of music and demons around us all blurred together and I fell into Mazie.

"Something's wrong," I tried to tell her, but she was no better off than I was. Except she seemed to be enjoying herself, if the giant grin on her face was any indication.

Keeping hold of her, half so I wouldn't lose her, and half to keep myself standing, we made our way back to Penny, but she wasn't where we left her.

"Penny!" I tried calling, but there was no way she'd be able to hear me over the music.

Mazie swayed beside me in time with the music, her eyes closed as she moved her arms around above her. She would be no help.

My heart rate kicked up a notch as panic set in. Pushing Mazie onto a barstool, I looked her in the eyes and said, "Stay, Mazie. I need to find Penny."

She nodded her head, but I couldn't tell if she was agreeing with my command or moving with the music. Backing away, I bumped into someone, my ankle rolling and sending me sideways.

Strong hands caught me under my arms and put me back on my feet.

"Thank—" I ground to a halt as I turned and came face to face with Mr. Sexy. "Jayce?" I gasped.

He cocked his head and furrowed his brow. "Do I know you?" he asked.

Shit. Shit. Shit.

Shaking my head, I swerved to try and walk around him, but my head swam, and I couldn't quite see straight, so I bumped into someone else. Without stopping, I approached the curtained off area.

A hand gripped my elbow, and it didn't take much to pull me back in my current state, so I ended up spinning around and into Jayce's arms, catching myself against his chest. His eyes widened in surprise.

"Are you okay?" He searched my eyes as if he'd find the answer there, and maybe he did, because his lips pinched in concern.

My hands were still against his chest, and I was staring at his lips in a daze when I remembered what I was doing.

"I need to find my friend," I said. "Penny." Looking over his shoulder, I noticed Mazie was no longer on the stool I'd left her on. "Fuck." I pushed away from Jayce and tried to get around him.

"Wait," Jayce said, but I couldn't turn back.

Clarity was slowly returning to me, but not fast enough. Whatever had been in the drinks must have been one of the drugs that only lasted a short burst of time, thankfully.

"Mazie!" I called. She couldn't have gotten far.

"Emmy!" I heard her voice, but I couldn't see her. "Emmy up here!"

Tilting my head back, I cursed as she waved frantically from one of the cages, her smile as wide as when I'd left her. At least one of us was having fun.

"I guess you found your friend," Jayce said, coming up behind me. "Emmy, is it?" He smirked in amusement.

"Ember. Only Mazie calls me Emmy," I corrected. My wings weren't big enough to support my weight, so I couldn't fly, which meant Mazie was stuck up there until someone else brought her down.

"So that's Mazie, what happened to Penny?" Jayce asked. "Are we still looking for her?"

Shaking my head, I turned to him. "No. There is no *we*."

"Back off, she's with me," Penny growled as she strode up on the other side of Jayce.

He put his hands up and backed away. "Sorry. Didn't mean to interrupt girls' night." Winking, he disappeared into the crowd easily. People seemed to give him a wide berth even though he wasn't wearing his vest that night. Dominic's inner circle wore the leather vests, or cuts, when they were working. There was an image of a skull with two horns coming out the forehead on the back of the vest, along with *Southside* written underneath. Dominic was the only one who didn't still wear his cut, opting for suits and business attire ever since becoming the leader of the Southside drug ring.

"What the hell is she doing up there?" Penny groaned when she spotted Mazie.

"There was something in our drinks, didn't you feel it? It wore off quickly, but I think Mazie's still under its influence," I explained.

Penny scowled. "I didn't finish mine."

"Then where did you go? I assumed you were off in a corner, losing your mind or something." It wasn't like Penny to leave Mazie and I unattended.

"I had to pee," she said, but she didn't look me in the eye. "Let's get her down and get out of here. This place isn't for us."

It took us a while to find someone to get Mazie down from the cage, but once we did, she was almost sobered up.

"That was wild," she said once we were outside. "We should do this again sometime!" She beamed at us.

"We were drugged, Mazie!" I chided. "Thank Lucifer it didn't affect me as much as you, or who knows what might have happened."

"I wouldn't have let anything happen to either of you," Penny said. Her phone lit up as she unlocked it and opened her ride share app.

"You let *Jayce* talk to me," I reminded her.

Mazie gasped and gripped my arm, bringing her face close to mine. "*The* Jayce?"

"The very one." I couldn't help but smile. "And he was even more gorgeous up close."

"AGH!" Mazie groaned. "I missed him!"

"Jayce?" Penny asked, finished with ordering our ride. "As in one of Dominic's enforcers, Jayce?"

My stomach dropped. "Well, I didn't know that tidbit."

Penny pressed her fingertips to her brows, groaning. "We are so dead. If Dominic finds out, there is no way in *hell* he is ever letting you leave the house again."

"But he won't find out," I said. "Jayce saw me yesterday in the mansion and didn't say anything, so I don't think he'll say anything now. It's not like he knows who I am, anyway."

Penny's gaze snapped to mine. "He *saw* you in the mansion? Fuck, Ember! This isn't a game! We joke about Dominic killing me or Mazie, and he may not actually confine you to the mansion, but he *will* kill Jayce! He's done it before and—"

"What?" I reeled back. "What do you mean, he's done it before?" Remnants of my recurring nightmare flashed in my mind, but I refused to acknowledge them.

Rolling her shoulders, Penny stalked away. She sat on a bench and dropped her head into her hands.

Mazie put her hand on my back and guided me over to the bench, pressing lightly on my shoulders to get me to sit. Crouching in front of me, Mazie took my hands and squeezed them.

"Do you remember Grant?" she asked, wincing.

Grant. He had worked as a runner for my brother for years, as far as I knew. But at some point, he'd been killed, or left. I couldn't remember. The only reason I knew his name was because Maurice had mentioned him to me.

Mazie looked at the ground before she met my eye. "Well apparently, he saw you in the mansion and asked Dominic about it. The next day, he turned up dead across town on the border of Eastside. It was deemed a drug deal gone bad, but Penny and I know what really happened."

"What do you mean, *what really happened?*" I asked, even though I could guess exactly what they meant.

"Don't be so naïve, Ember," Penny said, sounding exhausted. "Your brother killed him or had him killed by one of his enforcers. Either way, he's dead because he found out you existed."

Grief mixed with guilt swallowed me, making me cold, even though it was stifling outside. "Jayce ..." I trailed off, not able to voice the fear clawing its way up my spine.

"He'll be okay, Emmy," Mazie said, her voice soothing as she rubbed my hands between hers. "We'll be more careful from now on, and we'll lay low for a while."

"You're right, it will be okay," I said, though the words sounded hollow.

Our ride arrived and Penny ushered us inside, taking the front seat so she could monitor the driver. We went to Mazie's apartment to wait until the sun rose.

When I was finally home in bed, I cried myself to sleep. Even in my dreams I couldn't escape the guilt that ate away at me.

It had been nine years since our parents had died, and I still had nightmares about the night Dominic killed the ones responsible. I'd outgrown being read stories by Maurice, so he told me all the family business gossip instead.

I swung my legs as I sat on the counter licking brownie batter from a spoon.

"The meeting will be ending soon, you should get back upstairs before your brother learns you were down here at all," Maurice said.

I dropped the bowl and spoon into the sink and hopped off the counter. "Don't forget to bring me some of those when they're finished cooking."

"Mhmm," Maurice hummed, waving absentmindedly as he cleaned the kitchen.

Sneaking up the stairs to my room, I paused at the top, staring down at the entryway below. If I waited there long enough, Dominic's crew would come out of the room on the left and see me.

*It would be a relief to no longer need to hide, but
Dominic insisted that I'd be in danger if the other drug lords
knew I existed. I may not care about my own self-preservation
all that much, but Dominic was the only family I had left, so I
refused to make his life harder than it already was.*

*I turned to my room and left the stairs behind. But I
went straight to my window to watch when all the demons left. I
imagined elaborate lives for all of them, since I couldn't have a
life of my own.*

*For a brief moment, I could have sworn one of
Dominic's crew members locked eyes with me, but there was no
way they could see me in the darkness of my room.*

My dream brought back the night Grant had seen me at
my window. I didn't know it at the time, but a few days after that
particular night, Maurice told me about Grant's demise.
Though, he said an Eastsider had killed Grant. Not my own
brother.

Weeks passed without seeing Mazie or Penny. I kept
making excuses, like I wasn't feeling well, or I had things going
on at home. I knew they'd see through the excuses, but they
didn't pressure me.

I didn't attempt to sneak looks at Dominic's meetings
and didn't even ask Maurice for updates.

Finally, on a Friday when Mazie would normally come
over for sleepovers, she showed up and forced her way into my
room.

"That's it," she said. "No more moping. This is no way
to live your life."

I pulled my pillow over my face and groaned into it.
"What life?" I asked, though it came out muffled.

Mazie jumped onto my bed and ripped the pillow from my grasp, throwing it across the room.

"Harsh," I commented, turning on my side, away from her. "I can't live like this Mazie. Grant *died* because of me."

Leaning over me so I was forced to look at her, Mazie put one hand on my side table to balance herself.

"No," she snapped. "Grant died because of your brother. Not you. You can't blame yourself for your brother's actions."

Sighing I rolled and she fell back onto the bed, sitting cross legged instead. She pulled me into a sitting position and kept my hands in hers.

"We're going out tonight. No excuses." She quieted a little and added, "I'll even let you dance with someone other than me for a few minutes."

"What about Penny? Dom won't let me out if she's not with us," I said, as if I actually planned on leaving my bed.

"What *about* Penny?" Penny asked.

I whipped my head to the door where she stood, leaning against the frame, smirking.

"I'll admit, it was nice not going clubbing for a couple weeks, but then I started to miss you two weirdos." She ran and jumped onto the bed, surprising both Mazie and I and dissolving us all into a fit of laughter.

Dominic stomped down the hall and appeared in my doorway. "What the hell is going on in here?" I thought he'd be upset, but he seemed amused for once.

"Why don't you come out with us tonight, Dom?" I asked, though I knew there was no chance of that ever happening.

Shaking his head, he confirmed my thought by saying, "I can't. I'm meeting up with some friends."

"To play cards?" I asked. That was the only thing he ever did with his friends. It seemed boring to me.

"You have friends?" Mazie teased.

"Yes, and yes." He leaned against my doorframe much like Penny had.

"Whose house are you playing at?" I couldn't help asking.

"Jayce. You've never met him," he answered.

My pulse spiked and I inhaled sharply. "Well, I've never met *any* of your friends," I said, trying to appear normal.

"And you never will." He shook his head. "I do it to protect you, Em. Remember that." Pointing at me, he spun out of the doorway and stalked down the hall.

"At least we don't have to worry about bumping into Mr. Sexy tonight," Mazie said, keeping her voice low so Dominic wouldn't overhear her.

A wave of disappointment washed over me. I knew it was for the best, and I hadn't truly *wanted* to see him, because it would be dangerous if he found out who I was. But ...

Mazie shifted, hopping off the bed and diving into my closet.

"Hey," Penny said softly, putting her hand on my knee. "It will get better. Life won't always be like this." Her gaze traveled around the room and back to me.

I tried my best to enjoy my night out with Penny and Mazie, but it was dampened by the constant reminder that I had to go home and start the cycle again: go to bed, wake up, find some tedious tasks to fill my day, go to sleep, and do it all again. Over and over and over. Never making new friends or having a deeper connection with anyone other than the two demons my brother had literally bought for me.

Monday night, Dominic had another meeting. He had meetings every Monday and Thursday. Mondays were with everyone in his drug ring and Thursdays were for lieutenants only. Which meant Jayce would be in our house that Monday night.

"You're staying in your room tonight, right?" Dominic asked from my doorway while I laid on my bed, a book in front of my face.

Sighing, I lowered my book. "I know we've talked about it countless times, but have you ever *actually* considered letting me be a part of the family business?"

"Of course I have. But the risks outweigh the benefits. You know that, Em." He came further into my room for once, sitting at the end of my bed. "When our parents died, I promised myself I'd never let anything happen to you. They kept you secret for a reason, so I'm only continuing with what they would want."

Kept me secret. Like I was some object instead of their daughter. Sometimes I couldn't help wondering if Dominic would be more lenient if I'd inherited our mother's power. But I couldn't have those thoughts or else bitterness soon followed.

"They're gone, Dom. We don't need to keep pretending they never made any mistakes. Like any other demon, our parents were far from perfect." I put my book aside and shifted onto my knees. "Just because they got caught up in a turf war doesn't mean the same thing will happen to us."

"It took me *years* to fully diffuse that situation. One wrong move and things could go back to how they were. The Eastside sector is volatile at best. If they found out about you, they'd jump at the opportunity to use you against me and try to take over our territory." Dominic pressed his hand to the comforter between us. "There's too much going on right now. Maybe in a few years ..."

"Years?!" I fell back onto my pillows and groaned. "Dom this is killing me! I'm so *bored.* All I want to do is help you, and you won't even let me do that."

"I'll find something for you to do that won't put you in harm's way. Something that will keep you out of sight, and on the sidelines, but keep you occupied." It was a hollow offer, but I nodded anyway.

"Fine," I said, not looking at him. "I'll be here if you need me." Pulling the comforter up over myself, I closed my eyes and waited for him to leave.

It took a few seconds, but he sighed and stood, the bed shifting with him. "I love you, Ember, and all I want is to keep you safe."

I kept my mouth shut. There was nothing more I could say to change his mind right then, but I'd find something. There had to be some way to convince my brother to let me become a part of the family business, and I would make it my mission to figure it out.

Chapter 5

Jayce

I twisted the gold ring on my index finger as I waited for the rest of the crew to show up. Dominic was seated at the head of the table, a pained expression on his face as one of his lieutenants, Nyle, talked to him.

The seats were filling up at the massive oval table, there were never enough for all twenty of the main crew. There were more demons who worked for Dominic, but not all of them needed to be at the meetings. His lieutenants each had their own groups they kept tabs on.

The demons who attended the meetings were the only ones who got to wear the cuts marking them as a part of Dominic's crew. We all wore them tonight, though Dominic's hung on the wall above him, retired there once he took over as the leader.

"Do you think we'll get out of here early tonight?" Oliver asked as he took the last open seat beside me.

"Why, you got a hot date?" I asked, quirking my eyebrow.

Sighing, Oliver stretched out his legs and relaxed into his chair. "If only. My last date was with that guy I met at The Mausoleum, remember him? He tried to get me to have a foursome with him, which I was down for, except one of the four was one of my exes." He shuddered.

I couldn't help laughing. But I remembered the guy who he was talking about. They met the night I met Ember. Ember and I had interacted for less than a minute, but something about her had struck me down deep. Maybe it was the way she'd said my name as if she knew me, even though we'd never met.

Shaking my head, I asked Oliver, "Which ex?"

"Bianca." He scowled.

"Now that we're all here," Dominic's voice rose above all the others and everyone fell silent. "I know some of you are still worried about the drop in business, which is valid. Last week we were almost back to our usual numbers, and there was another dip this week. Jayce has been monitoring The Mausoleum, where there seems to be an uptick in drug use, mostly due to their specialty drinks, but he'll let us know if anything else comes up there."

I zoned out as Dominic went over a few other spaces he had people frequenting. We spent enough time together, I already knew everything he was reporting on.

"Tomorrow I'll be attending an auction on the Westside, hosted by Jericho," Dominic said, and my focus snapped back to him. "The drug lords from all of the factions will be there, so I can test the waters and see if anyone knows anything about certain demons pushing the boundaries."

"He shouldn't be going alone," I murmured, leaning closer to Oliver.

"Nyle will be attending with me," Dominic said, as if he'd heard me. "And that's everything for tonight. You're all dismissed."

I waited for most of the group to file out of the room before weaving my way toward Dominic.

"Jericho invited you to the westside?" I asked, shaking my head. "That's a trap if I've ever heard one."

Dominic lifted his hands. "It seems like he's trying to remind us of his stature. An *auction* of all things? He wants us to remember who has the most money and the most influence." He rolled his eyes.

"If it goes south, you should have more than Nyle with you," I said, casting a glance over my shoulder to make sure the lieutenant wasn't around anymore.

"If I show up with anyone other than my plus one, I'll seem weak. They'll think I'm afraid of them, or that I don't trust them. I can't have that. Besides, I'm stronger than Jericho." Dominic put his hand on my shoulder. "Don't worry about me."

He veered around me to walk out of the room with the rest of the stragglers. Oliver and I were meant to stay as anonymous as possible, since we were Dominic's enforcers, so it made sense he wouldn't bring us with him, but it still irked me.

My phone vibrated in my pocket, and I ignored it. The only demon who would be texting me that wasn't at the mansion was Victoria, and I couldn't deal with her at the moment. The good thing about her was she could take a hint, and she wouldn't pester me. She'd find someone else to keep her occupied.

In the foyer, Oliver and Dominic were the last two remaining from the meeting. I joined them by the front door.

"I'll be at The Mausoleum tomorrow," I said. "But if you need me, I can easily be in Westside within twenty minutes."

Oliver's eyes widened. "Me too! I mean, I won't be at The Mausoleum, because it's my night off, but I'd *love* to rough up some Westsiders." He put his hands together in front of him, pleading. "Please tell me we're going to get to—"

"No!" Dominic said, laughing. "No. We're not fighting *or* killing anyone. I'm sure Jericho has no underlying scheme for the auction. I'll be fine." He pointed at me and then Oliver. "And you two will remain in Southside."

Sighing, Oliver conceded. "Yes, sir."

"Yes, sir," I mocked.

Dominic opened the front door and ushered us out.

When I pulled into my parking garage, I checked my phone to see my text from Victoria.

Vic: *It's been so long since I've seen you, just wanted to make sure you're still alive*
Can I come over tomorrow night?

She was right, it had been a while. Well, longer than usual for us. I hadn't seen her since before I met Ember ... But that had nothing to do with anything.

Shaking my head, I texted her back.

Me: *See you tomorrow*

That would help reset my mind and remove Ember from it. It wasn't like I'd seen her since that night at The

Mausoleum. She'd probably been in Southside for one night and I'd never see her again.

Later that day, I woke up mid-afternoon and headed to The Devil's Brew. Grace wasn't working, but Luca, who was almost equally as skilled of a barista, was. He wasn't as chatty, but sometimes it was nice not to have to talk when I'd just woken up.

I couldn't help the nerves whenever I thought about Dominic going into Westside territory without more backup than *Nyle.* It wasn't that Nyle wasn't capable, but they'd be surrounded by enemies. Not only Westside, but Eastside, and any other sector that deigned to show their faces. Northside tended to keep to themselves, and most of the outer sectors didn't care about the drug business. They had other commodities they specialized in.

It wasn't like the four main sectors had never gathered before, but it was rare. It had only happened twice since Dominic took over for his parents, and one of those events was arranged by Lucifer to ensure that the hatchet had been buried between Eastside and Southside.

Dominic was probably right, and the auction was a show of wealth on Jericho's part. But that thought did nothing to quell my nerves. So, I headed to The Mausoleum early to keep my mind occupied, taking my car and omitting my cut to keep a lower profile.

I headed straight for the bar, ordering a drink free from any additives, and watched everyone who came through the door.

As I finished my drink, I received a text from Dominic.

Dom: *No need to go to The*

H. M. Huntress

Mausoleum tonight
Take the night off

It was strange that he would bother telling me to stay away. He knew I had nothing better to do than be at The Mausoleum, since my entire life revolved around my job.

I ordered one more drink, figuring I'd leave once I finished it. The last sip was mostly water from the melted ice by the time I got to it. I glanced at the opposite end of the bar and had to do a double take.

Leaning over the bar, wearing a tight leopard miniskirt and a black leather top, was Ember. Her short, pink hair was hiding most of her face, but I knew it was her. My entire body heated. I debated leaving without saying anything to her, but the nagging thought that I may not see her again won out and I headed her way.

Chapter 6
Ember

Sitting at my computer, I scrolled through news article after news article, reading anything I could about the Eastside sector's drug ring. They were the most violent of the groups, from what I'd heard and read.

Dominic's ring, the Southside sector, mostly stayed out of the tabloids and public eye. Obviously, in Hell, drug dealing was a widely accepted business and a position working for one of the drug lords was highly coveted, but it still didn't do to have your name plastered all over the Sector Wide Times. A bad reputation meant demons were less likely to buy from your business. If they were afraid you might get violent with them, they'd hop on the train over to another sector and buy there.

Demons wanted to stay alive, so they tried to stay away from the worst of the trouble. And Eastside happened to be involved in a lot of avoidable trouble.

I wouldn't put it past them to encroach on Southside territory and cause a drop in our sales over the last month. But I also wasn't going to rule out the Westside drug ring. They generally kept to themselves, not causing too much trouble, like Southside, but their boss was more ruthless than any other. One of the few times Westside made headlines in the Sector Wide Times, their boss had slaughtered an entire group of his own drug runners because he was unsatisfied with their productivity.

A knock on my door made me jump and slam my laptop shut.

"Come in," I squeaked.

My door swung open, and Maurice came in with a plate of mini sandwiches.

"Lunchtime," he said, putting the plate on my desk. "You didn't come down, so I figured I'd bring some food up for you."

I smiled at him and took one of the sandwiches. "Thank you! I got so caught up, I forgot all about lunch." It was almost six o'clock on a Tuesday night.

Leaning on the edge of my desk, Maurice crossed his arms and nodded to my closed laptop. "What are you working on today?"

I finished chewing and swallowed before saying, "Research."

"Hmm," he mused, bobbing his head as if he knew *exactly* what kind of research I was doing. "You know, I overheard Dominic saying an Eastsider was caught trying to sell drugs over on Fifth street. Might be worth *researching.*" He winked and pushed off my desk, heading back to the door.

"Thank you!" I called after him.

Fifth street. Where The Mausoleum was. I wondered if they might be trying to sell undercover of the chaos of the club. There was only one way to find out.

Pulling out my phone from my hoodie's front pocket, I texted my group chat with Mazie and Penny.

> **Me**: *Round 2 of The Mausoleum tonight? I'd like to experience it without he drug induced panic attack*

Mazie: *ABSOLUTELY!*
Penny: *I've gotten no better offers*
Mazie: *AND YOU NEVER WILL*
I'll call and have us put on the list!

> **Me**: *Meet at the mansion at nine?*

Mazie: *Perfect!*
Penny: *I'll be there*

I danced over to my closet.

"Not that," I said, flicking through my clothes. Turning around, I walked to the other wall. There were so many choices, yet nothing I wanted to wear.

"Ember?" Dominic's voice came from my bedroom.

"In here!" I yelled.

A few seconds later, he walked into my closet, dressed in a black tux. "I'm headed out," he said.

I put my hands on my hips and raised my eyebrows. "Where are you headed dressed so *fancy?*"

"An auction over on the Westside." He did a full turn with his arms out. "Do I look okay?"

"You look great, but why Westside? Isn't that like, a conflict of interest or something?" I spotted a leopard print mini skirt laying beneath a pile of clothes and ducked down to grab it.

"It was an invitation from Jericho Blane himself. Far be it for me to turn him down and risk another turf war when we barely survived the last one." Dominic crossed his arms and picked at the cufflink on his sleeve.

Barely survived. Well, that was a stretch. Our parents *hadn't* survived.

"Be careful, okay?" I shimmied the skirt over my leggings. "And call me if you need me." I knew he wouldn't, but maybe someday he would.

"Yeah, yeah. You too." He waved his hand dismissively and left my closet.

Kicking off my leggings, I straightened and buttoned my skirt. I grabbed the first black top I saw, a leather cropped halter and changed out of my hoodie. I flexed my wings, glad to have them free of the fabric of my hoodie.

Perfect.

To kill a little more time before nine, I sat at my laptop, searching for *Jericho Blane.* The drug lord of the Westside. The very same who was said to have killed that whole lot of drug runners.

His name was mentioned every so often in articles online, but not much was truly known about him. There were no pictures or addresses on where to find him. I had to imagine he lived in a mansion like ours, so he couldn't be *that* hard to find.

Not that I'd ever go looking for him.

Nine o'clock rolled around and I slipped on my thigh-high boots and met Mazie and Penny in the foyer.

"If Jayce is there, we're leaving *immediately,*" Penny said, poking my arm as if I needed the reminder. Her black, leather fingerless gloves meant she was in full-on bodyguard mode tonight.

We had to walk a block away from the mansion so the ride share driver wouldn't think any of us lived there. *Everyone* knew the mansion belonged to Southside's drug lord.

Mazie's outfit was similar to mine, but her skirt was black, and her top was leopard print.

"Matching!" she squealed, tucking her arm through mine as we headed for our ride. "Don't let Penny ruin your fun, she's in a mood tonight," she whispered.

"Duly noted," I whispered back.

Penny climbed into the back seat with us for once, her leather leggings sticking against my bare legs.

"Make sure to ask what you're ordering before drinking anything this time," Penny instructed. "Their drinks are purposefully made with different drugs, depending on the mood you're going for."

"Whoopsies!" Mazie giggled. "We learned our lesson the hard way, I guess."

We got into The Mausoleum easily enough, and the effect of the atmosphere had lost some of its luster now that we knew what to expect, but it was still impressive.

Mazie made sure to order us drinks without any fun toppings that time.

"I'm going to try to find a way back into one of the cages," Mazie yelled to me over the music before slipping into the crowd, leaving me alone with Penny.

Except, when I turned to where Penny had been only moments before, she was gone.

"What the hell?" I turned in a circle, but she was nowhere in my line of sight. "Fine. I'll start my investigation by myself." I sipped my drink and casually strolled around while trying to read the room.

No one stood out to me as a drug dealer, but that didn't mean much. They could blend in well with the rest of the demons. One thing that caught my eye was the curtained off section beside the bar. If I was someone who wanted to sell drugs in another sector's territory, that would certainly be a better place to do it than out in the open.

Leaning against the end of the bar, I sipped my drink and watched the curtains. They swayed every so often, but that could be the air of the AC moving them or the groups of demons using the area as a cool down spot.

"Trying to catch them on fire with your mind?" A familiar voice said at my shoulder.

I coughed, choking on my drink and whirled to find Jayce behind me. Trying to catch my breath while still hacking, I set my glass down.

"Sorry, didn't mean to scare you. Want me to give you the Heimlich or something?" He smirked.

Shaking my head, I took one long, deep, breath and finally managed to stop the coughing fit.

"I'm fine," I said, turning back around and hoping he'd walk away. I didn't want to have to leave if Penny happened to see him.

"I swear, you look so familiar. Are you sure we haven't met before?" he asked, clearly not taking the hint.

Clearing my throat, I glanced back at him. As much as I wanted to talk to him and get to know him and ... *Calm down, Ember,* I chided myself. Dominic would kill Jayce if he knew that he was talking to me. Not only that, but Jayce was also his enforcer, so he'd probably make him kill himself or something twisted like that. So, I'd do the right thing and walk away.

"No. Sorry," I said, striding toward the curtains. If I was going to figure out what was behind them, now was the time to do it. It gave me the perfect way to lose Jayce.

Pushing aside one of the curtains in the middle, I stepped through them and was immediately met with a wall of a demon. He towered over me, and his curved horns on the sides of his head made him even more imposing.

"Oh." I let out a huff as I stared up at him. "Sorry, I'm—
"

"Let her through," a smooth, amused voice said.

The massive demon moved aside and revealed a table with a cushioned booth at the back of it. A blue demon with horns that almost appeared to have been slicked back with his black hair, if that were possible, sat in the middle, both of his arms around females on either side of him. They were both reddish pink, like me, but they had horns and tails. My wings shifted as if they knew I was comparing them to these female's appendages.

My gaze flicked to a door on the right and back to the male at the table.

Tucking my hair behind my ear, I put on a smile and feigned shyness.

"Sorry, I stumbled in here and have *no* idea where I am," I said, giggling.

It seemed to work and the blue demon grinned, taking one of his arms from around the females and beckoned me forward.

"We wouldn't want a pretty thing like you getting lost, would we?" His eyes darkened and he stood, putting both hands on the table and leaning in toward me as I walked closer to him. "What's your name, beautiful?"

I hesitated, knowing I shouldn't give my real name, and blurted, "Mazie." It was the first name I could think of, and I knew she wouldn't mind me borrowing it.

"Perfect," he said, waving a hand to his side and motioning to the demon on his right to move. "Take a seat, Mazie."

The female demon shot me with a glare but stood and sat in one of the chairs on the edge of the platform the table was on. I sat beside the blue demon, even though every instinct told me to run.

"What's your name?" I asked, biting my bottom lip and looking up at him from under my lashes.

His black eyes met mine and he lifted my chin with his index finger, his sharp black nail digging into my skin.

"Enzo," he said. "Now, tell me, what did you *really* come in here for, Mazie?" He dropped his hand and draped his arm along the back of the bench seat.

I twisted the ends of my hair and leaned closer to him. "Well, I was hoping to find something a little stronger than what they have at the bar."

Enzo chuckled and shook his head. "And what made you think to come in here?"

I shrugged and rubbed my leg against his. "It's not very subtle, is it? The curtained off area," I pointed out. "Call it a lucky guess."

"Lucky indeed." He jerked his head to the demon who sat in the chair off to the side. "One, Portia," he commanded, and she hopped up, heading to the door at the back and disappearing through it.

"How much do I owe you?" I fluttered my eyelashes and hoped he would give me an actual price and not want something *else*.

Licking his lips, he dropped his hand to my knee and squeezed. "For a demon like you? First one's free. So long as you don't make yourself a stranger."

It sounded almost like a threat, but I nodded in agreement. What choice did I have at that point? I needed to know what he was dealing and if it was something Dominic should be worried about.

Portia returned and slipped a small bag with a single purple pill into my hand. She tugged me out of the seat and took her rightful place.

"Thank you," I said, waving and giving Enzo a wink before ducking back out of the curtained area. As soon as I did, a hand landed on my wrist and pulled me aside.

I yipped in surprise, almost dropping my prize before I shoved it into my cleavage.

"What is that?" Jayce demanded, his gaze on where I'd stashed my pill.

"Eyes up here, asshole," I snapped, gripping his chin and forcing the issue.

He rolled his eyes. "I mean what did he give you?"

Cocking my head to the side, and widening my eyes, I feigned confusion. "I have no idea what you're talking about."

Jayce's gaze drifted to the ceiling, and he took a deep breath. It was fun messing with him.

Lowering his gaze back to me, he said, "Please. What did he give you?"

If he thought I was giving up my win to him because he said *please*, he was wrong. I needed the pill to prove to Dominic I was useful for the family business. And I was, clearly.

"Sorry, but anything I have on me, I brought in with me tonight." It was hard fighting my smile, but I pursed my lips and shrugged. "Is that why you've been following me? Because you thought I was someone who would be looking for *drugs?*" I asked, a little offended at the realization.

Jayce took a step back and leaned against the wall, shaking his head. "Of course not, and I haven't been following you."

"Could've fooled me," I said, smirking. "What was your name again? Jayce?" Now that I'd completed my mission, I decided I may as well have a little fun before Penny found me and made us leave. Clearly Jayce didn't know who I was, so he was safe from my brother's wrath.

One night of fun, and then I could be satiated for a while.

"And you're Ember," he said.

I scrunched my nose. I'd forgotten I'd told him that tidbit the last time we'd met. If he told my brother he'd met someone named Ember at the club, it wasn't a big leap to figure out it was *me*.

Fuck it. I was tired of living my life in fear of being found out.

"Want to dance?" I asked him.

"What?" He acted as if he'd never been asked to dance before. And maybe he hadn't. If I didn't know who he was, I may have stayed far away like everyone else. Even without the vest marking him as one of the Southside crew, he had an intimidating aura.

"Suit yourself." I turned and strode away, making sure to sway my hips a little extra. It worked like a charm and Jayce was at my side, his hand sliding around my waist.

"You want to *dance* with me?" he asked. "After that?"

"Don't question it, or else I might change my mind," I said.

When we reached the dance floor, I looked up. Mazie was in one of the cages, dancing with another demon. Their tails were entwined, and they looked like they were having the time of their lives. Penny was still MIA.

I turned to Jayce, and he wore a slightly nervous expression, which I hadn't expected. He *killed* people for a living, yet the idea of dancing had him nervous? It seemed odd.

"Haven't you ever danced with anyone before?" I teased, walking my fingers up his chest.

"I don't really have time for that. I shouldn't even be doing this." He glanced back over to the curtained area, but I cupped his cheek in my hand and turned his gaze back to me.

"Loosen up, Jayce. You deserve a night off." Little did he know how well I truly knew that. My brother always had his men doing side jobs for him, so they had little time for themselves.

Though I wouldn't admit it to Jayce, I'd also never danced with anyone other than Penny or Mazie. I'd watched enough TV and danced on my own plenty to learn *some* things.

I started dancing, and Jayce stood awkwardly, rubbing his hand over the back of his neck. Sighing, I moved closer to him and took his hand, placing it on my waist.

"*Dancing* requires *moving*," I said. "Do what I do, okay?" It wasn't lost on me that I was trying to teach one of

Dominic's most brutal men to dance, but I'd yet to see that harsher side of him, and he'd agreed to this.

He rolled his eyes, but his small smile told me he would do as I told him to. His hand tightened on my waist as I stepped side to side, and he followed my movements.

Raising my voice to be heard over the music, I said, "Feel free to improvise at any time."

Holding his hand that wasn't on my waist out to me, Jayce twirled me out away from him, and pulled me back in, closer than I'd been before. My hand landed on his chest, and we continued swaying with the beat. His hand strayed to my lower back, and I put both of my arms up over his shoulders. He was a good six inches taller than me, even though I was a solid five foot six.

Our eyes were locked, and his smile grew. I bit my lip, hiding my smile and trying not to appear too eager. He was so much *prettier* up close, his long lashes brushing the tops of his light blue cheeks. And his lips ... I wanted to touch them.

"Eyes up here, beautiful." He caught me staring.

Looking for a distraction, I took his hand and spun myself out again, doing a twirl under his arm. He took me by surprise, and when he pulled me back in, he dipped me low and whispered in my ear, "I'll be taking this."

I faltered in confusion, and then he plucked the small bag from between my cleavage. It had slipped out enough for him to take without touching me.

Scrambling to grab it back, I righted myself and pulled down my skirt that had ridden up. "Mother f—"

"Sorry, beautiful. I need this more than you." He strode away through the crowd, toward the front door.

"You fucking asshole!" I yelled after him, trying to push my way to him, but it was as if the crowd had closed ranks and refused to let me through.

Chapter 7

Ember

"Ember!" Penny's voice startled me after so long without seeing her.

I turned to find her shoving her way to me. When she stood in front of me, she put her hands on her hips and gave me her best disappointed look.

"We promised we'd leave if Jayce showed up," she said. "Not dance with him and ... Where the fuck is Mazie?"

I looked up, but she wasn't in the cage anymore.

"Hi guys!" she chirped as she popped up beside me, nearly giving me a heart attack.

"Holy fuck, Mazie," I hissed. "Don't do that."

"Sorry." She grinned sheepishly. "What happened to Jayce?"

"You knew she was with him, and you didn't stop her?" Penny turned on her. "What is wrong with you guys?"

Mazie shrugged. "I didn't see you stopping her, so I thought we were on the same page of letting her live a little for the first time."

"I had other business I had to deal with," Penny snapped. "Let's get out of here."

Mazie and I shared a look as we followed Penny. She cut a path through the crowd easily. If only she'd been there to help me get to Jayce when he was escaping with my drugs.

Outside, the humid air made me immediately sticky and gross. Sweat from the club didn't mix well with the heat of Hell.

"Tell me everything," Mazie whispered, but Penny still heard her.

Sighing and rolling her eyes, Penny said, "Yes, we're dying to know what was so worth risking his life for."

I told them everything, starting with my research and what I'd planned to do. Much to my surprise, Penny didn't interrupt with any chastising remarks on how reckless I'd been.

"Was Enzo at least cute?" Mazie asked at the end of it all. "Because I need a new boy to root for since Mr. Sexy decided to betray us."

Gaping at her, I sputtered. "Not the point Mazie!" I took a breath and added, "But yes. He was conventionally attractive for an older demon."

"So, we need to beat Jayce to your brother," Penny said, surprising me again.

"You want to help me?" I asked.

She nodded slowly. "We have an advantage here, since you *live* with Dominic. I'm assuming Jayce will approach him tomorrow."

"Yes!" Excitement filled me. "The lieutenants' meeting is on Thursday, so he'll want to fill in Dominic before then."

Our ride pulled up and Penny went to the front seat, Mazie and I to the back.

Leaning forward so I could talk with Penny, I asked, "Will he believe me if I don't have the, you know what?" I tried to remain vague since we had an audience.

"Once *he* shows up and corroborates your story, your brother will have no choice but to believe you," Penny said.

Our ride dropped us off at Mazie's. It was a safe spot within walking distance of the mansion, but we could go inside in case anyone was watching and hang out for a while.

"Dominic is at some auction tonight over in the Westside sector, so he won't be home until the early morning," I said. We entered the apartment building and took the elevator to the fourth floor.

"What if Jayce meets him there?" Mazie asked.

Penny shook her head. "Jayce is an enforcer which means he has to lie low. He can't burst into parties he's not invited to; it would draw too much attention. He'll wait until the morning to drop by, or maybe even tomorrow night."

Mazie unlocked her door and let us inside her apartment, flipping on the lights as she made her way to the kitchen. She pulled out a box of Pop Tarts and tossed them to me.

I took a package out for each of us and left the remaining one on the counter.

"Don't you know where Jayce lives?" Mazie asked, dropping onto her couch and draping her legs over the arm. "He's your brother's best friend."

I sat down beside her, and kicked my boots off, pulling my legs up beneath me.

"Dom has never mentioned where Jayce lives, just that he goes there to play cards sometimes," I explained. "Besides, if I showed up at his house, I'd have some serious explaining to do as to how I found him."

"I may or may not know *exactly* where to find him." Penny smirked, her eyebrow cocking.

"And you've been holding out on us?!" Mazie exclaimed. "Penny, I don't know what's gotten into you, but I'm liking it. Let's do a heist and get the drugs back!"

"How do you know where he lives?" I asked Penny.

"I may have followed him home after one of the meetings. Being your bodyguard, I make it my business to know where everyone lives who may become a problem." She shrugged as if it was no big deal to be *stalking* people. "His apartment is within walking distance from here."

"*Apartment?* I assumed he'd at least live in a house if my brother deigns to go there for card games." My brother was particular about where he went and who he was seen with.

"Well, less of an apartment, more of a penthouse. You'll see," Penny said. "You two should change into something more ... Flexible."

I glanced down at myself. "What, a miniskirt and a halter don't scream *kick ass spy outfit* to you?"

Mazie didn't miss a beat. She ran into her room and started digging through her clothes. Her clothes closet was in the living room, so I assumed she had something specific in mind. She came back into the living room, dressed head to toe in black, and held a similar black, skin-tight body suit out to me.

"I've been waiting to pull these out for a while. I got them a few months ago on a two for one deal!" She grinned.

"It's a good thing we're similar sizes," I said, taking the body suit and holding it up to myself. It didn't *look* like I'd be able to squeeze myself into it, but Mazie had, and like I'd said, we *did* have a similar body type and size.

She twisted her hair up into a top knot bun and covered it with a black beanie.

"If we don't dissolve into puddles by the end of this, I'll be shocked," I murmured. The heat would have no mercy on us in these outfits, but they were perfect for blending in with the night.

After a few painstaking minutes, I managed to get the body suit on. I couldn't quite breathe in it, but it fit. The zipper up the front wouldn't zip all the way on mine like it did for Mazie, so I left it partially unzipped.

"All right, let's get going before the sun starts to rise and we lose our advantage," Penny said, leading the way out of Mazie's apartment and down the street, in the direction of the mansion. Instead of taking the turn that would take us back to the mansion, we crossed the street and went in the opposite direction.

You could tell the second we crossed into the wealthier district. The streets were clean of any trash or debris, there weren't any loiterers, or really *any* demons on the streets. Anyone who lived on this side would be either driving a fancy ass car or chauffeured around by someone driving a fancy ass car. Even though I lived in a mansion, whenever I went anywhere, I wasn't allowed those luxuries because it would pin me as someone who could afford them, and people would ask questions.

We passed a few luxury apartment buildings and Penny ducked down an alley between two of them, pulling Mazie and I along with her.

"This is the one," she said, pointing up.

At the top of the apartment building, there was one massive window overlooking the street. The windows were tinted, so there was no way of telling if anyone was home.

"Come on." Penny hurried down the alley to a door at the back end of the building. Taking out her lockpicking tools, she made quick work of the door and ushered us inside. Some places in Hell were well protected, but apartment complexes were not one of those places. Dominic's crew kept the peace in Southside for the most part, but it was still *Hell.* Demons were going to do what they wanted to do.

I gaped, looking around as we stepped through the door into a whole other world. The mansion was nice, and we had plenty of fancy décor and niceties, but this was *top tier.* The plush carpets were pristine and looked so comfy you could sleep on them. There were exotic plants decorating the hall we'd entered, making it look like we were entering a jungle.

"What is this place?" Mazie asked, gazing around with her jaw dropped. She ran her fingers along one of the fronds of a nearby plant. None of them were *real,* of course. Real plants couldn't grow in Hell.

"Don't touch anything," Penny hissed. "They frown on that here. Come on." She opened a door marked, *stairwell,* and we began our climb.

Flight after flight of stairs, I reconsidered how badly I wanted to get this pill back. Sure, it would help me prove to my brother I was able to help him and the family business, and I could be of use. But was that really necessary?

I huffed, trying to regulate my breathing.

"Is it too late to say I changed my mind?" I asked, pausing to put my hands on my knees and catch my breath.

"There's only like, ten more flights," Penny said, barely sounding winded.

We'd gone twenty flights, and we had ten more. I didn't think I would make it.

"Next time, I don't care about the risk of being seen, I'm taking the elevator," Mazie said, leaning over the railing as she huffed.

We pressed on, and by the grace of Lucifer, made it to the thirtieth floor. There was a special keypad next to the door that would lead us into Jayce's foyer.

"Well, that's going to be a problem," Mazie murmured, squatting against the wall as she wheezed from exertion. I was right there beside her.

"Hardly," Penny said, entering a six-digit code on the pin pad.

It lit up green and Mazie and I both gaped at Penny.

"How did you figure *that* out?" I asked.

She put her finger to her mouth, shushing me, and opened the door, peeking inside before waving us forward.

The penthouse was dark except for the light coming in through the window from the hazy night. It was an open concept space, with no doors. The kitchen flowed into the living room space, and a wall with a doorless entryway led to the bedroom. I could see the end of the bed from where we stood, and it looked like there was someone in it.

If I had to guess where Jayce would keep something as important as evidence of another drug ring selling in our territory, I'd say he'd keep it close.

Penny must have guessed the same thing, because she headed toward the bedroom, not making a sound. I followed her and stopped in the entryway, looking over at Jayce as he slept.

I inhaled sharply. He was *not* alone. A beautiful, purple-haired demon sprawled beside him; her arm slung over his bare chest.

"What an ass," Mazie whispered behind me, making me jump.

I whirled, my eyes wide, and slapped my hand over her mouth. Glancing back, I let out a sigh of relief when Jayce and his girlfriend, or whoever she was, remained asleep.

Penny was going through the dresser, so I shuffled through the items on top of the side table. When I opened the drawer, Jayce stirred and I froze, but he didn't wake. The pill was still in the small baggy from Enzo, sitting right on top.

Grabbing it, I held it up for Penny and Mazie to see.

We backed out of the room, but the girlfriend groaned in her sleep, her eyes fluttering. Penny and Mazie kept moving, but I froze again.

When she seemed to settle back into a deep sleep, I backed the rest of the way out of the room, muttering, "Sweet dreams, asshole."

Once we were in the safety of the stairwell, we let out a collective breath of relief.

"Penny, can you hold it? Believe it or not, I don't have any pockets in this thing." I patted the body suit for emphasis.

She nodded, taking the pill, and slipped it into her jacket pocket.

The way back down the stairs was so much easier than the trek up had been. When we reached the bottom, we practically ran down the hall to the exit and threw open the door.

The sky was beginning to lighten.

"Who was that girl in there?" Mazie asked. "Didn't Jayce dance with *you* at the club? How could he?"

As much as I wanted to agree with Mazie, I hardly knew Jayce. He had every right to sleep with whomever he wanted.

"He only danced with me to steal the pill," I reminded her, discomfort swirling in my gut. Just because I barely knew Jayce, didn't mean I hadn't been creating endless romantic stories for us in my head, with the help of Mazie, that all came crashing down the moment I saw that demon in his bed.

I couldn't help but be disappointed, even if I was pissed at him for what he'd pulled at the club earlier.

"It's for the best. Now the two of you can move on to a new obsession," Penny teased.

Instead of going back to Mazie's, we separated, and Mazie went home while Penny escorted me to the mansion.

"I should talk to Dominic alone. I don't want him blaming you or Mazie for my choices tonight," I said to Penny.

She shook her head. "You don't need to protect us, Ember. We're the ones who are meant to keep *you* safe. So, if Dominic thinks we failed, then we deserve whatever punishment he doles out."

"No. I need to do this," I countered. "Otherwise, he'll think you did all the work and won't believe I'm capable of being an asset to the family business."

"Fine. I shall leave you to your fate, but make sure to text me once you're finished talking with Dominic. I want to know what he says."

We went in through the back door, not bothering to be quiet since Dominic wouldn't have anyone over that day. He didn't seem to be home yet, so Penny left me to obsess over what I would say to convince him to let me start working for him.

I grabbed a snack from the kitchen, noting that Maurice wasn't there. He was probably sleeping. My next priority was getting out of the bodysuit. It took me way too long to peel it off my body, but I succeeded and pulled on my sweatshirt and silk pajama shorts, which were far more preferable.

It was only once I was settled into bed, writing out a whole slew of different openers for my conversation with Dominic that I realized I'd forgotten to get the pill from Penny.

> **Me:** *PENNY YOU HAVE*
> *THE PILL!*
> *Can you bring it back here*
> *pretty pleaseeee I'll owe you!*

Penny: *Oh HELL*
Penny: *You're going to hate me...*
Penny: *There's a hole in my jacket pocket's lining ...*
But try talking to Dom without it
You're still a bad ass
and can tell him it's all my fault
we don't have the evidence

Well fuck. This would make my argument much weaker. But, like Penny said, I could do this. It was time for me to take a stand and *make* my brother listen to me. I'd proved to myself I was capable by getting that pill to begin with, now I needed to prove it to Dominic.

Maybe he'd give me a chance to get another pill from Enzo. Of course, another one would cost me, since only the first one was free. Not that we didn't have the money, but I hated the idea of giving business to a rival drug lord.

The front door slammed downstairs, and I jumped out of bed, running to the stairs to see Dominic storming through the foyer. Darkness seemed to cling to him and swirl around him as he moved, and I ducked out of sight. He was *not* in any kind of mood to hear about my dangerous exploits of the night. But if I didn't approach him before Jayce did, then I'd lose my advantage.

I could at least check on him and feel out whether he could handle my news or not.

Taking the steps two at a time, I headed for Dominic's meeting room where I'd seen him disappear. The doors were shut, and something thudded against the wall, followed by cursing.

Placing my hand flat against one of the doors, I leaned in and called through it, "Dom? Is everything okay?"

The movement inside stopped, and I wondered if he was waiting until I left. But the door creaked open, moving away from me as he opened it, looking eerily calm.

"Everything's fine, Ember, go back to bed," he said.

He started to shut the door, but I stuck my foot out, stopping it.

"Don't lie to me, Dom. I want to help you." I pressed my hand against the door, pushing it back open. He was already across the room, his hands in his hair as he paced behind the meeting table.

"What's going on?" I asked. "Did something happen at the auction?"

He huffed a laugh, slamming his hands down on the table, and hung his head. "Yeah. *Something* happened."

Taking a seat at the opposite end of the table, I straightened and put on my best serious face. If I wanted Dominic to let me help him with the family business, it started here.

"Tell me everything," I said.

A long, weary sigh preceded his explanation. "The auction was nothing more than an opportunity for Jericho to practically shove in my face that he's been getting away with selling in Southside territory for *months* now without being caught."

My lip curled. "Why would he do that? Why not *keep* selling under your radar instead of telling you?"

"That's what I can't figure out." He dropped into his chair at the end of the table. "I can't tell whether he wants me to retaliate and cause bigger issues, or if there's something else going on."

"What do *you* want to do?" I asked.

"Obviously I want to stop him, but that could mean playing into his game." Leaning back, Dominic stared at the ceiling.

"What if you don't make a move right away," I suggested. "What if, instead, we find out a little insider information. Like what he *wants* you to do, so we can do the opposite."

Sitting forward, he looked straight at me. "You keep saying *we* as if you're going to have anything to do with whatever I decide." He cocked an eyebrow and pursed his lips.

"About that," I drawled, smiling sheepishly. "I may or may not have already, unknowingly, started this process for you."

He threw his hands up. "What the fuck do you mean *unknowingly?* Ember, were you approached by one of Jericho's men?"

I twisted my hands in my lap. "I may have been the one doing the approaching."

"Fuck, Ember!" He ran his hand down his face. "Do you *want* to get yourself killed? Because that's what is going to happen as soon as they learn who you are!"

"They won't!" I leaned forward, slapping my hands on the table. "No one knows I exist; you made damn sure of that."

His eyes narrowed. "What's that supposed to mean?"

"*Grant.*" I drew out the name. "You killed him because he almost found out about me."

Dominic's gaze shot to the ceiling. "Can we not talk about this? I've told you time and again, I will do *whatever* it takes to keep you safe. What happened to Grant should come as no surprise to you."

I threw my hands up. "Shouldn't it? He was your *friend.* We may be demons, but I never thought we killed in cold blood."

"Then you're naïve and have no place in the family business," he stated bluntly.

That hurt like a punch to the gut. But I wouldn't let him deter me or talk me down again.

So, I dove into my story. "I met Enzo, whom I'm assuming is one of Jericho's men, at The Mausoleum last night and created an in for us. I got a pill from him, but Penny lost it. I can get another, though. He's expecting me to come back."

Dominic wouldn't look at me. He stared at the wall as he swiveled his chair to the right, away from me. "What do you expect me to say to that Ember? Good job? Get out there and get yourself killed? Because that's exactly what's going to happen."

"But if you have proof of Jericho selling in your territory, then people won't blame you for retaliating against him. It will keep our business in good standing and get Jericho back to where he belongs on the Westside. Because once the Eastside catches wind of what Jericho's doing, you know they'll jump at the opportunity to stir up trouble here again." I held my breath, waiting for his response.

"You don't know what you're talking about," he said.

I wanted to scream, but I remained calm. "Yes, I do, Dom. And you know it. Ever since Eastside killed our parents, and Lucifer helped you retaliate, they've been itching to get back in here. They keep testing your boundaries, seeing how far you'll let them go." I folded my hands on the table. "Like last year, at the Festival of Lilith, when they were selling in the crowds."

"Ember, stop," Dominic ground out. "You're not going to impress your way into this. I know what Eastside is doing every second of every day. They're small pawns in this game."

"I don't think so!" Putting my hands on the table, I pushed myself to my feet. "They may be more disorganized than us or Westside, but they're no less threatening to our business here. We need to deal with Westside quietly and swiftly before Eastside becomes emboldened."

"Ember, I swear to Lucifer—"

I scoffed, crossing my arms. "What's he going to do for you?"

"Let me handle this!" Dominic snapped.

"No. I'm done sitting aside and watching you fumble the business our parents worked so hard to build for us. You can either let me help, or I'll do it behind your back."

He turned in his chair, glaring at me.

The front door opened and slammed for the second time that morning, and loud footsteps stomped toward the meeting room.

For the first time ever, Dominic didn't yell at me to hide, or race to meet whoever entered before they'd see me. Instead, we remained locked in our stare down until Jayce stormed into the room.

He did a double take when he saw me standing opposite Dominic and stopped beside me.

"You," he spat, scowling. "What the fuck is this? What is she doing here?" He turned to Dominic who raised his eyebrows and returned his gaze to me.

"You two know each other?" Dominic asked.

"Hardly," I said before Jayce could get a word out. "He happened to be at The Mausoleum last night and tried to steal the pill from me after I got it."

"Wait, she's working for *you*?" Jayce asked, his brows puckering in disbelief.

I gave him a cocky grin.

"I thought I told you *not* to go to The Mausoleum last night," Dominic said to Jayce.

"I was already there when I got your text, trying to get the evidence I needed to prove Westside was selling there," Jayce explained.

Dominic waved his hand toward me. "And Ember beat you to it."

"Apparently. Though I did get the pill from her, and then she broke into my apartment this morning and stole it back." He turned to me and added, "I have cameras."

"Oops," I laughed. "Should have seen that coming. How was the Mrs. this morning? Not too upset you had to fondle me to get that pill from me?"

Dominic's stare turned lethal, but he said nothing. Jayce still didn't know exactly who I was, and I knew Dominic would want to keep it that way.

"I didn't even touch you," Jayce snapped.

He didn't deny the demon meant something to him or *was* someone to him.

"As much as I'd love to sit here and listen to the two of you bicker," Dominic cut in. "I have more important things to attend to, like *sleep.*"

Feigning a yawn, I nodded in agreement. I had way too much adrenaline pumping through me to actually be tired.

Pointing at me, Dominic said, "Jayce, meet your new partner. Ember, don't get him killed please."

"What? No!" Jayce argued.

"He's an asshole!" I chimed in.

Dominic gave me a look, and I backed down. This was my shot, and he wasn't giving me another one.

"Fine," I grumbled. "Does this mean I'm an enforcer now too?" Killing people wasn't at the top of my *must try* list but learning how to shoot a gun could come in handy.

"No," Dominic and Jayce said at the same time.

Jayce continued, "I don't trust her, how am I supposed to work with her?"

"*You* don't trust *me*?" I gaped at him. "You're the one who tricked me into dancing with you so you could steal from me! All while you have a girlfriend back home."

Jayce was starting to lose his appeal, maybe I'd be able to wipe out all those stupid stories I'd created in my head about him after all.

"You two need to work this out because it's happening whether you agree to it or not." Dominic stood. "I'll need you to bring me some actual evidence before we start trying to gain intel."

I cringed and felt Jayce's gaze on me.

"You don't have the pill you stole back from me?" Jayce asked, the judgment clear in his tone.

Scrunching my nose, I gave Dominic a death glare. "Well, not exactly. I gave it to Penny to hold onto, because my outfit was too tight for pockets, and she lost it." I had no shame pinning the blame on Penny.

Jayce huffed a laugh. "And you expect me to work with her?" he asked Dominic. "She's already fumbling."

"As I said. You two can work this out. I'm going to bed," Dominic said, striding past me and Jayce without sparing either of us a glance.

Jayce turned to me, scowling. "How did you even weasel your way into Dominic's crew? He's never mentioned you before and now suddenly, after I see you with one of Jericho's men, you're here. How do I know you're not a spy for Jericho?"

I lifted a shoulder. I didn't care much about what he thought. "I guess you'll have to *trust me,*" I sneered.

"Which I don't."

"Not my problem." Turning on my heel, I strode from the room. As I approached the stairs, I realized I couldn't go up them or else Jayce would wonder why I wasn't leaving. He couldn't know I lived there. So, I angled for the front door instead.

"Is that what you wear to a business meeting?" Jayce asked as he followed me across the foyer.

I glanced down at my sweatshirt and shorts. "You saw what I was wearing last night and this morning on your cameras. My body needed a break from being constricted."

I thought I caught him smirking out of the corner of my eye.

"So, you don't wear shoes?" he asked.

I looked down at my white painted toenails and cursed inwardly. "Um, I must have left them—"

"It's okay, you can admit you're sleeping with the boss. Why else would he let you work for him without going through all the hoops he made all his other runners go through?"

"Oh my god! NO!" I shuddered and made a gagging noise. "Ew, ew, ew."

Jayce laughed. "I'm sure Dominic would love to hear how disgusting you think he is."

I shook my head vigorously. "Trust me, he'd say the same of me. We're friends nothing more."

"Hm. Whatever you say."

"I'm going to find my shoes." I turned and headed back the way I'd come. I knew there'd be no shoes in the meeting room, but hopefully Jayce would leave quickly.

"I'll see you tonight at eight o'clock," Jayce said.

I turned back. "Why?"

Jayce lingered in the doorway and said, "Because if you were listening, we're partners now, and we have work to do. Where should I meet you?"

"Oh." I let out a huff. "Um, Bellerose Apartments down on—"

"I know where they are. See you tonight."

Chapter 8

Jayce

At least I knew where I'd recognized Ember from. If she was friends with Dominic, I'd probably seen her around before. But now I was stuck with her as a partner after she stole my chance to prove to Dominic I wasn't wasting my time at The Mausoleum. Not that he thought I was, but I hadn't had anything to show for weeks of frequenting that club, and Ember had swooped in and ruined everything.

On top of that, she'd broken into my apartment. What kind of ...

Deep breaths, I reminded myself. *Don't let her get to you.*

If Dominic truly trusted Ember and thought we could accomplish this mission together, then I'd do my best to work with her. But if she jeopardized the mission in any way, I'd make sure she never worked for Dominic again.

Victoria was gone when I returned to my apartment, and I couldn't help but imagine Ember standing in my bedroom, seeing Vic and I together. I'd lied when I told her I had cameras in my apartment. It wasn't a hard guess as to who would have stolen the pill from me, since Ember was the only one who knew I had it.

What was baffling was how she got in. I'd make sure to question her about that, but first I'd be changing my lock combinations and installing better security.

After a decent day's sleep, I woke to my alarm at six p.m. I had two hours before I had to be at Ember's place. For some reason, the thought of being alone with her for the first time made me tense and a little anxious. The fact that killing people never made me nervous, but Ember did was baffling.

I pulled on a pair of dark blue jeans and a plain black button up, rolling the sleeves to my elbows. It was my outfit of choice when I wasn't wearing my cut. Not too casual, but not too formal. I never knew when I had to be on my game in this business, and the black helped disguise any blood spatter.

My hair was easy enough to deal with, the waves taming with minimal product and a quick run of my hands through it. Most days I didn't bother with the product, but this was a business meeting, so I felt it warranted a little extra care.

It had nothing to do with the fact that I was seeing Ember. I had no further feelings toward her other than annoyance and suspicion.

I picked up my phone as a text came in.

Unknown: *It's Ember - my apartment is number 407 - top floor!*

Clenching my jaw, I chose to ignore how my pulse ratcheted up at the sight of her name. I typed out, *About to head out, see you soon,* and then deleted it. It sounded too friendly. I didn't want her to get the wrong idea. So, I sent a thumbs up instead.

I could have walked to Ember's apartment, it was so close, but I drove my Hellcat and parked on the street. It was too fucking hot outside to be walking anywhere.

When I reached the front door, I texted Ember to let her know I was there, and she buzzed me in. Unlike my apartment that took up the whole top floor of my building, Ember's was one of many on the top floor.

I stepped off the elevator, and number four hundred and seven was directly across from it. When I knocked, Ember opened the door and turned away quickly, letting me come in and close the door behind me.

She was dressed in jeans and a T-shirt, which was much different than anything else I'd seen her in. It still looked annoyingly good on her.

Glancing around, I noted the apartment was small, but the layout was not so different from mine. The kitchen and living room were one big area, but she had a door leading to what I assumed was the bedroom.

I cleared my throat, trying to ease some of the tension, and said, "This is where you live."

"Is there a problem with that?" Ember asked, stopping behind the kitchen counter and turning to me.

I didn't answer, taking a seat on one of the stools on the other side of the counter.

"What's so important this couldn't have been a text?" Ember asked, crossing her arms.

"I've been keeping an eye on The Mausoleum since it opened. Clubs pop up all the time around here, but something about this one seemed off," I explained.

"And you realized Jericho is having Enzo sell from inside the club?" she asked.

I frowned, not liking that she had more information than I did. "Enzo?"

"That's who I got the pill from. Jeez. One night and I'm already way more on top of this than you." She scrunched her nose. "Are you sure you're up for this task?"

"Buying drugs from these guys is easy. Getting information from them is a whole other story," I said, trying to hide my annoyance. "We're going to have to be extremely careful not to tip him off that we're onto him, or else he'll be gone, and we'll have to start from scratch."

"Easy enough. He thinks my name is Mazie, and that's all he knows about me. I'm pretty adept at hiding my identity." She dropped her gaze to the counter and bit her lip.

"Getting evidence on this guy isn't enough," I continued. "We need to know exactly what Jericho's plans are and why he's selling in Southside territory. He never does anything without reason."

"Got it." She jerked her head in a severe nod.

I rolled my eyes. "You need to take this seriously."

"I am! It's not my fault you make it all seem so boring."

"I'm telling Dominic this isn't working out," I said, taking my phone from my pocket.

"No!" She reached across the counter, putting her hand over my phone. "I'm taking this seriously. I promise."

Where her fingers touched mine, my skin lit up, soaking up the sensation of *her*.

Working to control my breathing, I pulled my phone away and broke our connection. I set my phone face down on the counter and said, "Fine."

Ember smiled. "So, I'll be careful not to reveal too much to Enzo. I'm assuming we'll be paying him a visit tomorrow night?"

"If that works for you," I said. "We can head to the bar, and you can get another pill from him. If we can at least get that, we can prove it comes from Jericho. Those pills are his own creation." Each drug lord had their own signature concoctions along with the basics.

Ember nodded. "I had a feeling. I've never seen them around before."

"You spend a lot of time in the clubs?" I asked.

She pursed her lips. "Mm, I don't think that's any of your business."

"We're *partners*. It's important I know some things about you. Like how often you go out or meet other drug dealers in clubs," I pointed out. Any information she had that could give us an advantage would make this whole mission go more smoothly.

"I go out often enough," Ember said. "But no, I don't seek out drug dealers normally. Last night was an exception."

"Right." I found that hard to believe after she'd gotten into Enzo's good graces so easily.

"Do *you* go clubbing often?" she asked.

"No."

She stuck out her tongue and curled her lip. "This is why I don't want to share anything with you. What *do* you do for fun?"

I fought a smile. "That would be unrelated to our work, so officially not your business."

"Ew. If we're done talking, you can leave." Pointing at the door, she turned and strode to the living area, plopping onto the couch.

"I'll pick you up tomorrow at nine," I said.

"Make it ten. Don't want to seem too eager for Enzo." She waved as I walked out the door.

I could have sworn I heard her grumble, *asshole*, and I smirked. It would be better for everyone involved if she kept that perception of me. We were partners, and nothing more. Though, I wasn't sure who needed more convincing. Her, or myself.

Oliver waited for me beside my car, his arms crossed as he leaned against it, staring at the sky. He didn't wear his cut tonight, so his wings were on full display. They weren't nearly as big as Dominic's, so they could be tucked beneath his clothes like Ember did sometimes. *Shit.* I was already learning her habits and I hardly knew her.

"What are you doing here?" I asked, flipping my keys in my hand. "Stalking me now?"

Pushing off my car, he shrugged. "I was walking by and was curious why your car would be parked outside of a place like this." He flicked his gaze back to the apartment building. "You hardly ever park your car on the street, so I figured it had to be something worth risking your precious baby for." He ran his hand along the hood of my Hellcat.

"Where were you coming from?" I asked, ignoring his obvious jab.

"Bar down the street. But the real question is, where are *you* coming from? Hot date?" Oliver smirked.

Unlocking my car, I got in the driver's seat and Oliver hopped into the passenger seat.

"Sure, I can give you a ride," I said sarcastically. "You headed home?"

"Are you not going to tell me who lives in that apartment building?" Oliver frowned. "Because I'll keep asking until you do. You know I won't be able to stop thinking about it otherwise."

I started my car and pulled out of the spot, heading toward Oliver's house.

"If you must know, Dominic gave me a partner to help deal with a situation at The Mausoleum. I was meeting with her tonight to discuss the logistics of our assignment," I explained. Knowing Oliver, he'd be confirming it all with Dominic, because he couldn't stand being lied to or being left out of the loop.

"*Her?* Who is she? Someone I know from the usual group?" Oliver was practically bouncing in his seat.

"Her name is Ember, and she's a friend of Dom's apparently. Though I'd never met her until a few weeks ago."

"You've been working together for *weeks?*" Oliver gasped. "And you didn't tell me until now?"

Groaning, I shook my head. "No. I met her a few weeks back, that night you and I went to The Mausoleum. I didn't see her again until last night, when Dom made us partners."

"Oh." Oliver let out a long breath. "Good. So, Ember, eh? Sounds cute, is she cute?"

Gorgeous, I thought. But I said, "She's annoying."

"Well, I'll have to meet her. She's not friends with Dom on Hellbook, so I can't find anything out about her that way," he said.

I glanced over at his phone as he searched for her online. A part of me wanted him to find her so I could know more about her. But another, stronger part of me didn't want him to find her because then he'd get to know her before I did.

I shook my head, refocusing on the road. None of that should bother me. But I couldn't help the relief I felt when he put his phone away, unsuccessful in his search.

"You have to let me come with you on one of your runs with her," Oliver said. "My life is boring right now without any hits. Let me live through you."

"That sounds more like you mooching off my own excitement," I pointed out, turning down Oliver's street.

"So, you admit, she's exciting, not annoying. I knew you weren't telling the whole truth," he said, poking my bicep.

"That's not what I meant, and you know it. Trust me, she's annoying."

I pulled my car into Oliver's driveway. His house was small, but gaudy. There were gargoyles on the roof, a wrought iron fence surrounding his backyard, and other gothic touches.

"Whatever. I'll meet her eventually." Oliver opened his door and climbed out, sticking his head back in to say, "Thanks for the ride," before slamming the door shut.

My phone buzzed with a text, and I pulled it out.

Dom: *Eastsider down on Perkins st.*
Goes by Trent, purple demon with
green hair.

Excitement shot through me. My first hit in weeks. I almost called Oliver back to come with me, because I knew he was itching for a kill too, but this one was mine. If Dominic had wanted Oliver to take care of it, he'd have texted him instead.

Revving the engine, I pulled out of Oliver's driveway and sped down the street. Perkins Street was on the other side of Southside, but I could make it there in less than fifteen minutes if there weren't too many people on the road.

It was always hit or miss that time of night, since it was when most demons were out and about, but a lot of demons in Southside walked rather than drove. Most cars on the roads were ride shares and easy to swerve around.

I parked my car a block away from Perkins Street and double checked my glock was fully loaded. It wouldn't take more than a single bullet, but I liked to be prepared for any scenario.

Most likely, Trent wasn't alone, but he was my primary target. Take him out, and the rest would scatter and spread the word not to encroach on Southside territory again. It always worked for a little while, and then the threat was pushed to the back of their minds, and they'd try again. It kept me employed, at the very least.

There were a few clubs on Perkins Street, so the sidewalks were bustling, which was the perfect cover for me. I blended in with the crowd, and once everyone heard a gunshot, they'd scatter, and I could get lost in the shuffle. Anonymity was key when it came to my job. If no one saw you coming, then they wouldn't fight back or run.

I kept my hands in my jean pockets as I walked, scanning the area for any purple demons with green hair. It was a combination that should stand out among the rest.

Spotted. Standing in the shadow of one of the clubs, a tall, lanky demon with green hair smoked a cigarette while another demon beside him chatted with what I assumed was their next customer.

I watched and waited while they made their deal, and the assumed customer handed over a wad of cash, too big to be for a single pill. The green haired demon took over, waving their customer down the alley.

Moving across the street so I could get a better look, I walked past the alley as if I was another club patron. I made it to the club door as Trent and his customer returned from wherever they'd gone, and she walked away with a smile on her face.

He was definitely my target. So, I passed the club and walked to the crosswalk, waiting for a big group to cross with me, and stayed with them as they walked parallel to the entrance of the alleyway.

I slipped into an alcove where I wouldn't be seen and pulled out my glock from the waistband of my jeans. Trent had resumed his position leaning against the side of the club with his cigarette hanging from his lips. I took aim and fired, and he dropped.

As I'd guessed, chaos broke out and I was able to slip into the next crowd that passed by without any issues. There were no police to contend with in Hell, so I had no worries about that. I simply had to remain discrete so the other sectors wouldn't know who to look for when trying to find Dominic's enforcers. Once an enforcer's identity was leaked, they became a target. Take out the enforcers, and it makes it much easier to sell in rival territory.

When I got back to my car, I texted Dominic that Trent had been taken care of and headed home. I felt more relaxed than I had in a while, as if pulling the trigger had released some built-up tension in me. Until my thoughts turned back to Ember, and the tension returned.

Chapter 9

Ember

The next night, I got ready at Mazie's apartment. It was the first time I'd be going out without her or Penny, and I was terrified and excited at the same time.

Standing in front of Mazie's closet in my underwear, I stared blankly at the clothes.

"Do you want me to be there, just in case?" Mazie asked, watching me from where she sat at the bar in her kitchen.

Shaking my head, I said, "No. I can handle this. I have to prove to Dominic I can do this."

I'd avoided telling Penny too much about what had happened with Dominic because I didn't want her to worry. Mazie was a worrywart enough, but Penny could be weird about me going out in public. So, to save her from herself, I decided I'd tell her about my first mission *after* the fact.

"Well, I'm only a text away if you need anything. I'll be catching up on some paperwork tonight," she said, and went back to typing on her computer. She worked for an organization in charge of overseeing demons who visited Earth and was always dealing with disgruntled demons who'd been rejected for visitation.

Pulling a black slip dress from Mazie's closet, I held it out to her. "Can I wear this? I'm thinking skintight isn't the vibe for my first night of work."

She giggled. "But lacy satin is? Not that I'm saying no. It will look great, and Enzo will most likely ask you to join his entourage while you're wearing that."

"Sold. That's exactly what I need. I need him to spill all of Jericho's secrets to me."

"Then grab those boots right there," she said, pointing to a pair of black thigh high stocking boots. "You won't even have to say a word and he'll spill anything and everything." She winked. "Here, let me steam the dress for you."

I laid it on the couch and sat down to pull on the boots.

Mazie plugged in her steamer and hung the dress off her curtain rod, peering out the window as she did. "Ooh! Jayce is here!"

A few seconds later the doorbell rang, and Mazie buzzed him in from her phone.

"Do you think his girlfriend will mind you two being partners?" Mazie asked.

"Not my problem," I said. I could only worry about one demon at a time, and that night, my focus was solely on Enzo and getting any information from him that I could.

The knock on the door announced Jayce's official arrival, and Mazie waved to me to get it as she picked up the steamer.

I strolled to the door and opened it, not bothering to greet him before strolling back to the couch and dropping down onto it.

"Welcome to our abode," Mazie chirped. "Sorry for the mess, Ember gave me short notice that we'd be having a guest."

Jayce seemed to be on edge standing in the doorway and avoided looking at me. He wore black jeans and a black button up with the sleeves rolled up to his elbows. I hated to admit he looked as sexy as ever.

"Is everything okay? Or are you going to stand in the doorway the whole time?" I asked.

"Do you always answer the door wearing *that?*" He waved a hand at me but refused to look.

Mazie burst out laughing and cursed as she got hit with a bit of steam. "Damn steamer."

Leaning forward and resting my elbows on my knees, I cocked my head to the side. "What's wrong Jayce? I've fully embraced my sexuality and I'd walk down the street like this if I wanted. Do you have a problem with that?"

He met my gaze. "If it doesn't bother you, then it's fine by me." Closing the door behind him, he walked to one of the barstools and perched on it.

"All done," Mazie said, breaking the tension in the room. She held the dress out to me, free of wrinkles.

Slipping it over my head I shimmied into it.

"Bra or no bra?" I asked Mazie. She studied me, pursing her lips as she considered.

"No bra. The straps stand out too much."

I turned so she could unhook my bra for me and slid it off and out of my dress, flipping my curled hair off my shoulders. It was long enough to be annoying again.

"Ready," I announced.

Jayce was at the door before I could even grab my purse, clearly anxious to go.

"Don't get into too much trouble, you two," Mazie called after us.

Once the door shut, Jayce waved ahead of himself. "After you."

Jayce had his own car, so we didn't need to wait for a ride share, which was a first for me. Neither Mazie nor Penny had a car. I had been looking forward to riding his Harley, but I assumed that would draw too much attention. Enzo couldn't know who Jayce was.

Jayce had parked his car on the street outside of the apartment building, and he opened the passenger door for me.

"Are you trying to get on my good side or something?" I asked, not trusting the gesture.

"Just accept it," he said.

"So bossy," I muttered as I climbed into his, obviously well taken care of, shiny blue Hellcat. I only knew the type of car because Dominic used to have a very similar one. But Dominic was always getting new cars to make sure no one recognized him when he went out.

When Jayce got in the car, he started talking right away. "We need to be on the same page tonight," he said. "You're going to approach Enzo and get another pill, and then we'll hang out for a little while, so we don't arouse suspicion before we leave."

"Easy peasy," I said, pulling down the visor to apply my lip gloss with the help of the mirror. "Get Enzo to spill all Jericho's secrets and get out. Got it."

Jayce groaned. "No. Not tonight. We need him to trust you before he'll do that."

I cast him a side eye and laughed, flipping the visor back up. "Have you *seen* me tonight? I'm sure I can get a little more out of him than a single pill."

"I don't doubt it, but we need to play it safe."

"Bleh. Boring, but fine. Get the pill, get out. Got it." I wouldn't go out of my way to wrench any secrets from Enzo, but I would listen carefully to everything he and his crew said. Names of places and people would be helpful in figuring out other areas they were selling in Southside.

We pulled up to the club and Jayce paid for the valet to park his car.

I gripped my clutch purse and stood tall as I faced down my first night on the job. Jayce glanced back at me.

"Are you coming or what?" he asked.

When I caught up with him, he gave his name to the bouncer who let us in ahead of the rest of the line. I was getting a big head from always being let in like that.

Once we were in the actual club, we headed to the bar first. I figured we should grab a drink and do some mingling rather than head straight to Enzo, in case any of Jericho's other men were watching.

Jayce and I sat at the bar, sipping our drinks and killing time.

"So, how did you and Dominic meet?" he asked. Of course he wanted to go there first.

"I'm assuming you're going to find some excuse why this is work related, so I won't bother saying it's none of your business," I said, giving him a knowing look. He lifted his shoulder. "We've known each other since I was little. He's kind of like a brother to me." I figured I'd keep it as close to the truth as possible so I wouldn't slip up later.

"That explains why you were disgusted when I said I thought you two were hooking up." He laughed. "Makes sense, I guess. Why did you want to start working for him now?"

I took a long sip of my drink, thinking through my answer before saying, "It's something I've been considering for a while, but since I heard about the trouble going on with a dip in sales, I wanted to help. It's the least I could do after all he's done for me."

"Hm."

"How did *you* meet Dominic?" I flipped the questioning, even though I already knew the answer. I'd shared enough about myself, and I didn't want to reveal too much.

"My parents worked for his parents and they kind of forced us to be friends when we were younger," he said, chuckling.

A pang of jealousy shot through me. I'd never been allowed to have friends or play dates when I was little because people couldn't know I existed. So, my friends were Maurice and Serena until my brother hired Mazie and Penny.

"So, you and Dominic must be about the same age, then," I said.

"He's two years older than me. I'm twenty-nine." He paused taking a sip from his drink and then asked, "How old are you?"

I considered lying, and saying I was older than I was, but there was really no point. "Twenty-one."

"Not what I was expecting," he said, not giving away any sign of surprise.

"Why? Do I look older? Or younger?" I grinned and turned my head from side to side.

Rolling his eyes, Jayce said, "Not answering that."

I shrugged and hopped down from the barstool. "Fine. I have some seducing to do. See you on the other side."

Turning on my heel, I sashayed over to the curtained area. This time, the large demon with the horns was outside of the curtains. I flashed him with a pretty smile, and he let me inside, either recognizing me or assuming I was the type of demon his boss would want to see.

"Mazie," Enzo drawled, using the fake name I'd given him, his gaze raking me up and down. "I wasn't expecting to see you again so soon."

Biting my lip, I clasped my hands, pushing my chest out. "What can I say? I couldn't stay away."

The two female demons on either side of him weren't the same ones who'd been there the first night, but they seemed equally annoyed with my presence.

"Ladies." Enzo turned his head slightly to the demon on his right. "Give us a moment alone, please."

A thrill went through me. Without them around I had a better chance of getting information out of him. Or at least I could find a way into his inner circle.

Setting my clutch down on the table, I took a seat on Enzo's right, sitting close enough that our thighs pressed together.

I'd told Mazie he was conventionally attractive, but that wasn't even close. He was almost as attractive as Jayce. He wore a full suit, but it didn't hide the muscles underneath.

The hand that gripped his glass, of what I assumed was whiskey, or scotch, because he seemed that type, tightened for a moment. The veins and tendons bulging in a way that made me want to see his hand wrapped around me.

Fuck, Ember. Focus. I chastised myself.

Lifting his free hand, he brushed a knuckle across my cheek. "Are you here for more?"

"More?" I breathed, barely able to comprehend what was happening as my body heated and I leaned in closer.

"Mm." He smirked, knowing exactly the effect he was having on me.

Taking a deep breath, I nodded, not trusting myself to speak.

"What about your boyfriend out there? Does he also expect something?" His smirk slipped away, and his eyes darkened.

Thinking quickly, I put my hand on his thigh and my chin on his shoulder. "He's a little protective of me, but he likes to watch." I winked.

"Are you ..." He paused, clearly questioning my intentions. Hell, I didn't even know what they were anymore. But I couldn't fail my mission from Dominic this early on.

Tracing my lower lip with his thumb, he leaned in, and I closed the gap, pressing my lips to his. At first, I worried he might push me away, and then I'd have lost my chance at getting close to him, but instead, his hands gripped my waist, and he helped me to straddle him.

Enzo leaned to the side. "Draco," he called, and the large demon from outside poked his head through the curtains, not appearing surprised by what he saw. "Bring in the boyfriend."

My face heated and I put my arms over Enzo's shoulders, kissing him again to hide my reaction. If Jayce was smart, he would play along and not ask questions. This was a test, and Enzo would be watching Jayce closely, despite his hands being all over me.

"Here he is," Draco said.

"What—" Jayce started but stopped quickly.

Turning my head, I said, "I hope you don't mind I told him your secret. That you like to watch."

To Jayce's credit, he didn't react. Instead, he crossed his arms over his chest, leaning back against the far wall and jerked his head in a nod. "Carry on."

Enzo smirked and gripped my chin with his thumb and forefinger. "Eyes on me, Mazie," he demanded, and I obeyed.

I couldn't lie, knowing Jayce was watching, made the whole thing much hotter.

Grinding against Enzo, he hardened beneath me, and I hesitated, not sure how far we would take this. I was willing to go as far as I needed to, but a small part of me wanted my first time to be a *little* more ... Special, for lack of a better word.

"Boss, sorry to interrupt, but there's someone here to see you," Draco announced.

Enzo pulled away from me, sighing in resignation.

"Send them in," he said, sliding me from his lap and grabbing my clutch from the table. He opened it and dropped something inside, handing it to me. "Sorry to cut our fun short, but I'll be seeing you again." His gaze flicked to Jayce, and he smirked before kissing me.

I slid off the cushioned bench and Jayce stalked over, putting his arm around my waist and catching me off guard by digging his free hand into my hair and kissing me fiercely.

It was dizzying and I didn't want it to stop, but he broke away and pulled me from the curtained area before I could even catch my breath.

A gorgeous feminine demon wearing a suit much like Enzo's slipped through the curtains as we exited them. All I heard before the sound of the club drowned them out was Enzo asking, "What do you want, Celia?"

Jayce pulled me aside, away from the crowds near the bar and out of range of Draco.

"What was that?" I asked him, touching my fingers to my lips where I could still feel his lingering kiss.

"I should be asking you the same thing!" he retorted, his jaw taut. He was *upset.* "You were supposed to be getting drugs from him, not riding him."

I laughed and opened my clutch, showing him what Enzo had dropped inside. Two purple pills in a small bag, like the first had been.

Jayce's mouth snapped shut, but he didn't seem any calmer. "That wasn't the plan."

Shrugging, I said, "The plan changed."

He shook his head. "If we're going to be partners, we need to be on the same page."

"Well, we are now. And we got what we came for so, you're welcome." I flipped my hair and grinned. "Are we not going to talk about you kissing me, though? Because that was *not* part of my plan."

"I had to make sure Enzo believed I was actually your boyfriend. I'm sure you know what happens if he finds out you were lying."

"Right. Good thinking." I bobbed my head, trying to play off that his kiss hadn't rocked my world. "Should we dance? Or drink? Or both?" Without waiting for him to respond, I weaved through the crowd to the bar and ordered a shot of tequila.

Taking the shot helped distract me from all the crazy thoughts swirling in my mind.

Jayce came up behind me, placing his hand on my waist and whispering in my ear, "We're being watched." He feigned a teasing grin as his eyes flicked to Draco.

I turned into his touch and draped my arms over his shoulders, pressing my chest against him and looking up into his bright blue eyes. "What now?"

He ducked his head down into the crook of my neck and his breath tickled the sensitive skin there making goosebumps rise along my arms.

"We should probably report back to Dominic," he said.

Right. This was a job. I was supposed to be keeping a level head and proving myself to Dominic, not losing myself in fantasies.

Keeping his arm around my waist, Jayce led me toward the door. Once we were outside, he dropped his arm. The valet brought Jayce's car around, and when we were both inside, Jayce turned the music up loud enough that we couldn't have a conversation.

Clearly something was bothering him.

"We shouldn't tell Dominic about how I got the pills," I yelled over the music. It was some kind of punk-metal band I'd never heard but didn't mind. It reminded me of the music Dominic listened to.

The vein in Jayce's neck became visible for a second before he jerked his head in a nod.

"Is everything okay? You seem upset," I said.

He turned the music down. "I shouldn't have kissed you."

"Because of your girlfriend? I'm sure she'd understand it was part of the ruse." I wasn't entirely sure that was true, but I would think she might be more understanding knowing the whole story.

"What?" He shook his head, keeping his eyes on the road. "No. I don't have a girlfriend."

"So that beautiful demon in your bed the other night ..." My face heated.

"Not a girlfriend."

"Then why are you worried about kissing me? No one will find out, if that's what you're worried about." Enzo had been my first kiss, and Jayce my second, so it was possible I was a bad kisser and that's why he was regretting it.

He turned the music back up and I surmised it was the end of our conversation.

Staring out the window, I let out a sigh of relief as we pulled up to the mansion. Of course, after we updated Dominic and gave him the pills, I'd have to let Jayce bring me back to Mazie's to keep up *that* ruse.

It was weird walking up to the front door of the mansion and using the doorbell. Maurice opened the door, letting us in, and acting as if he hardly knew me. Dominic must have told him about my newfound status. I felt a little guilty I'd been too busy to tell him myself.

Dominic met us in the meeting room, taking his usual seat at the head of the table.

Jayce and I sat in two empty chairs on the opposite end of the table.

"How did the night go?" Dominic asked.

In answer, I pulled the bag with the two pills from my purse and slid it down to the end of the table.

"And I think I have an in with Enzo," I said. "The next time I see him; I'll try to get some information out of him about other locations they might be selling. Though, a demon named *Celia* went in to see him after I left."

Tilting his head, Dominic said, "I'm pretty sure that's the club owner's name. I'll look into it." He turned his attention to Jayce. "Were you satisfied with Ember's performance tonight, Jayce?"

I nearly choked on my spit and had to cough to recover. Dominic gave me a look but didn't comment on my reaction.

Jayce cleared his throat and nudged my boot under the table. "She did well. Enzo suspected nothing."

Oh, right. That performance. My job *performance.*

Breathing in and out slowly, I returned my heart rate to normal.

"Perfect." Dominic folded his hands on the table. "Then you two will continue working together on this. I'd like to have it wrapped up within a few weeks. Jericho will grow suspicious if we don't respond in some way before then."

"Will do," Jayce said.

Chapter 10

Jayce

Fuuuuck.

I was in over my head.

Sitting in my car outside Ember's apartment after dropping her off, I stared blankly at the road. I considered what would happen if I let myself go down this treacherous path I'd veered onto by kissing Ember.

Not only was Ember eight years younger than me, but she'd said Dominic was like a brother to her. Which meant he would most likely kill me if he ever found out what had happened that night.

So, it couldn't happen again. I needed to distance myself from her. When I was home, and far enough away from Ember that I could think straight, I texted her.

> **Me:** *We'll skip a night at the club. Enzo will get suspicious if we keep coming back night after night*

That way I could have a night away from her, hopefully finding someone else to occupy my thoughts. But the way she'd melded to my body when I kissed her ...

Jesus, stop thinking about her, I chastised myself.

When I'd seen her on top of Enzo, I could have torn the whole club apart. I'd never been consumed by so much jealousy and rage before over anyone. Victoria told me about her dates or outings with other demons all the time, and it never bothered me.

And then there was the way Ember had opened the door at her apartment in nothing but her underwear and those boots. I'd never seen anything as stunning as that image. It was burned into my brain, and I was getting hard just thinking about it.

Fuck. I needed something to take my mind from her pronto.

Calling Oliver, I waited three rings until he picked up.

"Did you read my mind?" Oliver asked. There were voices and music in the background, meaning he was most likely at a bar. "I was wondering how your first night with your new partner was going."

"You seriously need to get your own life," I joked. "Where are you? I need a drink." I ran a hand down my face.

"I'm at Fever Dream. What was that?" His voice moved further away, and he laughed as he talked with someone. "Sheila says she'll have a mule waiting for you," he said when he came back on the phone.

"And a shot or two," I requested. "I'll be there in five."

"Oof, rough night?" Oliver asked, but I hung up without answering. He'd be hounding me when I arrived, so there was no point dealing with him over the phone too.

Oliver was my best friend, other than Dominic, but he grated on my nerves most days. Weirdly enough, I didn't mind because I knew he only did it because he cared. If he suddenly stopped pestering me, I'd know something was wrong.

There was no valet at Fever Dream, unlike The Mausoleum, so I parked in the back lot.

"There he is!" Oliver cheered when I walked through the door.

The dim lighting helped to disguise the fact that the place needed some serious renovations. There was low music playing, but the chatter from the patrons almost drowned it out.

In the back left corner, there were two pool tables, and to the right, a couple dart boards.

"I saved you a seat," Oliver said, patting the barstool beside him. There were two shots and a mule waiting for me, as promised. I downed the shots before sitting.

Sheila sidled over and flung her cleaning rag over her shoulder before leaning on the bar in front of me. "Rough night?" she asked.

"Something like that," I mumbled, lifting the mule mug to my lips and taking a sip. It was a strong one, and I nodded to her in thanks. "This is perfect."

My phone buzzed in my pocket, and before thinking, I pulled it out, groaning when I saw Ember's name on the screen.

Ember: *Fine. But we should
really discuss our fake personas
Like who are we as a couple?
Do you even have a name?*

Oliver peered over at my phone and attempted to snatch it away, but it was in jest. "Partner problems already? Need me to step in and take over for you?"

The thought of Oliver kissing Ember popped into my mind, and I tightened my grip on my mule.

"No," I snapped. "I mean, we're not having problems, it's ... Complicated."

Oliver groaned. "Jayce, you know I love complicated. Come on, give me the details before I have to beg for them." He winked, and the insinuation was not lost on me.

Oliver had asked me to join him in bed on multiple occasions, and though I'd never taken him up on the offer, I knew it was always on the table.

Shaking my head, I typed out a response to Ember.

> **Me:** *Give me any name*
> *I couldn't care less*

Maybe it was rude, but I needed to make sure to draw a thick, uncrossable line. We couldn't become more than partners.

Ember: *Mazie dated a Brock a few months back that seems like an overprotective boyfriend kind of name*

> **Me:** *Brock it is*

Ember: *Do we live together?*

> **Me:** *No*

Ember: *How long have we been together?*

Me: *Three months*

Ember: *Ok. And how far
are we willing to go?*

I paused, lifting my gaze from my phone to find Oliver
staring at me.

"I've never seen you so engrossed in your phone before.
What's happening to you?" He smirked. "You said her name
was Ember, right?"

I lay my phone face down on the counter and nodded.

"I *need* to meet this demon." Oliver sipped his beer and
pointed to my phone. "What are you two talking about?"

"Logistics," I said. "We—" My phone vibrated, shaking
the glasses on the bar. It vibrated a steady rhythm, meaning I
had an incoming call. *She wouldn't.*

Oliver picked up my phone and showed me the screen.

"She can't seem to get enough," he said, pressing the
answer button before I could stop him. "Good evening," he
drawled.

Reaching out, I tried to wrestle the phone from his grip,
but he ducked out of the way and danced out of reach.

"I'm Oliver, Jayce's best friend. Don't let him convince
you otherwise, there's no one else."

I chugged my mule. If I had to endure this, I'd be doing
it as far from sober as possible.

"Tell me about yourself, Ember, because Jayce has been
tightlipped every time I try to ask him about you." Oliver's
brows raised. "Oh really? Tell me more." Holding my phone
out to me, Oliver said, "She wants to talk to you. Go figure."

"I'll kill you," I said to Oliver before taking my phone
and pressing it to my ear. "Hello?"

"Hi," Ember said. For the first time, she sounded unsure. "I wouldn't have called if I'd known you were busy. I assumed you'd be at home, I guess."

An image of her in that black slip dress flashed in my mind and I wondered if she was still wearing it. I readjusted in my seat and cleared my throat.

"It's fine. I'm at Fever Dream with Oliver, so I'm not busy."

"I've never been there. But Oliver seems like fun! You'll have to introduce us some time." The uncertainty had disappeared from her voice. "That's not why I called though. You didn't respond to my text, and I wanted to make sure you didn't think I was trying to pressure you or anything. I meant how far we were willing to go with Enzo. Like I'm fine going as far as it takes, but I don't know—"

"Absolutely not," I snapped, but then I remembered who we were and that this was all a part of our mission. The alcohol was starting to go to my head. "I mean, you shouldn't have to do that."

"I appreciate your concern, but I can handle myself," Ember said. The sound of fabric brushing against fabric came through the phone and I assumed she was in bed.

She could be in my bed if I wasn't trying so hard to keep her at arm's length, I thought, immediately cursing myself for it.

"We should talk about this later," I said. *Talking about this is not doing me any good right now.* I hoped it was dark enough in the bar that no one would notice the bulge growing in my jeans.

"What does that mean? Not doing you any good?" Ember asked. I'd said the quiet part out loud on accident.

Shit, what did Sheila put in that mule? It was hitting me harder than most drinks. Even with the two shots, I could normally go a lot longer before I became so out of sorts. It might also have something to do with who I was on the phone with, but I refused to believe she could have such an effect on me.

"Sorry, I was talking to Oliver. I'll call you later, okay?" I didn't even know where Oliver had gotten to. He wasn't anywhere in my line of sight.

"Okay. Talk to you later, then." She hung up and I let out a sigh of relief.

"You lied to me," Oliver said, dropping back into his seat.

I slammed my hand on the counter and gasped, "Jesus, Olly. Where the fuck did you come from?"

Laughing, Oliver shook his head. "As if I'd go far enough that I couldn't hear your every word?"

"Right. So, what is it I lied about?" I asked.

"She's *hot.* I could tell from her voice." He pumped his eyebrows.

"I never said she wasn't, I said she was annoying," I reminded him. "And how can you tell from her voice?"

"It was the way she said my name, all seductress like." He narrowed his eyes and smirked. "I could tell from that, and the nudes she sent me." Taking his phone from his pocket, he shook it in front of me, and as if on cue, Ember's name came up on the screen.

I snatched his phone from him. "What the fuck?" I yelled, though the bar was loud enough no one even glanced our way.

Oliver leaned back on his stool, gripping his sides as he laughed. "Oh my god, you've got it bad for this demon," he gasped between fits of laughter. "Go ahead and look at the message."

Grinding my teeth, I glared at Oliver. Curiosity got the better of me and I opened the message from Ember.

Ember: *Does Jayce know you stole my number from his phone? Should I be concerned?*

I threw the phone at Oliver, and he caught it against his chest.

"You're fucking crazy. Don't text her again," I said. "I mean it. She's close with Dom and he'll kill you if he finds out you're messing with her."

Oliver's smile faded and he glanced down at his phone. "Shit. You think she'll tell him?" He shook his head and shrugged. "Dom won't hurt me. He'll make you do it, and we both know how that would go." His smile came back, and I wanted to slap it off his face. But Oliver was right: I didn't have it in me to hurt him.

"She doesn't know you and she's going to think you're a stalker or something. If you scare her too bad, she might quit, and I'll lose my partner." Though, maybe that was exactly what I needed. "On second thought, text her all you want."

"Oh no, I'm not scaring her off until I have the chance to meet her. You think my curious mind could handle never seeing her after she got you all in a tizzy?" He cast his eyes down to my crotch and I groaned inwardly.

"Fuck off. It's been a while. Vic's been busy with work, and I haven't seen in her weeks," I grumbled, not sure why I felt like I needed to justify myself to him, and it wasn't even true. I'd seen Victoria earlier that week.

"Say the word and I can—"

"No, Olly. We're not going there," I said, holding up my hand to stop him.

"Can't blame me for trying." He winked at me.

"I can, actually. I think I'm gonna head home." Pulling out my wallet, I left a few bills on the counter. "See you next time, Sheila," I called to her. She waved from the other end of the bar.

"Don't worry, I won't steal your girlfriend," Oliver said. "Unless she asks me to."

I rolled my eyes and left. I'd had my fill of Oliver for the night. Sometimes I wondered if he ever got on his own nerves with his antics.

Chapter 11

Ember

Mazie stared at me, grinning. I'd had my phone on speaker while talking with Jayce and she'd been hanging onto every word.

When Jayce dropped me off at Mazie's, she'd been practically foaming at the mouth, bouncing in her seat waiting for all the details of my night. Her jaw dropped when I told her about my interaction with Enzo, and then she dramatically slid to the floor, pretending to die, when I told her about Jayce *watching*. I left out the kiss with him.

"It's not fair you get to do all this under my name, while I'm actually cooped up working at home alone," she'd said.

So, I'd started texting Jayce with her and then called him. As much as I wanted to say I did it to placate Mazie, I'd wanted to hear his voice again.

When Oliver texted me, I wasn't all that surprised. From our one conversation I'd gathered he was either super protective of Jayce, or super nosy. Either way, I could respect that. So, I responded before going to bed.

When I woke in the afternoon, Mazie brought me home so I could shower and get ready. I was meeting Penny for an early dinner at one of our favorite spots, Tastes of Southside. It had been killing me I hadn't told her what I was up to, but I planned on updating her on everything.

She beat me to the restaurant, already at a table when Dominic dropped me off. It was something he never would have done before, but he was being a bit more lenient with all his former rules.

Penny and I almost matched, both wearing leggings and crop top sets, but hers was black, as always, and mine was light purple. Seeing her out of her usual bodyguard garb was jolting, but when I did, it felt like I was seeing the real her.

Taking a seat across from her at our little two-demon table, I waited for her to say something first.

"So?" she prompted. "What's the update?"

Our waitress popped over to our table at that moment, so we ordered our food and coffee, and then I started my story.

"Dominic is letting me work for him," I said, figuring that was as good a place to start as any.

Her eyes widened, but she didn't interrupt me.

"I went out with Jayce for the first time last night, and we were able to get two more pills from Enzo at The Mausoleum."

"Why didn't you tell me you were going out with him?" She didn't *sound* angry, but her pinched and taut features said otherwise.

"I didn't want to worry you. And a part of me thought you might try to talk me out of it," I admitted.

She sighed. "I probably would have." Her phone buzzed on the table, and she shot off a quick text before putting it back, face down. "Sorry. Tell me everything that happened."

So, like I'd recounted it all for Mazie, I recounted it for Penny. This time, though, I didn't leave out the kiss with Jayce at the end. I'd known Mazie would have made a whole thing of it, and I wasn't in the mood for that last night. But Penny would be more level-headed.

"Wait ... One more time. You made out with Enzo, in front of Jayce who proceeded to kiss you after, in front of Enzo?" Penny asked.

"Well, he said it was to make it look real that we're dating. But of course, afterward he told me he shouldn't have kissed me. So clearly, he regrets it." I toyed with the ends of my hair, twirling some of it on my finger.

"Yeah, it may have been a heat of the moment kind of thing. But, Ember, you've never kissed anyone before this." It wasn't a question. Penny knew everything about my life, down to my favorite brand of toothpaste.

We paused as our server placed our coffees in front of us.

"Well, no," I said. "But it's not a big deal. Enzo was a *great* first kiss. No regrets there." It was true, there wasn't a single part of me that regretted finally having my first kiss, no matter who it was with. I was thankful Enzo was at least a good kisser.

"If you're fine with that, then I won't let it worry me. Don't let him take any of your other firsts, though, okay?"

I shrugged. "I'm fine with doing whatever I have to do for this mission. I'm comfortable with who I am. When it comes to sex, so long as you both consent and feel good about it, why does it have to be a big deal?" I'd had plenty of time to think about it. *Too* much time. I was ready.

"You're not wrong, but still. Sometimes it's important to think about *who* you're doing it with. But if you want to go there with Enzo, don't let me hold you back." Penny wrapped her hands around her mug and sipped her coffee.

It wasn't that I *wanted* to go there with Enzo, but I'd be lying if I said I hadn't thought about it. He was a runner, or more likely a lieutenant, for Jericho, but if he wasn't, I didn't know if I'd have even given him the time of day. Not because he wasn't attractive, but because he wasn't the type of guy I normally gravitated toward.

If I was honest, Jayce fit that type better, despite their many similarities. Enzo came on much stronger than Jayce and had that overbearing kind of aura. I scrunched my nose thinking about it.

"I'll be careful, I promise," I teased. "And I won't do anything you wouldn't do."

Laughing, Penny said, "That's an awfully short list, but I appreciate the sentiment. Just, don't hide anything from me, okay? Even if you think I'll worry."

"All right. I'll be sure to tell you about all my upcoming ventures. We'll probably be going back to the club tomorrow. Jayce said it would be too obvious if we went back tonight."

Penny nodded. "He's right. At least he's smart enough to know that much. But the two of you should really get your story straight. If Enzo questions your relationship at all, you'll lose him. Even if he doesn't suspect you're working for Dominic, he won't be taking any risks."

"We've gotten a few details figured out, and Jayce said he'd call me to go over the rest." I pulled my phone out to see if

I had any missed calls, but there was nothing. Sighing, I put my phone back in my purse.

After eating, Penny walked me home. Dominic was out, and Maurice was taking a nap, leaving me alone once Penny left. It was strange to be back in my bedroom after everything that happened the night before. Being at Mazie's was becoming more *normal* for me. In my bedroom, it was almost like none of that other stuff had ever happened. It felt like I'd dreamt it all and was back to being stuck in the mansion.

Until my phone rang, and my two worlds collided. Jayce was facetiming me. In a panic, I ran to my bed, leaning against the headboard. There was nothing to give away that I was in the mansion rather than Mazie's apartment, but it was better to be safe.

Jayce's face popped onto my screen and before I could say anything, he was talking.

"Sorry, I didn't mean to facetime, and once I realized what I'd done, you were already answering." He ran a hand over his hair, ruffling it.

I smiled. "It's okay." He was always so *serious,* it was nice to see him more disheveled. Like he'd already seen me.

"Glad to see you're fully dressed this time," he commented, his gaze flicking to something off screen.

"I'm happy to undress for you, if that makes you more comfortable," I joked. "Though you're one to talk." His phone dipped low enough I could see his bare chest, with tattoos peeking from the corners of the screen on his pecs. I bit my lip.

He looked down as if he'd forgotten he wasn't dressed. "Oh, shit, yeah. Like I said, I wasn't meaning to facetime."

"Well, now we're even." Though I wouldn't mind if he dipped his phone camera a little lower ...

"Right. So, we needed to finish our conversation from last night," he said. He almost seemed like he didn't want to bring up the topic we'd been discussing, so I decided to rip off the band aid for him.

"The question of how far we're willing to go," I said.

His eyes narrowed slightly, and his jaw clenched.

"Like I said last night, I'm willing to go as far as I need to for this," I said, playing with the ends of my hair. "But preferably my first time won't be with Enzo."

"If things start to stray into that territory, I'll make sure to get you out before anything happens," he said. "Wait, *first* time?" His gaze snapped to mine from whatever he'd been looking at off screen.

"I could have fooled you, huh?" I teased, fluttering my lashes. "My brother always told me I'd be a great actress." My breath hitched when I realized my slip up.

"You don't need to do any of this if you don't want to, Ember," he said, not saying anything about my *brother* comment, thankfully. That could spiral quickly.

"I don't mind, honestly. Enzo was a great first kiss," I laughed.

Jayce dragged a hand down his face. "Jesus, Ember. Have you never left your apartment or something? I can't even imagine a demon like you never kissing anyone until *yesterday.*"

I furrowed my brow, irritated. "A demon like *me*? What's that supposed to mean?" I wasn't sure how to take that. "Just because I'm comfortable with my body and my sexuality doesn't mean I'm throwing myself at every guy I see."

Jayce sighed. "That's not what I meant."

"If there's nothing else we need to talk about, I have other things to do today," I said, my finger hovering over the end call button. Jayce had a knack for pissing me off.

"Ember, I didn't—"

"I'll see you tomorrow night." I ended the call.

Instead of stewing alone in my room, I went down to the kitchen to see what we had for food. I made myself a plate of leftover lasagna.

Maurice came in while I was eating.

"Good afternoon, Ember," he greeted me and went to the sink to start washing the dishes.

"Hi Maurice! Do you want an update on my newfound status as an official member of the Russo empire?" I couldn't help smiling. All I'd ever wanted was to be included in the family business.

Maurice nodded as he continued the dishes. "Tell me everything."

So, I did. I left out a few of the saucier details, not particularly wanting to share those with someone who was almost like a parental figure for me.

"And we're going back to The Mausoleum tomorrow night," I finished.

"It sounds like you're doing a great job. I'm proud of how far you've come in such a short time," Maurice said, turning to me.

Warmth flared in my chest. I'd never had someone tell me they were proud of me before. There'd never been an occasion to.

"Thank you," I said, beaming.

Once I finished eating, I went back to my room. Dominic was there, sitting at my vanity, when I arrived, which was surprising. I hadn't heard him come in, and he never hung out in my room, even when I was in it.

"You're never home now that you work for me," he said, a slight strain to his voice, despite his smile. "I don't know how I feel about it."

Flopping down on my bed, I lay on my stomach at the foot of it, facing him. "Don't worry, I'm in for the night."

"Good. Every time you're out I can't help but worry."

"You don't trust Jayce to keep me safe?" I asked, honestly curious how he felt about our partnership, even though he was the one who stuck us together.

"I've always trusted Jayce with my life, so I trust him to keep you safe as well. But he can't control everyone around you, or *you* for that matter," he teased. "So, I still worry."

We sat in silence for a minute. I considered our new dynamic, and even though I still had rules to follow, things were so much different. Better.

"Things are changing," I mused.

"Indeed, they are." Dominic stood and walked to the door. "I hope you're ready for it. You can always change your mind, Ember. I wouldn't fault you if you decided to walk away from the family business."

I stuck my tongue out at him. "Not happening, Dom."

He huffed a laugh and turned into the hall.

I texted Jayce the next night.

> **Me:** *I have to check in with Dominic tonight, you can pick me up at his mansion*

It wasn't that I didn't want to see Mazie, but it was easier that way.

I decided to keep my outfit simple and went with a basic little black strapless body-con dress, and my heeled combat boots. Thankfully Serena wasn't busy and helped me with my makeup.

Brock: *Pulling up now*

I'd put Jayce in my phone as the fake name I'd come up with for him in case Enzo saw my phone at some point.

I hurried down to the foyer with my clutch purse in hand. Dominic was in the kitchen with Maurice and promised to stay out of sight until we were gone. Otherwise, he and Jayce would get talking and could reveal things that might be contradictory to my story.

Jayce didn't bother coming inside, so I'd worried for nothing. Neither of us spoke while we rode to the club. There was still tension between us from the way we'd ended our last phone call.

We arrived at the bar and immediately something was wrong. The curtains to the VIP area were drawn wide open and a demon who was most certainly *not* Enzo occupied the table with a whole entourage of demons I didn't recognize.

"He's not here," I murmured.

Jayce stepped up beside me, letting out a long sigh. "We couldn't expect him to be here every night. That would draw too much attention."

"So, what now?" I deflated. I'd never prove myself to Dominic if I couldn't get the information we needed from Enzo. And I definitely couldn't do that with the key player missing.

"We come back tomorrow night," Jayce said.

"And if he's not here again?" I scrunched my nose. I didn't want to worry, but it was hard not to.

"Then we'll come back the next night. I've been doing this longer than you, Ember. They *always* come back to the hot spots."

"All right. So, what are we doing tonight? We can't just leave, in case one of his crew is here and recognizes us." I scanned the dance floor and the bar, but I didn't see anyone from Enzo's entourage. That didn't mean much though, my focus had been elsewhere when I'd been with him.

"I don't think we have to worry about that. Come on, let's get out of here." Jayce turned and led the way to the door. I cast a longing glance back at the dance floor but followed him.

When we were in his car he said, "I can bring you home now."

He meant Mazie's, which would have been fine, but she'd expected me to be out for a while and had someone over. And I couldn't go *home* because Dominic had invited a few friends over, also expecting me to be out all night.

"Mazie has someone over, otherwise I'd be happy to go home early," I said. "But I can always hangout in a bar for a few hours, I guess." Even though I'd promised Dominic I wouldn't go anywhere or do anything alone. Maybe Penny would be able to meet me out.

Jayce's phone buzzed in the cup holder and Oliver's name flashed on the screen. Groaning, Jayce picked it up and answered the call.

"What now?" he asked. It made me wonder if Oliver had been lying to me when he'd told me he was Jayce's best friend.

Jayce glanced over at me and then back at the road.

"Yeah, fine. Our night has taken a turn, so we've got nowhere else to be." Moving the phone away from his ear, Jayce asked me, "You okay with hanging out with Oliver at Fever Dream tonight?"

My heart raced. I'd never *hung out* with anyone besides Penny or Mazie. Excitement and nervousness warred within me.

"Yeah, that sounds good," I said.

He lifted the phone back to his ear. "We'll be there in ten." Dropping his phone back into the cup holder, his hand brushed the edge of my thigh. "Sorry," he mumbled.

I glanced at him, noticing a tinge of red on his cheeks. It was hard to tell in the dark if it was a flush or from the lingering red of the night sky.

He turned up the music before I could respond. It was a heavy metal band that time. There were very few metal bands I listened to, so it wasn't a surprise I didn't recognize the one playing.

"Who is this?" I yelled over the music, trying to make conversation despite the awkwardness in the car.

Jayce turned the music down on his steering wheel. "What?" he asked.

"Who is this?" I asked again, pointing to the radio. Normally it would say the name of the band on the screen, but Jayce must have turned his screen off, because it was black.

"Oh, Alpha Wolf. I can change it if you want, I know it's an acquired taste," he said, smirking.

I shook my head. "No, I kind of like it. Can I pick the next song?" I reached for his phone, and he nodded.

He had no passcode for his phone, which seemed strange. I didn't know anyone who didn't keep their phone locked. Opening the music app, I typed in one of my favorite heavy metal bands, Netherwalker. They only had a few songs, but I loved them. It was way out of my usual repertoire for music, but it was one of those songs I heard once and I couldn't stop listening.

"Dominic used to—" *Fuck.* I stopped midsentence, realizing my mistake. "I mean, Dominic mentioned he listened to heavy metal and I was curious, so I looked up some bands and I didn't hate it."

"You and Dominic are pretty close, huh? It's weird I've never heard him mention you."

"Well, we're not as close as you two are, I'm sure." I tried my best to remain casual so he wouldn't suspect anything.

Thankfully the song changed and distracted Jayce from our conversation.

"This is not what I would have expected you to put on." He laughed. "I love this song."

Grinning, I turned up the music. Mostly so we couldn't go back to talking about Dominic.

When we arrived at Fever Dream, I had to do a double take. It was a run-down dive bar I would never be allowed to go to. Penny and Mazie always made sure the places we went were 'safe.' I tried to convince them they were what made any place safe for me so we could try some new places, but they never agreed with me.

Jayce pulled into a small dirt lot behind the bar and when he turned off his car, there were no lights to see by. If I wasn't with Jayce, I'd be put off by the lack of illumination. But maybe that was the point. The cloak of darkness meant it was a great place to do any shady things that were frowned upon, even by Lucifer's standards.

"You're not planning on killing me here, right?" I joked, though I gripped my clutch tighter than necessary, trying to remain calm.

Jayce chuckled. "Are you scared, Ember? Do you want me to hold your hand while we walk inside?"

I looked at him, his face barely illuminated by the dashboard lights. "If you wouldn't mind, that would help, yeah," I said.

He blinked and sucked a breath through his teeth, making a quiet whistling sound. "Come on." Turning, he climbed out of the car.

I followed suit and had a mini panic attack when I shut the door and was met with nothing but darkness and somehow, even darker shadows. It seemed like even what little light the red sky usually provided didn't reach this place.

"Ember," Jayce said, much closer than I'd anticipated.

Jumping, I swatted him with my clutch. "Jesus, Jayce. I thought you were still on the other side." As tough as I wanted to seem, I'd still been sheltered my whole life in the mansion. This new freedom would take some time to get used to.

Jayce held his hand out to me, and I grabbed it a bit too quickly.

"Thank you," I mumbled. "I swear, I'm not usually this jumpy."

Jayce tugged my hand, and we started toward the bar.

"Are you afraid of the dark?" he asked.

"Not necessarily. I'm more afraid of the demons who might be hiding in the dark," I said, glancing left and right to make sure I hadn't accidentally summoned said demons.

"Have you taken self-defense classes?" he asked.

"No. I know a few basics, but nothing substantial," I explained. My brother had hired Mazie and Penny to keep me safe, so I was never taught how to keep *myself* safe.

Jayce furrowed his brow. "Seems like something you should learn, especially now that you're working for Dom."

"I guess so," I said. We paused outside the door to the bar.

"As much as I think you should stay far away from Oliver, he's a great self-defense teacher. He used to teach kickboxing and self-defense classes before he worked for Dom."

"You think he'd teach me?" I asked, excited at the idea of doing something *other* than going out to clubs or restaurants.

"I'll ask him." Jayce pushed open the door.

Fever Dream was nothing like any other bar I'd been to. The lights were low, there was rock music playing from a jukebox, and there were pool tables and dart boards. I'd always wanted to learn to play darts. We had a pool table in the mansion, so I knew how to play, but once Dominic got too busy to play with me, I stopped playing altogether.

All the tables were full, but there was only one demon at the bar. He was chatting with the bartender, a short, stocky demon with gray, frizzy hair and dark brown eyes.

"Here we go," Jayce said, letting go of my hand and walking toward the one patron at the bar. "Oliver, meet Ember." He waved a hand toward me and Oliver swiveled on his stool to look at me.

I vaguely recognized him from the times I'd watched people leaving the mansion from my window. He was much more attractive up close. He was a darker shade of red than me, and his hair was black, like Dominic's, but shorter. His tail twitched behind him, spade-tipped like Mazie's.

"Ember," Oliver said, grinning. "Welcome to Fever Dream."

I glanced between him and Jayce. It was interesting that Jayce had said Oliver was the better fighter when Jayce was more muscled. Going by looks, I would have put money on Jayce winning in a match, but that proved how little I knew about physical fitness.

Stepping up to the bar in front of Jayce, I faced Oliver. "Nice to meet you, officially," I said.

"And you," Oliver said. "I'm surprised, really. Jayce made it seem like you were so unattractive he was embarrassed to be seen with you."

"Oh, fuck off, Oliver," Jayce snapped. I glanced back at him and cocked my eyebrow.

Oliver's hand came up under my chin and he lightly turned my face back toward him. "Don't worry, I didn't believe him for a second."

Jayce's hand struck out around me, gripping Oliver's wrist. "Don't fucking touch her."

"Oooh." Oliver lifted both of his hands in the air, leaning back on his barstool. "I see how it is." He winked at me.

Jayce cleared his throat. "I meant unless she says it's okay."

I pursed my lips, trying to hide my smile. Taking a seat on the stool between Oliver and Jayce, I crossed my legs, trying to ease the ache between them from the way Jayce's words had turned me on.

"Sheila," Jayce called to the bartender, and she came over to us from the other end of the bar. "Can I get a mule? And whatever she wants."

I perked up. "I'll have a mule too, please."

"Which type? You can be basic, like Jayce, and get a Moscow Mule, or switch it up," Sheila offered, waving a hand to the line of liquors behind her.

"What type is it if I want rum instead of vodka?" I asked. I'd always preferred rum over vodka.

"If it's dark rum, a Dark an' Stormy. You want that?" She grabbed a mule mug and a highball glass from beneath the counter.

I nodded. "Yes, please."

Oliver sipped his beer and leaned closer to me. "How do you like being partnered up with Jayce?" he asked.

"Fine," I said. I assumed Jayce hadn't told Oliver about our kiss, because we'd agreed to keep it from Dominic, and Oliver seemed like a gossiper. "He's a little bossy sometimes."

Oliver laughed. "He is! I'm glad I'm not the only one he likes to boss around." He peered around me to Jayce. "Don't let him think he's won, though, or else it will go to his head."

"All right, I think we're done talking about me when I'm *right* here," Jayce said.

Sheila placed our drinks down and Jayce grabbed his, leaving his seat. "I'm going to play some pool."

"Oh!" I turned and hopped off my seat, grabbing my drink, too. "Can we play darts instead? I've never played before."

Oliver walked ahead of us, looking back to say, "Darts it is."

There was one free dart board, and Oliver retrieved the darts from it and the surrounding wall.

Jayce and I stood beside one of the tall tables.

"Ladies first," Oliver said handing me three darts.

I left my drink on the table, moving away from it, though unsure what I was supposed to do other than try and hit the board with my darts.

"Jayce, why don't you give her some tips," Oliver said, and then a bit lower added, "Or else I will."

I faced the dart board, pretending not to hear, and didn't look to see what Jayce would do, but a moment later, he came up to my right side.

"Step up to the white line," he directed, a bit stiffly. "You can back up if you need to, but don't cross the line."

I nodded, gulping back my nerves. Something about him being so close and *helping* me spiked my heart rate. All I could think about was how his hands felt when he'd dug them into my hair and—

"Ember," he said, as if I'd missed something.

I cleared my throat and looked at him. "Sorry, I was distracted. What did you say?"

"Are you right-handed or left-handed?" he asked.

I lifted my right hand with the darts in it. This was something I didn't need instruction on. Putting two of the darts in my left hand I lifted the remaining one in my right and aimed it at the dart board.

Easy enough, I thought. Until I threw the dart, and it hit the wall below the board.

"Whoops," I laughed. "Guess my aim's not as good as I thought."

Jayce moved behind me and placed his hand on my elbow. If I took a step back, I'd be pressed against him. My entire body warmed at the thought.

"Lift your arm a little higher," he said, putting pressure on my elbow as I lifted it. Goosebumps arose from his touch. I hoped he didn't notice. "And put a little more force behind your throw."

Utilizing his instructions, I threw another dart, and it hit the edge of the board, bouncing off.

"It takes practice, but you'll get it," Jayce said. He didn't try to direct me again, but he also didn't move from behind me. I almost wondered ...

Taking a slight step back, his warmth radiated into me, and butterflies erupted beneath my ribcage. He still didn't move. I threw the final dart, and it stuck in the bottom of the outer ring on the board.

Squealing in delight, I turned, forgetting how close Jayce was in my excitement, and stopped mere inches from him.

He smiled. "Like I said, you just need more practice."

"Now, let me show you how the pros do it," Oliver said, nudging me aside and breaking the bubble that had formed around Jayce and me.

Jayce walked back to the table and picked up his drink, taking a long swig from it. I did the same, sputtering a little from the rum. Sheila made a *strong* drink.

"You watching, Em? I'm only doing this to impress you," Oliver joked.

"All eyes are on you, Olly," Jayce said, though his gaze flicked to me. I pretended not to notice.

Two hours and two drinks later, I was toast. Normally it took a bit more than three drinks to make me start stumbling, but Sheila made her drinks far stronger than I was used to.

I sat at the bar and put my arm down to use as a pillow while I rested my eyes.

"Me thinks the princess needs to return to her castle before she turns into a pumpkin," Oliver mock whispered to Jayce, but I heard him loud and clear.

"Cinderella wasn't a princess at first," I mumbled, not bothering to open my eyes. "And *she* didn't turn into a pumpkin."

"That's right. I was testing you," Oliver said. "Now, Jayce, get poor Ember home."

I laughed. Hangovers weren't really a thing for demons, unless you drank so much you were still drunk the next day, then you might be a bit cranky. So, at least I didn't have to worry about that.

"Come on, Ember. I'll drive you home," Jayce said.

"Mm, can't yet," I reminded him. "Mazie has company. I can sleep here while you two ..." I waved my hand in the direction I thought the dart board was. My eyes were still closed, and I truly could have fallen asleep with my head on the bar.

"I'm not going to let you get a kink in your neck from sleeping on the bar," Jayce said.

"Ha, you said kink," I teased, finding it far too funny. Oliver laughed along with me.

"Hilarious. Come on. You can nap at my place until I can take you home." Jayce stepped up beside the stool I sat on.

"Hm. How do I know you're not trying to get me alone in your apartment so you can kill me?" I cracked an eye and poked Jayce's chest.

He took my hand and held it. "Because I could have killed you in the parking lot earlier, and I didn't. That and Dominic threatened to kill *me* if anything happened to you."

I sighed. "Of course he did. Fine. Take me home." I sat up and the room shifted with me. "Oof."

Bracing myself on the counter, I stood and took a step. Once we started moving toward the door, I stumbled and had to grab a barstool to catch myself.

Jayce took my arm and put it over his shoulders. I thought it was odd, until he scooped down and lifted me into his arms, one arm at my back and the other under the backs of my knees.

"I can walk," I protested half-heartedly.

"Sure you can." His chest vibrated against me as he talked.

I placed my hand on his sternum, and he stiffened beneath my touch.

Oliver skipped ahead of us and opened the back door.

"You've received my stamp of approval, Ember," Oliver said, amused. "Next time, I'll make sure Sheila goes a little lighter on your drinks, though."

"G'night, Olly," I said, waving.

Jayce chuckled.

The wave of heat from outside hit me and I groaned. "I hate how hot it always is." My eyes closed of their own accord.

When the car door opened, and Jayce placed me into the passenger seat, going so far as to buckle my seatbelt for me, I blinked slowly, only half awake. When his arm grazed the front of my body, I shuddered.

"You okay?" he asked, hesitating with his face hovering in front of mine.

I closed my eyes and bit my lip, nodding. "Mmhm." I couldn't trust myself not to lean in and kiss him or say something stupid. He'd said he regretted kissing me the other night, after all. I didn't want to give him anything else to regret now we were becoming friends.

Once he had shut my door and gone around to his side of the car, my body had calmed down slightly.

He climbed in and I turned my head to look at him as he started the car and backed out of the spot. The air coming through the vents, though not cooled yet, was helping keep me awake.

"Are we friends now?" I asked him.

"What?" He kept his eyes on the road as we turned onto it.

"Oliver said I got his stamp of approval. Does that mean we're friends now?" I clarified.

The music filled the pause in our conversation, and I almost forgot I'd asked anything.

"Do you want to be friends?" he finally responded.

"Not unless *you* want to," I said. "I don't want to waste my time on someone who doesn't want me around."

He either sighed or laughed softly. The music was loud enough I couldn't tell which. I peered at him through the dark, the only light in the car coming from the dashboard, and thought I saw a smile.

"Yeah. We're friends, Ember." The amusement was clear in his tone.

"Good." I turned my head and pillowed it on my arm, trying to get comfortable enough to close my eyes and take a quick power nap.

Chapter 12

Jayce

Ember would be the death of me. Literally. Because Dominic would absolutely kill me if he knew the thoughts I was having about her.

Kissing her had been the biggest mistake of my life, because now I knew what she tasted like, what she felt like against me, and I couldn't stop thinking about it.

If I wasn't already in Hell, I'd be going there.

And I'd told her we were friends ... Fuck, it was almost like I *wanted* to continue torturing myself. But it was better than *not* being around her at all.

I pulled into the garage for my apartment building and parked. Ember was sound asleep in the passenger seat, and I almost didn't want to wake her. But sleeping in that position for too much longer would bring a lot more aches and pains for her in the morning, and the thought of her being in pain was intolerable.

When I got out of the car and slammed my door shut, I assumed it would wake her, but when I got to the passenger side, she was still sleeping against the door.

Easing the door open, she moved with it until the motion snapped her awake and she stared up at me with wide eyes before realization set in and she smiled sheepishly.

Unable to stop myself, I smiled back. "We're here," I said, as if it wasn't obvious.

She stretched her arms, shaking out the one that had been her pillow, and turned so her long legs draped down to the ground. "I feel better already."

"Think you can walk?" I asked, half hoping she'd need me to carry her again.

She nodded, so I stepped back and gave her space to get out of the car.

"I might need a little support, but I can walk," she said, propping herself up with the car door.

I slipped my arm around her waist too easily. Her intake of breath told me she also hadn't been expecting it. I'd reacted without thinking. I shouldn't be that comfortable touching her, especially after yelling at Oliver for touching her earlier.

"Sorry, do you want me to—" I started to move away, but she caught my arm.

"No, this is fine." She leaned into my side.

We walked inside and she didn't stumble once.

In the elevator, Ember broke the silence between us. "I'm so happy we don't have to use the stairs this time."

"How could I forget, you've already been here," I said, shaking my head. The elevator stopped on my floor and the doors opened. "I would offer to give you a tour of the place, but since you already broke in and showed yourself around, I guess that's unnecessary."

"Ha ha. As if I would let you steal my hard-earned evidence so easily." She pulled away from me and sat on the bench in my entry way. I hesitated, unsure whether she'd want me to keep helping her, but she started taking off her shoes and I figured she'd have a much easier time walking without heels. So, I entered the kitchen area and poured us both a glass of water.

She came around the corner and headed for the couch. I brought her the water once she was seated, and she drank it greedily.

"Oh my god," she moaned.

I backed away, walking behind the couch so she wouldn't see the effect she'd had on me.

"I didn't realize how much I needed this," she said. She tucked her legs up under her, and her dress rode up with the movement, revealing more of her thighs.

Sitting down, I avoided looking at her.

"Do you want something to eat?" I asked. "We could order something, like pizza."

She shook her head. "No, I think I'd fall asleep before anything got here." Setting her glass of water onto the coffee table, she nuzzled back into the couch, stretching her legs toward the center of it. I was tempted to reach out and pull her legs onto my lap to have an excuse to be in contact with her, but I didn't. We were *friends*, and that wasn't something a friend would do.

Her phone buzzed and she checked it, typing out a response before setting it back down. She noticed me watching her and said, "Just letting Mazie and Penny know where I am in case you change your mind and decide to murder me." She gave me a sweet smile.

Standing, I grabbed the throw from the back of the couch and handed it to her. "Get some rest. I'll be in my room if you need anything."

I would have offered Ember my bed, but the couch was almost more comfortable. I'd made sure to pay top dollar for the best of the best when furnishing my apartment. Dominic paid me well enough, and I wasn't going to be uncomfortable if I could avoid it. That and she was asleep almost instantly after lying down.

Before I went to bed myself, I refilled her glass of water and mine. In my room, I stripped down to my boxers and climbed into bed. I wasn't worried about Ember seeing me, since I'd wake up long before her. I was way too light of a sleeper.

I think I jinxed myself, because I woke to Ember knocking on the frame of the entryway of my room.

At first, I didn't remember why she was there, and I sat up quickly, throwing my legs over the side of the bed, thinking something was wrong, but then the night came back to me.

"Are you always so eager to get out of bed in the morning?" Ember teased. Her gaze dropped to my boxers and a blush reddened her pink cheeks. "Is it all right if I make some food? I didn't want to go rummaging in your cabinets without permission."

I ran my hand through my hair and nodded. "Go for it." My voice was still rough from sleep, so I cleared it. "I'll be out in a second."

She turned away and said, "Take your time."

I went to the bathroom attached to my bedroom and turned on the shower. Dropping my boxers, I stepped under the stream of the hot water. My imagination got the better of me, and I pictured Ember walking into the bathroom, shimmying out of her little black dress and stepping into the shower behind me, her pretty, pink hair getting slicked back from the water.

I fisted my dick, imagining it was Ember, reaching around from behind me. My hands were much bigger than hers, so it kind of ruined the image, but it didn't take long for me to finish even with that hindrance.

Leaning my arm against the shower wall, I rested my forehead against it, letting the water cascade over my back.

Friends definitely don't do that, I chastised myself.

When I'd collected myself enough to face Ember, I dressed in jeans and a hoodie, rolling up the sleeves, and joined her in the kitchen.

"What are you making?" I asked, totally normal, as if I hadn't just masturbated to her in the shower.

"I have bacon in the oven, and eggs here." She flipped one with the turner. "We can either eat them as is, or if you have some kind of bread, we can do sandwiches."

"I'm a little surprised I had either of those in my fridge. Did you check the dates?" I asked, only half joking. Sometimes Victoria brought food over for herself, so it was possible she'd bought them, but I couldn't remember the last time *I* had.

"Yep, both good," she said. "But I'm guessing that means you won't have bread?"

I shook my head. "I eat out mostly."

She sighed dramatically and smirked. "I'll survive without, I guess."

Sitting at the bar facing her, I let myself get a good look at her. She'd wiped off her makeup from the night before, and her hair was a little more unkempt, but she was equally as beautiful. The dress seemed out of place for cooking in the kitchen, but it wasn't like she had a change of clothes.

"So, if Enzo is at The Mausoleum tonight, what's our plan?" I asked. "Are we going behind the curtain together?" The reminder of what had happened behind that curtain before had me wishing I never asked.

Friends, Jayce, I reminded myself.

She chewed her bottom lip, clearly thinking about her answer. "Mm, we go in together," she said. "You can pay attention to anything going on around us while I do my thing."

She said it so casually as if her 'thing' wasn't seducing Enzo into giving her information. Nausea spoiled my appetite at the thought of it. But this was the job. We'd promised Dominic information, and this was how Ember and I, well mostly Ember, had agreed we'd get it.

"Right," I said through gritted teeth. "What's our code word if you want to get out of there?" I wasn't about to let her get herself into anything she'd regret. If I thought it was going too far, code word or no, I'd risk the entire mission to get her out of there.

"How about 'please?'" she answered as if she'd had that already in mind.

"Please?" I echoed. "You wouldn't say that otherwise?"

She shook her head. "I can't see myself ever begging anyone for anything, especially Enzo. So, seems like a good word I could throw out without it being obvious."

I'd like to make you beg for— I stopped my thoughts from going there. *Friends, Jayce,* I reminded myself, yet again.

"Okay. Please it is," I said, trying my best to keep a straight face.

After we ate, I brought Ember to her apartment so she could shower and get ready for our night. I had a feeling Enzo would be back and we'd actually have to work.

When I went back to pick her up, she was wearing the same brown, corseted, leather dress she'd been wearing the first night I'd met her. It left nothing to the imagination.

"Hey, Jayce!" Mazie greeted me from inside the apartment, waving around the corner as I stood in the hall outside the door.

"I'll see you later, Maze!" Ember said before shutting the door behind her.

During the ride to the club, neither of us spoke, and I turned the music up to try to diffuse the tension.

Once we sat at the bar, Ember broke the silence between us.

"At least we know he's here," she said, nodding toward the closed curtains. "I guess we may as well get this over with."

Slipping off her stool, she strolled over to the curtained area and approached Draco. I followed her, trying to seem as nonchalant as possible.

"Is Enzo in tonight?" Ember asked, winking. "I missed him last night."

Draco grinned and pulled the curtain aside, letting her pass. He waved me through behind her.

Chapter 13

Ember

I stepped through the curtains with Jayce at my back and tensed when I saw Enzo. As ready as I was for whatever happened, there was still the fear of him figuring out who we really were.

"I was wondering when I'd see you again. After our former meeting, the past few nights seemed ... Lacking," Enzo said. "Come. This is my last night here; we'll make the most of it." He stood, his entourage standing with him, and made his way to the door at the back of the room.

Jayce tried to catch my eye, but I stared straight ahead, feigning confidence. I didn't want him to think I couldn't do this.

Following Enzo, I asked, "You're not going to be here after tonight?"

The room we entered was lit with dim purple and blue lighting, and smoke filled the air. People lounged around the room on couches and a more subdued kind of music played over the speakers.

"Time to move on," he said, leading us to a half-moon couch with a round ottoman in the center.

"Where will I be able to find you?" I asked, pouting as he sat down and took my hand, pulling me into his lap. He cast a glance at Jayce, who said nothing but sat to the left of us, so I was facing him.

"I'm not sure yet, but here." He handed me a phone. "Put your phone number in, and I'll find you next time I'm in town."

I entered my number and handed the phone back to him. "You won't keep me waiting too long, will you?" I asked, widening my eyes and looking at him from beneath my lashes.

Digging a hand into my hair, he pulled me in for a kiss.

A hand gripped my thigh, and I assumed it was Enzo, until he broke away and said, "I was wondering when that protective side would come out to play."

Glancing down I saw Jayce take his hand back, his blue eyes darker than I'd ever seen them. I gave him a warning glare. We couldn't give Enzo any reason to doubt us. I should have guessed it was him from the coolness of his rings digging into me. Enzo didn't wear rings.

"Let's make things a little more interesting, shall we?" Enzo snapped his fingers at a demon walking by. "Three," he demanded.

She reached into the apron she wore and took out three purple pills, handing them to Enzo. He popped one into his mouth, swallowing it, before handing one to me and one to Jayce.

144

"Something to calm your boyfriend's nerves," he said, looking pointedly at Jayce.

"It's Brock," Jayce said, remembering the fake name I'd given him, and tossed the pill into his mouth, swallowing it.

Slowly, I put my pill in my mouth, but before I could swallow, Jayce leaned forward and kissed me. His tongue surprised me, until I realized what he was doing. He swiped the pill from my mouth and took it into his.

Enzo chuckled. "Now it's a party."

Jayce rubbed a hand over his face, and I figured he was taking the pills from his mouth. "It's about damn time," he said.

Lifting my legs, I placed them over Jayce's lap, while I kept my eyes on Enzo. Jayce rested his hand on my calf.

Enzo's eyes were closed as he tightened his hold on me, apparently feeling something from the pill he'd taken. I tried to relax and pretended to be feeling the effects as well.

"Mm," I mused, letting my hands trail up his chest and over his shoulders. "I'm going to miss this."

He opened his eyes and kissed me. Clasping my hands at the back of his neck, I held him there for a few seconds longer. When he pulled away, he trailed his lips down my throat, and across my exposed collarbone. I leaned my head back and let out a small moan, grinding my ass against his hardening length. A thrill shot through me as Jayce's hand traveled up my calf, but then his grip tightened and he pulled on it, making me squeak in surprise.

"My turn," Jayce growled. Enzo raised an eyebrow, but he didn't argue.

Instead, Enzo shifted me onto the couch, so I was between them. He pulled one of my legs onto his lap and gripped my thigh. If anyone looked our way, they'd be able to see up my dress. Thankfully I'd chosen to wear underwear that night.

Jayce cupped my cheek and turned my head to face him, giving me a long look, as if searching for something. I gave him a slight nod to let him know I was okay with this.

Like the last time, he kissed me fiercely, as a jealous boyfriend might. I dug my hands into his hair, savoring every second of our kiss. While Enzo's hand trailed up my thigh, my core heated in anticipation. Except his hand never made it to the destination.

"Enzo, you have a visitor," Draco's voice registered, but neither Jayce nor I made any move to break apart.

Enzo sighed and stood, leaving us to meet his visitor, I assumed.

Instead of stopping things like we should have, Jayce lifted me, pulling me over to straddle him and kissed me again. His hands trailed down my back and over my wings, to my ass. I ground against him as I'd done to Enzo.

My dress was riding up, and I assumed my thong was on display for the whole room, but I couldn't bring myself to care. Jayce gripped my ass, and he hardened beneath me.

His mouth left mine and followed the same path Enzo's had, but something about his kisses had me lighting up in every sensitive place. If he wanted to finish what Enzo had started, he'd find me slick and ready for him.

But suddenly, Jayce pushed me off his lap onto the couch and stood, leaving me breathless and aching for more.

Breathing heavily, I stared at Jayce's back, pulling my dress down to cover myself.

"We should go," Jayce said gruffly, moving away from the couch.

"Right." I stood and grabbed his hand. He still wouldn't look at me, but he didn't try to pull his hand away. We had to keep up appearances, after all.

"You can leave through here," a pretty demon said, pointing to a backdoor.

"Thank you! Can you tell Enzo I said goodbye and I'll be anxiously awaiting seeing him again? My name's Mazie," I chirped.

"Of course," she said, smiling.

Jayce pulled me out the door, clearly eager to be out of the club. The air outside was slightly cooler for once, and it calmed the adrenaline pumping through me.

Surprisingly, Jayce didn't drop my hand once the door closed behind us. He kept hold of it until we found his car and I was inside it.

When he sat down in the driver's seat, he stared straight ahead for a few seconds, not doing anything.

"It doesn't have to mean anything," I said, my voice sounding overly loud in the too quiet car. Would it hurt if Jayce said it didn't mean anything? Sure, but at least I was the one to say it first.

"We shouldn't do this, Ember." He leaned his head back against the headrest, staring at the roof of the car.

"I can go alone when Enzo comes back to town. I can handle it if it's too much for you." I pulled on the hem of my dress, trying not to let my emotion leak into my voice or show on my face.

There was so much going on in my body, I wasn't even sure how I felt. I was still hot and tingling from our interaction but also hurt from the sting of rejection. None of it was supposed to be real, it was all supposed to be a part of the plan to get information on Jericho. But my body didn't know the difference between real affection, or fake.

"You're not seeing him alone," Jayce snapped.

"Okayyy, so then have another of Dominic's runners go with me so you don't have to do this anymore," I offered as an alternative.

"No," he said forcefully.

I threw my hands up in frustration. "You don't want to be my partner, but you don't want anyone else to help me, so I don't know what you expect me to do here."

"I never said I didn't want to be your partner." He finally looked at me.

"You said we shouldn't do this. I said it doesn't have to mean anything, so why is there an issue?" I asked. He was infuriating.

"Because I fucking *want* you Ember, and I know I shouldn't."

I inhaled a sharp breath, giddiness bubbling up in me.

"Dominic is trusting me to keep you safe. He'd kill me if he knew what we've been doing." Jayce shook his head.

Shifting in my seat, I faced him and leaned closer. "He doesn't need to know." I smirked.

"Fucking hell," he sighed. He lifted a hand and brought it to the back of my neck, his thumb stroking beneath my hair as his gaze searched for something in mine.

I put my hand on his thigh and leaned in, closing the distance between us and kissing him. This time it was much softer and slower than our first kiss.

Having the console between us was a bit of a problem. It jammed into my ribs making me uncomfortable.

"Hold on," I gasped, pulling back.

"We don't have to do this," Jayce said, brushing a lock of hair behind my ear.

Shaking my head, I huffed a laugh. "That's not it." Lifting a leg, I eased my way over the console to straddle him. The steering wheel dug into my back, but it was better than the console being between us.

"Oh." He grinned, looking up at me. His hands gripped my waist. "Hold on." He leaned forward, pressing against me, and reached behind himself, taking his glock from his waistband and setting it on my seat.

Okay, that's hot, I thought, ducking my head to kiss him. I pressed my hand to his chest, moving it down slowly between us. Taking one of his hands from my waist, I guided him to my thigh, and then up, beneath my dress, hiking it up.

"Needy little demon, aren't you?" he mused, toying with the edge of my thong.

"Mm. You have no idea." I'd been dreaming of this moment since the first time I'd seen him. But none of those fantasies came close to how he *actually* felt, his cock hardening against me as he teased me over the thin fabric of my underwear.

"Watching Enzo touch you was the hardest thing I've ever endured," he said. "I don't know if I'll be able to watch him do it again."

I ground against him, moving as much as the steering wheel at my back would allow. "I couldn't tell," I teased, leaning down to kiss him.

He pulled my underwear aside and groaned into my mouth when he found me already wet for him. His thumb rolled over my clit, making circles in the slickness.

"So fucking wet. Perfect," he murmured, pumping his index finger inside me.

Letting my head fall back, I moaned in delight. I moved with him, and he added another finger alongside the first, curling them against my tight walls. His fingers filled me better than mine ever could.

"Fuck," I gasped, biting my bottom lip. My nails dug into the front of his shirt as he moved his fingers in and out of me faster, curling them each time and bringing me close to the edge. "More," I begged, riding his hand.

He chuckled. "Not tonight, beautiful. Your first time won't be in the front seat of a car." With his free hand, he pulled my head forward, bringing my mouth to his. His tongue swept inside, and he swallowed my moans as I came all over his hand.

Pulling out of me, he licked his fingers clean and then kissed me again so I could taste myself on him.

I leaned back, accidentally pressing the car horn and jolting in surprise, getting a groan out of him as I slid forward on his lap.

"Whoops." I climbed back over the console, handing him his glock, and sighed as I settled into the passenger seat.

Jayce took my hand and kissed it.

My phone buzzed and I took it out to look at it.

Mazie: *I'm so sorry, I have company again tonight, but Penny said you could stay with her!*

"Well, looks like I'm not going home tonight," I laughed, showing the text to Jayce.

"You can stay at my place again. And I'm not trying to get you in my bed, I promise," he said lifting his hands in surrender.

"I think we proved we don't need a bed but thank you. That would be great."

He started the car and pulled out of the parking lot.

Glancing at his lap, I could tell he was still rock hard, and I wanted to alleviate his tension like he'd done for me. I reached over and started unbuttoning his pants.

He gripped my hand and made me pause. "What are you doing?" he asked, his eyes widening in surprise.

"Give in Jayce. I promise, I think I know what I'm doing." I winked. We both knew I had no idea what I was doing, but I'd watched enough videos and read enough books to have *some* idea. It couldn't be that difficult to figure out.

Releasing my hand, he let me unbutton and unzip his jeans. I slid my hand beneath his boxers and freed his impressive length.

He inhaled sharply, gripping the steering wheel tighter as he drove. Leaning across the console, I licked his shaft and relished his shudder, knowing I held the power in this situation. I took him into my mouth, coating his cock in my saliva as I bobbed up and down. I took it slowly at first, his groans telling me I was doing something right, and then I sped up, using my hand at his base since I couldn't take him all the way into my mouth. Unlike the characters and actors in those books and videos I'd seen, I *did* have a gag reflex.

His hand gripped my hair, and the car jerked forward as he lost control for a second. After he came, I sat up, swallowing and using my thumb to swipe a drop from the corner of my mouth. His eyes were glued to me, tracking my every movement.

I helped him back into his boxers, zipping and buttoning his pants, before leaning back in my seat, grinning in satisfaction.

He wore a grin that matched mine.

When he parked the car in the garage for his apartment building, neither of us made any move to get out.

"I want you to know that you staying here doesn't mean we have to do anything or even sleep in the same bed. I never want you to feel like—"

I put my hand on his arm. "Jayce, I understand. I don't feel pressured, or uncomfortable, I promise. Can we go inside?"

He nodded and we finally got out of the car, heading for the entryway to the apartment complex.

That time, when we stepped off the elevator, the lights were already on in his apartment.

"Jayce?" A feminine voice came from the kitchen, and I froze. "I was starting to wonder if you'd ever come home."

Her footsteps came toward us, and in a panic, I backed into the elevator right before the doors closed. I caught a glimpse of Jayce's slack jaw and wide-eyed look before the door closed between us.

"Oh my god," I huffed, wrapping my arms around myself. "I'm so stupid. *I don't have a girlfriend, Ember,*" I mimicked him and feigned vomiting. "The fuck you don't. Booty calls don't hang out in your apartment when you're not there." I bit my lip. "I don't think." It wasn't like I'd ever been a booty call, so how would I know? It seemed strange, though.

The elevator dinged as it passed each floor, on its way back down to the lobby. Someone must have called it, because I hadn't thought to press any buttons.

I dug my hands into my hair, groaning. "Fuck, fuck, fuck. This is so fucked up."

The elevator stopped and the doors opened, revealing the lobby and an older demon waiting. I stepped out, letting her have the elevator to herself. There was no way in *hell* I was going back up there.

I'd walk home. It wasn't that far.

By the time I was on the street, I had about five texts from Jayce, but I deleted them all before reading them. I didn't want his excuses or his pity.

The night was still young and there were plenty of other demons out once I reached the main strip of road Mazie lived on. My phone buzzed in my clutch, and I ignored it.

Even though Mazie had someone over, I knew if I told her what was going on, she'd kick them out in a heartbeat. But I didn't want to ruin her night too. As much as I wanted to shorten my walk and go to her apartment, I went toward the mansion.

I was used to walking in heels from all the times I'd walked to Primetime, but it didn't stop my feet from hurting. My entire body was weary, and I wondered if that was from my release earlier, or from the fact that I knew I'd have to face Jayce again *eventually.*

There was a bar between my house and Mazie's apartment that I'd only been in once before, and I decided to make a pit stop there. I deserved a drink, and I needed to get the taste of Jayce out of my mouth.

There was no dance floor or loud music at this bar. The music was more like background noise while people chatted amongst each other at their tables. The lighting was dim, but nothing like the backroom at The Mausoleum. It was a much more comforting vibe.

Taking a seat at the bar, I ordered a Dark and Stormy, with an extra shot of rum on the side. I set my clutch on the bar, putting my phone face down beside it. I tapped my fingers on it, considering responding to Jayce so it would stop vibrating, but I wouldn't give him that.

"Rough night?" The bartender smirked as she handed me my drink and poured my shot.

I had no idea how I looked. After everything, I hadn't thought of touching up my makeup or even running my fingers through my hair.

"Something like that," I mumbled, taking the shot.

"I'll keep 'em coming." She winked and left to tend to another patron.

Pulling up my camera on my phone, I used it as a mirror as I made myself a bit more presentable. I didn't look as bad as I thought, but I could see why the bartender had thought I'd had a rough night.

It hit me that for the first time in my life, I was out in public *alone.* I straightened in my seat, very aware of the fact that anyone could approach me and I didn't have my security blanket of Penny, Mazie, or Jayce to scare them away.

It was simultaneously thrilling, and terrifying. Even if there was no way anyone would guess who I was, it was still dangerous to be out alone. At least in a bar full of other demons it would be a *little* harder for someone to kidnap or murder me.

I finished my mule, somewhat calming as the alcohol dulled my senses.

"Let me buy your next one," a demon said as he sat down on the stool beside mine and waved down the bartender.

I looked him up and down. He reminded me of Dominic, with his domineering vibe and dark hair. But he wasn't as muscular or tall. His face was slightly round, giving him a soft, kind look. *He doesn't seem the murdery type,* I thought. But maybe that was the exact thing I should be wary of.

"Why not," I said, shrugging. "What's your name?"

"Peter. And yours?"

"Mazie," I lied. Best not to give any real information while I was at my most vulnerable.

My phone buzzed between us, and I sighed, flipping it to see *Brock* across the screen. His fake name seemed much more fitting now.

"Someone you don't want to talk to?" Peter asked.

I nodded. "Ex-boyfriend." May as well embody the role fully. "He won't take the hint and leave me alone."

"I can answer it, if you want," Peter offered, shrugging. "He might take the hint then."

Sliding my phone over to him, I said, "Knock yourself out."

Clearing his throat, he tapped the answer button on the screen and held the phone to his ear.

"Brock, is it?" he asked, pausing for a response. "Sorry to burst your bubble, but Mazie's with me tonight. Give up already." He handed me back my phone.

"Thanks," I muttered.

"I hope it helps. And I hope you don't mind me hanging around for a little while, I had kind of a crappy night myself."

"Oh?" I feigned interest. At least it would give me something else to think about. "I've burdened you with my problems, the least I can do is try and give you some insight on yours."

He laughed. "I've been trying to prove to my boss I can meet a quota without going into the clubs. So far, I'm not doing great."

I tapped my nails on the bar. "What's your quota? Maybe I can help."

He jerked his head to the side, indicating he wanted me to follow him. I grabbed my drink and hopped off my stool, walking behind him toward a booth at the back of the room. There were two other men sitting there.

Slowing as we reached the table, Peter turned to me.

"These are my partners," he said. "They don't trust me to hold onto the product." He smirked.

"Product? Are you offering me drugs, because you can say that. It's not like we're in *Hell* or anything." I laughed behind my hand, but he stiffened. This was another of Jericho's men. Any of Dominic's men wouldn't be afraid of being called out in their own territory.

"Right." He cleared his throat. "This drug isn't anything like what you've tried before, so we like to keep it on the down low, so we don't stir up any trouble."

"Mm, I'm sure it's great. So where are you hiding it?" I teased, looking past him to his partners. "I'd love to give it a try."

"Of course you would." He smirked.

"Mazie," Jayce's voice boomed across the room. At least he was smart enough to use my fake name.

Scowling, Peter turned to the door. "Ex-boyfriend?" he asked, and I nodded, heat flushing my neck and face. "Want me to handle him?"

I wanted to laugh in his face, there was no way he could take on Jayce, but I didn't do that.

"No, I can deal with him." I met Jayce halfway, steering him to the bar, where I set down my glass. "What are you doing here?" I asked, keeping my voice low.

"I've been calling and texting you and you didn't answer. I was worried," he said.

I scoffed. "You don't get to worry about me." Pushing past him, I headed for the door. I'd go to Mazie's if I had to. I wasn't staying another minute with Jayce.

While I walked, I shot a quick text to Dominic.

> **Me:** *The bar down the street that our parents used to love there's a demon named Peter selling for Jericho*

At least he might be able to do something with that information.

Jayce caught up with me and we walked side by side down the sidewalk.

"You didn't give me a chance to explain," he said.

"Because I don't want an explanation. I want to forget this night ever happened." The rum was dulling my senses and making my lips tingle. I touched them softly, reminded of how it felt kissing Jayce.

"Victoria wasn't supposed to be there."

I rolled my eyes. "Is that supposed to make me feel better? You told me you didn't have a girlfriend, and I believed you, like an idiot."

"She's not my girlfriend, I promise. Sometimes she comes over and we ..." He paused, so I decided to fill in the blanks for him.

"Have sex? She's your booty call, or fuck buddy, or whatever you want to call it." The bitterness in my voice was clear.

"If you have to put it in those terms, then yeah." He ran a hand down his face. "She knows the pin to get in, and she shows up sometimes."

"Like a girlfriend," I pointed out. "You know it's fine, really. I wasn't expecting you to stop seeing other people, or care about me more than a partner, just because we did what we did. You can go back to your life, and I'll go back to mine, and we can resume work as normal. Like I said before, it doesn't have to mean anything." Even though my heart was already invested, and it *did* mean something to me.

Jayce gently gripped my arm, making me stop and face him.

"I already told you that's not what I want," he said.

"Yes, but then we walked in on your girlfriend doing ... Whatever she was doing for you." I truly had no idea. I'd run before I could find out. "So, I'm giving you the chance to change your mind."

"I'm not changing my mind. Are you?"

"Maybe," I said honestly. I'd been blindsided by Victoria, and I wasn't sure I could take anything like that again.

"Let me take you to dinner," Jayce suggested.

"Right now? It's four in the morning." I bit my lip.

"Breakfast, then."

"We can't. I—"

A car pulled up beside us, and Dominic yelled out the window, "Ember, get in."

I looked between him and Jayce, in shock that he'd shown up. And he'd come from the opposite direction of the mansion.

"I sent you a job, Jayce," Dominic said.

Jayce perked up and seemed excited. I'd never killed anyone so I couldn't say for sure whether I'd be able to do it, but the idea of it didn't appeal to me at all.

Jayce pulled out his phone. "Got it."

Once I got in the passenger seat, the car started moving, leaving Jayce behind.

"Don't you think Jayce might question why you came and picked me up?" I asked.

Dominic scoffed. "He knows better than to question me. I needed to get you away from the bar. Jayce will take care of that Peter guy. It's a small play I can make toward Jericho without a full-on war starting. Enzo is a bigger pawn I'm relying on you for. Speaking of which, how did things go with him tonight?"

The entire night flashed across my mind, and I kept my face turned away from Dominic so he wouldn't see the flush on my cheeks.

"Fine, except Enzo said he'll be away for a little while. So, I gave him my number, and he's supposed to let me know when he's back in town," I said.

"Well, that throws a wrench in things. If he's gone for too long, we'll have to figure out Jericho's plans on our own."

I knew Enzo wouldn't be gone that long, but I didn't want to explain how I knew that to Dominic, so I stayed quiet.

It was a short ride to the mansion. Taking off my dress and shoes when I got to my room made me feel ten times better, and when I snuggled up in bed, it was like I could almost forget the events of the night.

Before I fell asleep, my phone buzzed on my side table, and I checked it quickly.

Jayce: *Raincheck on breakfast?*

I left his message on read so he could fret about that while I slept soundly.

Chapter 14

Jayce

In the chaos of all that had happened that night, I'd forgotten what day it was. Victoria and I had agreed when we first started seeing each other on a more regular basis that Sundays could be the day, if either of us needed more than sex, we could talk about our lives. So sometimes, if she'd had a bad week, she'd show up at my apartment on a Sunday and we'd eat food, and I'd let her vent. Every once in a while, I vented too, but I had Oliver for that, so I usually didn't have too much to share with Victoria.

When I returned to my apartment after finding Ember and taking care of Peter, Victoria was still there.

"You didn't text me before coming over like usual," I said, walking past the food she'd laid out on the counter and straight to the living area.

"I didn't realize you were seeing someone else," she said, leaning against the bar.

"I shouldn't have to worry about you being here ..." I trailed off. I was trying to put the blame solely on her, but she wasn't at fault. She'd always made sure to let me know if she started seeing anyone so we wouldn't have any awkward encounters.

I'd never had an occasion to do the same. Until Ember. But we were *just friends* until that night.

"From the glimpse I got of her, she's cute. I'm sorry I scared her away," Vic said.

"She wasn't scared away." I jumped to defend Ember, but there was no reason to. Victoria wasn't one to go against other females. "I mean, she thought you were my girlfriend."

She clucked her tongue. "Ah. That makes sense. If you want, I'll happily explain to her that I won't be a problem. I actually came here tonight to let you know I started seeing someone, and it's getting serious."

"You could have texted that," I said, dropping down onto the couch.

"Well, you won't have to worry about me anymore," she said, grinning. "But since I'm here, and I made food, tell me all about her."

I kept most of the details of me and Ember's relationship, whatever it was, to myself, but I gave Victoria enough to satisfy her intrigue. She told me way too much about her new boyfriend, Mark. I didn't comment on his boring name and let her talk as much as she wanted.

Once Victoria left, I yearned to text Ember and let her know things between Victoria and I were done. But she hadn't responded to my last text, so I refrained. I didn't want her to think I was being pushy or coming on too strongly.

Fuck. I felt like I was losing my mind. I'd never worried about that kind of thing before, but I didn't want to ruin things with Ember. I'd even go back to being friends, if that's what she wanted.

My phone buzzed and hope flared in my chest before Dominic's name came up on the screen. I'd texted him letting him know I'd finished the job with Peter.

Dom: *I dropped Ember off at her apartment. I had her fill me in on your night, but she didn't explain why you were at The Lounge after The Mausoleum*

Dread replaced hope, and a weight dropped in my stomach as I tried to think of a reason why we would have gone to that bar.

Dom: *It's a good thing you were. At least this will remind Jericho I have eyes everywhere in Southside*

Me: *Ember and I overheard talk at The Mausoleum that The Lounge was another good place to find the new drugs Enzo's been peddling*

I lied. At least it was a good enough reason for us to go there and would keep Dominic from asking too many more questions. He was my best friend, and I didn't think I could lie to him if he outright asked me if anything had happened between me and Ember.

A part of me wanted to tell him anyway. I couldn't imagine he'd care if two of his friends got together, even if he was a little unusually protective of Ember. But since I had no idea if anything else would ever happen between Ember and I, there was no reason to tell Dominic anything yet.

After a few crappy hours of sleep, I hit up the coffee shop and made my rounds with the usual hot spots for unsanctioned criminal activity before I went to Dominic's for the weekly meeting.

Ember still hadn't responded to my text. I assumed since she was working for Dominic, she'd be at the meeting, and I could try to talk to her either before or after.

Except she didn't show up to the meeting.

While Dominic talked at the head of the table, filling everyone in on what had happened over the weekend, I texted her.

Me: *Skipping out on meetings already?*

Ember: *I thought only seasoned runners went to the meetings?*
Either way, I got special permission to skip
You should try it sometime
it's liberating

Me: *I'm pretty sure Dom would notice if I didn't show up unfortunately*

Ember: *But you're his best friend*
If anyone could get away with it
it would be you

"Jayce." From the command in Dominic's tone, I'd guess that wasn't the first time he'd said my name.

"Sorry. Got a tip on a possible unknown dealer in Southside," I lied. It was becoming far too easy to do that.

"I asked whether you had anything else to add?" He cocked his eyebrow and scowled. He knew I hadn't heard a word he'd said.

"No, nothing. I think you covered everything." I had to fight to hide my smile. Dominic would not find my lack of attention funny, especially if he knew who had been distracting me.

He kept talking, asking the lieutenants for updates on their sectors.

> **Me:** *You should have seen the way he looked at me when he realized I wasn't paying attention. And you think he'd let me off easy if I didn't show up? Never*

Ember: *Whoops*

I put my phone away after that.

Once Dominic ended the meeting, I slipped out before he could catch me alone. Oliver caught up with me at the front door.

"You were texting her, weren't you?" he asked, wearing a shit-eating grin. "You're like a fucking kid in a candy store."

I scowled. "No. We're friends, nothing more. Dominic trusts me to keep her safe, not to f—"

"Jayce," Dominic called. "Hold on."

Oliver patted my shoulder. "Good luck, buddy." Then he slipped out the door with the rest of the group.

Turning, I faced Dominic as he approached. He waited as the last of the stragglers left and the door shut behind them.

"Sorry about in there, I can't play favorites in front of everyone," he said.

"Yeah, I know. But I shouldn't have been so distracted. It won't happen again." I knew it was hard for Dominic to balance his personal life and his status as the drug lord of Southside, and I didn't want to make that harder for him.

"I wanted to let you know that since Enzo won't be around for a little while, Ember's going to take a break. She's not ready for regular runs, and I don't want her taking on enforcer shit." He shrugged. "I'm going to give her some training before she does anything more."

"Oh," I huffed. I hoped my disappointment wasn't written plain on my face. "That makes sense. I told her Oliver could give her some self-defense training, though, which would be good for her to know when she starts doing the drug runs."

Dominic nodded slowly. "Yeah. I'll probably have her do that first, then."

"Right, well I should look into this tip I got." I had no idea if he believed me, but he didn't call me out on my lie.

After leaving the mansion, I went back to my apartment. Normally I'd meet Oliver at Fever Dream, but without Ember, it didn't hold as much of an appeal as it usually did. It had only been a day since I'd seen her, but I *missed* her. Which seemed odd to me. I'd never really missed anyone before, not even my parents after they up and left on my seventeenth birthday.

I put on one of those human TV channels when I got home. It was some family sitcom that made me laugh.

Ember: *Dom told me I'm
going to be training with Oliver
I'm assuming you have something
to do with that?*

Ember texted me and the sheer thrill it gave me was
almost concerning. She had a serious hold on me.

Me: *I may have mentioned it to him*
Ember: *Well, thank you.
Do you ever train with Oliver?*
Me: *Ha, no. Oliver wishes. Why?*
Ember: *No reason. I trust
Oliver to be a great teacher*
Me: *Butttt....*

Ember: *But nothing*
Me: *He is a great teacher,
and you can trust him*

Ember: *Well, I trust you, even
though I shouldn't
So I'll take your word for it*

That made me pause. *Even though I shouldn't.* She was
still thinking about what had happened with Victoria. It made
sense, since we hadn't really hashed that whole thing out yet.
And it wasn't something that could really be done over text.

My finger hovered over the call button next to Ember's
name. Whether the phone sensed my finger, or I'd accidentally
grazed the screen, it started calling her.

"Jayce?" Her voice had my stomach doing a flip.

"Uh, hi." *Oh my god. I sound like the twenty-one-year-old right now,* I groaned inwardly. "Hey, Ember," I said more strongly.

"Why did you call?" she asked.

"There's no one else." I figured I'd get to the point rather than waste her time.

She inhaled sharply. "What?"

"Before I met you, Victoria and I used to hook up, but we ended that. And she was the only one who I ever hooked up with regularly. There's no one else. I don't know what you want to do with that information, but I needed you to know. The only reason she came to my apartment Sunday night was to tell me about her new boyfriend." Maybe I was oversharing, but I'd rather she know everything before she made any decisions on where we stood.

Silence followed and I worried she'd hung up, but I waited.

"Okay," she said.

"Okay," I repeated.

"Is that all?" she asked.

"Yeah, I guess." I deflated. I don't know exactly what I'd been expecting her to say, but it wasn't that.

"Okay, I have to go but thank you."

The phone call ended, and I stared at the screen in disbelief for a while. I thought telling her Victoria and I had ended things would make things *less* awkward, but it seemed to have done the opposite.

I almost wished I'd waited to tell her in person so I could have seen her reaction, but waiting any longer would have driven me crazy. Now she knew and we could move forward, whatever that meant.

But two days passed without any word from Ember, and I wasn't going to be the one to text first. The ball was in her court.

On Thursday, after my workout, I was surprised to find a text from Ember on my phone with an image attached. It was a picture of her in lilac-colored leggings and a matching sports bra.

Ember: *Is this an okay thing to wear for self-defense classes?*

I had to imagine I looked like an idiot grinning at my phone in the middle of the gym. There were only a few other people there, but there were mirrors everywhere, so you could always see what everyone else was doing. It was one of the things I hated about the apartment complex's gym.

Me: *It's perfect
You starting that today?*

Ember: *Headed there now!
I'll let you know how it goes*

Me: *You'll do great*

And that was it. I didn't know whether this meant we were friends again, or something more, but I'd take it. Whatever *it* was.

Chapter 15

Ember

Every muscle in my body screamed as I lay on Mazie's couch. I'd never worked my body so hard in my life, and it felt amazing. Oliver hadn't gone easy on me, which I appreciated. People not knowing I was Dominic's sister had its perks. If he'd known, he probably wouldn't have let me break a sweat for fear I'd slip in it and break something, and then Dominic would kill him.

Since Dominic had his lieutenants over for a meeting that night, I wasn't allowed to go home. I had to sleep over at Mazie's, which was fine, except she wasn't home yet to keep me company.

I was trying to figure out what I should text Jayce while I couldn't move. He'd told me he wasn't hooking up with Victoria anymore, which I believed. And I appreciated that he'd told me, but I wasn't sure what that meant for us. We'd been friends for all of one day before we'd crossed that line, so I'd hardly gotten to know him.

He liked heavy metal and death core music, Moscow mules, bacon and eggs, and letting me ride him in his car.

Whoops. One of those things is not like the others. I laughed at myself, my abs aching with the movement.

Lifting my phone above me, I turned the camera on. Sticking out my tongue and scrunching my nose, I snapped a picture. The sports bra did wonders for my boobs, and the angle didn't hurt either.

I sent the picture to Jayce along with a text saying, *Oliver kicked my ass. I don't think I'll be able to move for a week.*

The anticipation from waiting for his response made each second feel like an hour. The adrenaline it gave me helped me get up, though, and I went to the fridge for a soda and a snack.

My phone chimed and I grabbed it as if my life depended on it, leaning on the counter and opening Jayce's text.

Brock: *At least you looked cute while he did it. And you'll be able to kick his ass before long*

I liked the thought of that.

> **Me:** *Well, I'm headed back tomorrow somehow. I don't think my body will let me*

Brock: *Do you need me to carry you there?*

> **Me:** *Would you?*

Brock: *Only if you say the magic word*

Me: *Sorry, not happening*
It shall remain our safe word
for when we're with Enzo

Brock: *I'll find something you'll*
be willing to beg me for

I nearly bit my tongue and choked on my own spit. I didn't respond immediately because I needed to craft the perfect response. I needed Mazie.

As if I'd summoned her, she walked into the apartment.

"Sleepover time!" she cheered. "I needed this." Flopping onto the couch, she dropped her bag on the floor and let out a long sigh.

"And I need *you.*" I joined her on the couch, picking up her head and placing it in my lap, before I handed her my phone and pointed to the text from Jayce.

"Holy shit!" she cried. "This is happening! Okay, okay, let me think. My brain is fried, but I can pull out a good response to help you. It's almost like I've been waiting my whole life for this moment."

It only took her a few seconds before she was typing out a text. She held it out to show me.

Me: *Who says I won't be the*
one making you beg?

I immediately blushed and squeaked, "Ah! I don't know if I can send—"

The *whoosh* of a sent text had ice filling my veins. The text was gone and unable to be unsent because it was already marked as *read.* He'd been waiting.

"If it gets too spicy, I'll have to leave this to you," Mazie said. "Don't want it to be weird. I see too many dick pics as it is."

"From who?" I asked. I'd never met anyone Mazie had dated in the past. It was too risky.

"You don't wanna know," she said, cringing.

"You'd think this would be easier. I mean, after Jayce and I ... Did what we did." It felt too weird to say it out loud.

Mazie had no problem with it. "You can say it, you sucked his dick," she stated, grinning. "I'm never going to judge you, Emmy."

"And I appreciate that, but I'm still not ready to talk so openly, even with you." After all my talk about being so confident with my sexuality, for some reason, it was harder than I thought to talk about what Jayce and I had done. Maybe because I wanted to keep it just for us.

"Fair enough. You'll get there." Mazie patted my knee.

"Do you think I freaked him out? He's not responding." I bit my lower lip, worrying at it.

"Oh, trust me, if he's not responding, he's busy doing something else." She pumped her eyebrows.

"Should I send another message? Like, a picture or something?" I asked.

"Now you're thinking!" Mazie hopped off the couch. "What are we thinking, like full frontal, or a tease?"

"Not full frontal!" I gasped before breaking into a fit of laughter. "Like, maybe getting ready to go out to the club or something to make him ... Jealous? Is that wrong?"

"We're demons, baby! Toxic is the name of the game. Come on, we are *so* doing this. Put on that dress you wore the first night you two went to The Mausoleum. Don't bother with shoes, we're not actually going anywhere."

I could agree with that. It took all my remaining energy to get out of my workout clothes and into that dress, but I managed it.

"Okay, let me fix you up." Mazie played with my hair, so it was strategically mussed and slipped one of the straps from my dress over my shoulder. "Now, pretend to be putting on one of my stilettos, and then put your hand out like you don't want me to be taking your picture."

I frowned at her, and asked, "Won't it be weird to send him a picture I didn't want taken?"

Mazie laughed and shook her head. "No, I'll send it as a group of pictures. Come on, just do it."

As I did as she directed, my phone chimed in her hand.

"It's an email, not him," she said. "I'm surprised it's taking him so long to respond. I'm either impressed, or worried for you."

It took me a second to catch onto what she was saying. "He's not doing *that.*" Though, I kind of hoped I *did* have that effect on him.

Mazie snapped a few pictures that turned out better than I'd expected, and then she took a few more of us together and sent them all off to Jayce.

"Shouldn't be long now," she said.

We flopped onto the couch.

"Are we doing too much?" I asked, laughing.

"Yes, but this is all the stuff you should have been able to do as a teenager, but you never did. So, I'm making sure you get these experiences *now.* Even if it seems like a little much." Mazie rested her head on mine.

174

"And you don't think Jayce will think it's too much? He's eight years older and probably thinking—"

"Don't even worry about what he's thinking," Mazie interrupted. "It doesn't matter. You're having fun and being yourself, and if he can't handle that, then he doesn't deserve you."

I knew she was right, but it didn't do anything to ease my nerves.

The chime of my phone woke me about twenty minutes later. Mazie was sound asleep beside me, so I draped a blanket over her and went to sit at the bar.

Brock: *You should meet me at Fever Dream Oliver and I just got here*

I bit my lip and glanced at Mazie. As tempting as the offer was, she seemed exhausted earlier, and I didn't want to wake her. I was also exhausted, and with as much freedom as Dominic was giving me lately, I wasn't breaking his rule of not going out alone. If he found out, he might never let me work for him again.

Me: *My ride fell asleep*

Brock: *Want to go for a bike ride?*

Goosebumps. I silently screamed in excitement so I wouldn't wake Mazie but then panic set in. I wanted to see him, but after our texts, I wasn't sure I was ready to be face to face with him. As hard as I tried to be so confident and sensual, this was all still new to me. It was different with him than it had been with Enzo because this was *real.*

But my excitement won out.

> **Me:** *To be honest, the only reason I've been hanging out with you is because I've been hoping you'd take me for a ride*

Brock: *Then you're in luck*
Pick you up in ten

I glanced down. A slip dress was probably not the best attire for riding a motorcycle. Running to Mazie's closet, I pulled on a pair of black jeans, a black tee, and one of Mazie's leather jackets. She had one in every color, so I grabbed the red one.

Mazie shifted on the couch but didn't wake, so I left her a note on the coffee table letting her know I was going out with Jayce, but I'd be back before morning.

Slipping out the door, I skipped to the elevator and couldn't stop smiling the whole way outside, fully rejuvenated from the adrenaline pumping through me. Even my muscles didn't seem as sore as before.

The heat of the night hit me like a wave, but it didn't bother me. I took a deep breath, relishing in the moment.

I heard Jayce's bike before I saw him coming down the street, but he wasn't alone. There was another Harley behind his, and I knew it was Oliver.

They pulled over in front of me and I had to bite my lip to stop myself from grinning and giving away my pure elation. I wanted to seem *somewhat* cool.

"He insisted on joining us," Jayce said, jerking his head to Oliver. "You ready to go?"

"Uh, yeah." I stepped closer to him, unsure whether I should get on the back, or what. But I swung my leg over the back of the bike, sitting on the cushioned pad behind Jayce.

I hesitated, knowing I should put my arms around him, but all the thoughts of our texts were swirling in my mind, and the heat of the night suddenly became unbearable.

Reaching a hand behind him, Jayce took my arm and pulled it around him, holding my hand to his abdomen.

"You're going to have to hold on," he said, chuckling. "I promise, I won't let you fall."

Becoming more comfortable, I put my other arm around him and leaned my chest against his back. None of us wore helmets, since we were all at least level three and durable enough to survive a fall.

Oliver revved his bike and pulled up beside us, shouting over the noise. "I'm not jealous at all. Jayce never lets me ride backpack."

In response, Jayce revved his bike, holding my hands at his front with one hand and keeping the other on the handlebars as he pulled back onto the road, speeding away from Oliver. A small squeak of surprise escaped me, and then I started laughing. He released his grip on me.

The wind whipped past us, cooling me down while Jayce heated me from the front. If I closed my eyes, it was almost what I imagined flying would be like.

I didn't often think about what I'd missed out on by my mother's power being taken instead of passed down to me, but it was moments like this that made me wonder what it would be like. Dominic didn't often fly, that I knew of, and I wondered if maybe it wasn't as enjoyable as I thought it would be. We didn't talk about it much, and I figured that was because he didn't want me to think I was missing out on anything.

When I opened my eyes, Oliver was weaving through oncoming traffic beside us. My heart raced as I watched him, but there weren't too many other cars on the road.

Oliver was in front of us, and he pointed to the right, veering down a side street, so Jayce followed. Pulling into an empty parking lot, Oliver and Jayce both parked and turned off their bikes.

"Got a tip on someone causing trouble at the nightclub down the street," Oliver said. "Dominic wants us to take care of it."

I took my hands from around Jayce and placed them behind me, bracing myself. Jayce turned to look at me.

"Are you okay if we go take care of this?" he asked.

This was their job, so I didn't want to keep them from it. And I was a little curious to see them in action.

I nodded. "Yeah. Let's go."

Oliver dismounted his bike, holding his hand out to me to help me from Jayce's. "You can wait outside for us. It could turn into a bit of a mess in there."

The thought of waiting alone outside of a nightclub in an area I'd never been was more nerve wracking than going in with them and dealing with whatever mess Oliver thought might happen.

Jayce stepped up beside me and seemed to guess my hesitancy as he took my hand in his.

"I know the night club owner, you can come in and hang behind the scenes," Jayce said. "You won't be alone."

The nightclub was a short walk from the parking lot, and we were let in immediately thanks to the bouncer recognizing the guys, or at the very least their cuts.

Inside it was dark with flashing lights and loud music, much like any other club I'd been to. Jayce kept hold of my hand as Oliver led the way through the crowd to the DJ at the back of the dance floor.

He hopped up beside the DJ and talked to him for a minute before coming back down to us.

"You're all set to go through that door there," he yelled over the music, pointing to a door beside the bar to the right of the DJ stand. "Don't come out until Jayce or I come and get you."

For some reason, I froze at the thought of leaving Jayce behind. There could be anything through that door. It could be like the back room at The Mausoleum, and I could come face to face with another dealer like Enzo. I wasn't ready for something like that. But I trusted Oliver.

Letting go of Jayce's hand, I wound through the crowd to the door. Once I stepped through it, a petite redhead with green skin and a purple long sleeve bodysuit hurried over to me and smiled.

"You must be Oliver's friend," she chirped and waved a hand to the room beyond. There were a few couches, but mostly there were tables with people playing cards or dice or other games. The room was *huge.*

"What is this place?" I asked, even though the answer was obvious. It was a gambling den. There was no reason to hide things like this in Hell, but they did tend to draw in the worst of the worst demons.

This place didn't seem nearly as scary as I'd imagined gambling dens would be. It was much brighter than the club area, and all the demons playing the games seemed in good spirits.

"This is Nova," she said. "I like to consider us a high-end gaming hall. But, in order to keep us on the higher end, we need your friends out there to take care of a few bad eggs for us."

"Oh," I huffed. That made sense. "What's your name?"

"Cecilia. But you can call me Cece." She smirked and winked. "Any friend of Oliver's is a friend of mine."

I stifled a laugh. "Right. So, what now?"

"Well, let me take you around and show you the different games." We started walking around the outskirts of the room.

"Do you know how long Jayce and Oliver are going to be?" I asked, not really interested in the games.

Cece lowered her voice and said, "I had a guy in here earlier counting cards and messing with some of my younger staff." She jerked her head to a young demon who was dealing cards at one of the tables. He was quick at shuffling and dealing and I was thoroughly impressed. "So, I called Dominic who forwarded me to Oliver. He's the one who usually helps us out here anyway."

"What are they going to do?" We paused beside a roulette table.

"They're going to make sure he never comes back here, or else, you know." She shrugged.

I narrowed my eyes. Maybe I did know, but it seemed extreme for what had happened. Unless there was something more I *didn't* know.

"You have to stay on top of demons like this or else they think they can get away with anything. Then we have a whole other problem on our hands." Cece shook her head, and I wondered how often she had to deal with demons causing problems.

"Right." I scanned the room. It made me realize how right Dominic had been when he'd called me naïve. After so long of being cooped up in the mansion, watching human TV shows, and only going to *safe* areas when I went out, I never knew what it actually meant to live in Hell. It was a ruthless, lawless place. Except, Dominic and his men were what took place of the law when Lucifer wasn't around.

"Come on. Let's get you a drink." Cece led the way to a smaller version of the bar that had been in the club area.

By the time we got our drinks and walked the rest of the perimeter of the room, Jayce came to let me know it was time to go. I didn't miss the blood stains on his jeans and hands. He noticed me staring and flexed his hand, his rings catching the light. I'd admired Enzo's hands when I first met him, but they couldn't compare.

Jayce didn't try to take my hand as if he thought I wouldn't *want* to hold his hand anymore. But it didn't bother me.

I handed my empty glass to Cece. "Thank you for keeping me company," I said, before turning back to Jayce and taking his hand. "Let's get out of here."

Pulling me closer, Jayce kissed my temple and put his arm around my shoulders. My skin tingled from his touch. I feared I was becoming obsessed with him.

"See you next time, Cece," he said, waving to Cece before steering us out of the gambling room.

We couldn't walk side by side through the club, so he held my hand as we squeezed through the crowd. Oliver was waiting for us outside, chatting with the bouncer.

"There's our girl," he said when Jayce and I appeared.

"*Mine,*" Jayce corrected, tucking me against his side and putting his arm around me, making me blush.

"Yeah, yeah. Come on." Oliver walked ahead of us back to the lot we'd left the bikes.

I was tempted to ask them what had happened with the demon they'd been called in to *take care of,* but I refrained. If it was anything like the movies I'd seen about crime bosses and gangs, I could guess what they had to do. I didn't need the details.

"I'm gonna call it a night," Oliver said when we reached the bikes. "And you should too, Emmy. We've got training tomorrow."

As if the mention of it reminded my body how tired it was, exhaustion washed over me, and all my aches came back.

"Olly's probably right," Jayce teased, leaning against his bike seat, as I stood in front of him.

Oliver started his bike and left us alone.

It was all too easy to take the few steps to position myself between Jayce's thighs and slip my arms over his shoulders. His hands gripped my waist, and he gave me a devilish grin.

"I should really get you home," Jayce said, reaching out to tuck my hair behind my ear.

"Mmhmm." I kissed him, losing myself in the feel and taste of him. This was something I'd never imagined I could have; *he* was someone I'd never imagined I could have. And here we were.

"Take me home, Jayce," I murmured, stepping back.

After Jayce dropped me back at Mazie's, I kept replaying that moment in my mind. For some reason, even though it was probably the most innocent thing we'd done so far, it had sparked something more in me than any other moment with Jayce had. And I couldn't wait to see him again.

Chapter 16

Ember

During training the next day, Oliver taught me how to disarm someone who was holding a weapon. The moves were simple enough, but remembering the sequence took me a few rounds of practice to learn.

It was kind of strange how professional Oliver was while we trained. He'd make jokes here and there, but mostly he was *serious.* I'd never have imagined he had it in him.

At the end of our session, I mentioned it to him. "You really take this training stuff seriously, huh?" I asked, still out of breath.

He shrugged. "Well, yeah. Before I started working for Dominic, it was my job. I had to take it seriously, and demons relied on me to teach them how to defend themselves."

"You're a great teacher."

"Tell Jayce that," he said, winking. "Make sure he knows what he's missing out on."

"I'll get right on that," I joked.

184

Picking up a towel and wiping his face, Oliver smirked. "Well, he'll be here any minute, so you can tell him then."

"Why is he coming here?" I asked, trying not to let my excitement show on my face.

"Cards with Dom tonight. We rotate whose house we play at, and tonight it's here."

"So, Jayce *and* Dominic will be here soon?" I could hide things from Dominic to an extent, but he wasn't stupid. He'd know something was going on if he saw Jayce and I together.

Before I could think too much about it, my phone buzzed, and I grabbed it from the table where I'd put it while we trained.

Unknown: *If you need a fix,*
come over to the Westside tonight
110 Brimstone St.

"Oh, shit," I breathed.

"Hm?" Oliver dropped his towel into the laundry basket beside the table.

"I think Enzo texted me. I mean, it's an unknown number, but ..." I showed him the message.

Oliver's eyes widened. "That seems like a text from a drug dealer. A little ominous and vague. I guess it will just be me, Kit, and Dom tonight."

"Who's Kit?" I asked.

"His real name's Chris. He's a low-level runner, but he's great at cards." A gleam in Oliver's eye told me Kit might be a little more than that, but I said nothing.

I tapped Jayce's contact in my phone. "I should call Jayce and let him know about Enzo in case he's not on his way here yet."

Oliver pulled out his phone and opened his *Find My Friends* app. "He's pulling in now." He showed me the little dot that was Jayce moving down the driveway. "Don't tell him I linked our phones, though. I did it for his own good."

"You sound like his mother," I teased.

"Yeah, well, when the two of you wind up stranded in a ditch somewhere tonight, guess who'll be the one to come to your rescue?"

A quick knock on the front door preceded the creak of it opening and closing. Oliver left the training room, which was also the weight room and kick-boxing studio. He had every kind of workout implement and machine I could think of.

"Jayce! Chop chop! You're needed elsewhere!" Oliver called.

"What are you talking about?" The annoyance in Jayce's voice made me laugh. Oliver was always getting on his nerves, but they were still best friends. It was cute.

"Emmy! Come tell him!" Oliver yelled at me.

Leaving the training room, I met them in the entryway. "Only my best friend calls me that, Oliver," I said.

Jayce smiled when he saw me, and I had to fight not to lose my cool.

Oliver shrugged. "You called me Olly the other night, fair is fair."

I *had* called him that, the night we'd been at Fever Dream, but Jayce called him that too.

"Fine," I said. "If I can call you Olly, then I'll allow you to call me Emmy. Deal?"

Oliver clapped once. "Deal. Now show him the text! Time is of the essence!"

Jayce's smile disappeared. "What text?"

Pulling up Enzo's text, I showed it to Jayce.

"We have to go, right?" I asked.

Jayce cleared his throat. "Uh, yeah. Oliver, let Dom know what's going on. I'll text you if anything gets sketchy."

"Go! Don't waste your time talking to me!" Oliver ushered us out the door.

Jayce opened the passenger door of his car for me, but he still hadn't really said anything to me yet, and I wasn't sure if I should be the one to break the ice. But I at least needed to make sure we were stopping at Mazie's apartment so I could change. I wasn't showing up to what was most likely a party in my work out wear.

"Can we stop at my place so I can change really quick?" I asked.

"Yeah. Enzo wouldn't expect us to arrive too immediately, otherwise he'd know we were waiting for him. Send him a message and let him know we might stop by."

Mazie wasn't home when we got to the apartment, but I had a key.

"Don't wear a dress tonight, or heels. Something feels off and we need to be ready to leave quickly if anything goes wrong," Jayce instructed.

I rinsed off in the shower, not letting my hair get wet, and applied a tiny bit of makeup. Even though Jayce said we didn't need to hurry, I couldn't shake the feeling we would miss Enzo if we didn't. I borrowed a pair of black skinny jeans and thigh-high boots from Mazie. They were probably one of her only pairs without a heel. I grabbed a black tube top I'd left behind one of our night's out and put that on.

"Ready," I announced when I stepped out of Mazie's room into the living room where Jayce waited on the couch. "Is this okay?" I spun around in a full circle when he looked at me.

"Can we talk for a minute before we go?" he asked, barely giving me a once over.

I furrowed my brow. "Is it the outfit? I can change."

He laughed. "No, you look gorgeous, as always. Come here." Putting his arm on the back of the couch, he waited while I walked over and sat beside him.

"What's up?" I asked, looking at my hands while I picked at one of the holes in my pants.

"Nothing's going to happen tonight," he said, and I looked up at him. "Enzo doesn't deserve to touch you."

"And you do?" I asked, smirking.

"Only if you say so," he said, remaining serious.

Without thinking, I leaned up and kissed him. Pulling back after enough to say, "I give you permission to touch me."

One of his hands dug into my hair, while the other gripped my thigh as he kissed me.

I moved up to my knees and swung one of my legs over Jayce's lap, straddling him. "I'm regretting not wearing a dress," I said between kisses.

"The things we want most we have to work harder for," he teased, pressing his lips to the side of my neck. "But like I said, nothing is happening tonight." He leaned back, looking up at me.

"Are you rejecting me?" I asked, trying to keep my tone light, but it stung a little.

He tucked my hair behind my ear.

"Are you kidding me? I've been imagining this moment for weeks. But we need to focus on Enzo tonight," he said.

I pouted. "Fine." Climbing off his lap, I grabbed my clutch from the table and headed for the door.

Jayce stood and took my free hand. I let him pull me back toward him. "I promise you, once we're done dealing with Enzo, I'll be happy to pick up where we left off." He grinned.

I took a step, closing the gap between us and rested my forehead against his chest. "You're just trying to make me feel better."

He tipped my chin up with his thumb, forcing me to look at him, and his voice lowered, coming out gravelly. "The only reason I'm not stripping these clothes off you right now is because Enzo doesn't get to see your just fucked look. That's reserved for me alone."

"Oh," I breathed, biting my lip as I smiled.

He kissed me and it felt like a promise of things to come.

Before we crossed the border into Westside territory, Jayce pulled into the parking lot of a bar and parked. We waited for a ride share to take us the rest of the way, in case anyone at the location we were headed decided to try and trace Jayce's car.

When we pulled up to the address Enzo had given us, we had to get out of the ride share because it was a gated mansion. No one uninvited was allowed inside.

We were buzzed in and walked down the long driveway toward the house. There were fancy cars lining the driveway when we got closer, and music thumped through the night.

"This is quite the event," I said. "I wonder why Enzo would invite us to *this*."

"I guess we're going to find out." Jayce seemed on edge, his eyes scanning our surroundings every few seconds. "Don't let yourself get separated from me. There's a lot of people here, and anything could happen."

We were met at the door by a large demon with huge ram-like horns. "Name," he asked.

"Mazie and Brock," I told him. "Enzo invited us."

He stepped aside without checking a list, which made me question why he bothered asking our names. Unless he'd been waiting for us.

I linked my arm with Jayce's, holding tightly to him as we moved through the entryway into the mansion. The lights were dim and there were demons everywhere.

"Don't drink anything," he murmured. There were demons holding trays of drinks in each room. Jayce took one to hold, so I grabbed one too. It would seem less suspicious if we at least pretended to be enjoying ourselves.

"I don't see Enzo," I said as we entered a large area that reminded me of a ballroom in a castle. There were even pillars like the ones at The Mausoleum.

"Come on, I don't think he'd be in here." Jayce steered us back to the smaller living area, which was still bigger than Mazie's whole apartment. This mansion put mine and Dominic's to shame.

There were so many demons in the mansion, we kept bumping into people, and with the lighting so low, it was hard to tell if I recognized any of them.

"I know you said we should stick together, but I think it might be easier to slip through the crowds and find Enzo if we split up. Then whichever of us finds him first can text the other and we can reconvene," I suggested.

Jayce didn't look too keen on that idea, but he nodded. "Yeah, you might be right. But text me *before* approaching him if you find him. Okay?"

"Will do," I agreed. We went opposite directions, Jayce toward the entryway to try the other side of the mansion, and me back toward the ballroom.

As I walked, I caught myself sipping the drink I'd been holding. "Fuck," I hissed, dropping the cup as if it had bit me. No one spared me a glance, too busy having fun or chatting with their groups. I'd drank at least half of the cup before I'd realized what I'd been doing, and I could tell there was more than just alcohol in that drink.

Amateur, I thought, shaking my head. If it was anything like the drink I'd had at The Mausoleum, it wouldn't take long to wear off, I just needed to find a place to cool down for a few minutes while the worst of the disorientation passed.

I veered down a hallway where no one else was going. There was a large double door at the end, and I paused outside of it, hearing voices inside.

"—and the horns. The power from those isn't as strong, but it will hold him over. If we don't find some more powerful demons soon, Jericho will be in trouble."

I blinked rapidly, both trying to clear my vision, and trying to understand what I was hearing.

"You'd be a better boss than him, anyway," a feminine voice drawled.

"Watch your fucking mouth," Enzo snapped.

Losing my footing, I bumped into a fake plant beside the door, and the pot screeched as it slid on the floor.

"What was that?" Enzo asked.

The right door slammed open against the wall, barely missing me.

"There's someone out here," Draco said, grabbing my arm before I could run. "That bitch from the club." Hauling me into the room that turned out to be a study, he shut the doors behind us.

"Rude," I muttered.

"Oh, Mazie," Enzo tutted. "I was looking forward to seeing you and you had to go and spoil it all by sneaking around in places you aren't meant to be."

"I-I didn't hear anything," I tried. "Someone gave me a drink, and I wound up down here." I forced a smile and tried to giggle like I was drunk.

"The problem is, I don't believe you." He waved two demons forward. "Take care of her, ladies."

In a panic, I yelled, "Wait! Brock is with me, he'll come looking for me!"

"Then I'll kill him, too," Enzo drawled. "Problem solved."

"No, please." I had to think quickly to save Jayce. I wasn't going to let *my* stupidity end his life. "He doesn't know anything, so there's no reason to have one more demon go missing. Let me dictate a text for you to send him from my phone. That way you know I'm not trying anything, and he can get out of here safely."

"I don't owe either of you anything. Why should I bother?" Enzo appeared bored.

I hesitated as a story wove its way through my mind.

"Brock isn't really my boyfriend," I started, knowing the only way through this was to reveal some truths. "He's been helping me as a favor. I'm close friends with his real girlfriend,

Ember Russo." I was probably royally fucking up, but I had no other ideas. I was already dead, so it didn't matter what they knew about me, or who they thought I was. "Dominic Russo's sister. Brock has no idea about the drug business, and he's only here to keep me safe while I try and get information on Jericho. I told him you were an ex-boyfriend I was trying to get a family heirloom back from. He'd do anything for Ember, and if anything happens to him, she'll be more than happy to make sure it's known that the Westside started a turf war." Lucifer frowned on turf wars since it usually meant breaking his one big rule. No killing higher rank demons.

Enzo scoffed. "Nice try. Dominic Russo doesn't have a sister."

I lifted my chin. "He does. She's the Russo family's best kept secret, and if you doubt me, text Dominic on my phone that I fucked up and let *you* know Ember exists and see how he reacts."

Enzo narrowed his eyes and tapped his fingers on his desk. "If you're telling me the truth, then you've handed me Southside on a silver platter."

What he didn't realize was once he had me killed, he'd actually have nothing.

"Fine," he snapped. "Give Georgia your phone. She'll text Brock while they take you away from here. I can't have blood staining my newly installed carpet." He sneered and waved his hand to the demon who I assumed was Georgia.

Georgia and another demon stepped up on either side of me, taking my arms and leading me out a back door to an SUV with blacked out windows. Draco followed, getting into the driver's seat while me and my two captors climbed into the back.

"Phone," Georgia said, holding her hand out to me. I passed it to her as the SUV jerked forward.

"Brock," I reminded her as she scrolled through my contacts. At least my forethought of putting Jayce under his fake name was paying off. One thing had gone right for me.

She started typing and I watched over her shoulder.

> **Me:** *I got sick and Enzo's driver*
> *offered me a ride home*
> *I'll text you when we get there*

"I wouldn't say that," I said, pointing to the screen. "Brock may not be my boyfriend, but he *is* overprotective. I'd start by saying, *please don't be mad.*"

Georgia let out an exaggerated sigh but added my suggestion to the start of the text. He'd probably have guessed something was wrong either way, but this way I could guarantee it.

We rode in silence for the rest of the trip. We wound up in the middle of nowhere, with no demons for miles around. Georgia got out of the SUV first, and when I followed her, the demon behind me shoved me so I fell flat on my face, scraping it and my arms.

Flipping over, I scrambled away from her, but Georgia was already at my back. "What exactly are you going to do to me?" I asked.

"Jules is going to kill you while I watch," Georgia said, grinning.

"Some kind of fetish or kinky thing?" I asked, trying not to let my terror show.

"Initiation," Georgia said. "Now shut up and stay still."

Yeah, as if I'd do that.

Jules stepped up to me, rearing her leg back to land a kick to my ribs. She wore steel toe boots, and now I understood why.

At the last second, I rolled away, getting clipped by her boot. It was painful, but manageable. I jumped to my feet, trying to remember what little training I'd had with Oliver. We'd only done one day of strength training and then a day learning how to disarm someone. Neither of those things would help me in that situation.

Fuck. Running was out of the question because the drug was still coursing through me and making my movements sluggish. Georgia and Jules would easily overtake me. But it might buy the time I needed for someone to show up, *if* anyone showed up.

So, I turned and ran. Georgia cackled while I assumed Jules took off after me, since I only heard one set of footsteps gaining on me. One second, I was running and the next, Jules tackled me to the ground.

I lifted my arms to cover my face while Jules pommeled me. Each strike stung worse than the last. She wore something on her fingers that made the blows more painful; more lethal. Most likely some kind of brass knuckles.

One of her strikes landed on my right wing and I screamed in agony.

She paused for a few seconds, and I tried to buck her off me, but when I went to move my arms to try and fight her, a punch near my right armpit left me breathless. Warmth spread from the impact point.

She hadn't punched me. She'd *stabbed me.*

Gasping as the pain hit, the adrenaline kicked in and I was able to shove her off me, but she took her knife with her. Blood seeped from the wound at an alarming rate.

"I'll leave you to bleed out and die here, alone, like you deserve," Jules hissed. I had no idea what she had against me.

Georgia had rejoined us at some point and dropped my phone out of reach.

They left me alone, as they promised, and I had nothing to do but stare at the dark red sky as I lay dying. But I wouldn't give up yet. As painful as it was, I crawled the few feet across the rocky ground to my phone.

My back throbbed, and I was pretty sure my wing was broken, but I'd worry about that if I survived. I was already feeling woozy from blood loss, which couldn't be a good sign.

When I held my phone, the screen lit up as it registered my face and unlocked. I opened my recent calls and tapped the first name: *Brock*.

It rang once before Jayce picked up.

"Are you safe? I got your text and had Oliver send me your location. Don't ask, that's a later problem. I'm not far from where it says you are." If I had to guess, I'd say angels sounded a lot like Jayce did to me at that moment.

A sob escaped me, and my ribs ached. I had to put my phone down on the ground and a wracking cough took over, blood mixing with my saliva as I spit it out.

"Fuck, Ember, I'm almost there. I swear to fucking Lucifer." He almost sounded as scared as I felt.

"Don't hang up," I managed to get out, pleading with him as another sob came and I dissolved into a fit of them.

"I'm not hanging up. I'm right here," he said.

I could hear the car through the speaker and the engine revved as the gears shifted.

"Fuck fuck fuck. I'm two minutes away." He sounded desperate and I wanted to console him, but I was too tired.

My eyelids were heavy, so I let them close. I tried to take deep breaths, but it was too painful, so they were short and gasping.

When a car finally pulled up, I couldn't bring myself to open my eyes. It all seemed far away, as if in a dream.

"Ember!"

I didn't answer; didn't want to or couldn't. A weight lifted from me, and it felt like I was flying, but then I was on a softer surface, something warm thrown over me. After that, I remembered nothing.

Chapter 17

Jayce

As soon as I got Ember's text, *Please don't be mad at me ... I*'d almost fucking lost it. We'd been separated for less than ten minutes and everything went to shit.

I left the party immediately, calling Oliver.

"What's Ember's location?" I asked when he answered.

"Why would I have that?" he asked, but we both knew he had *everyone's* location.

"Fuck, Oliver, give me her location, I don't have time for this." It was hard not to completely lose my shit, but I had to keep it together if I wanted to find her. Something told me she wasn't in the mansion anymore, but I needed to know for sure before I left.

"Right. She's moving away from your dot. Northeast," Oliver said.

Okay. That meant I needed a car. Moving from car to car, I found one that was unlocked. If they were stupid enough to leave it unlocked, then the keys should also be ...

198

I pulled down the visor and the keys dropped into my lap. The owner of the car must have assumed there wouldn't be anyone at the party dumb enough to try stealing a car when the whole area was gated and everyone was likely armed.

"Got a car," I told Oliver who was still on the phone with me. "Is Dominic with you?"

"No, we cancelled cards, and he stayed home to wait for an update from you."

"Don't tell him what's happening. I'll fill him in once it's over." I paused as I pulled up to the gate. "Do you think an Audi would survive ramming through a ten-foot-tall iron gate?"

"Absolutely not. The car would be undrivable after that," Oliver said.

I glanced at my phone, wishing Ember would call or text me again. Her text said she'd left, so did that mean I was expected to leave too?

Pulling up to the gate, I pressed the call button on the speaker set up at car window height.

"Name," someone crackled over the speaker. They were serious about who they let in *and* out.

"Brock." I didn't bother trying to come up with a last name. I couldn't imagine there would be too many demons named *Brock* at a party like this.

The gates opened and as grateful as I was, I had an inkling that meant things were more dire than I'd originally thought.

"What did you do, Ember," I murmured to myself as I pulled out of the driveway.

"I'm still here, by the way," Oliver piped up. "And I've shared Ember's location with you so you can have your GPS take you right to her."

Fumbling with my phone, I held it up, clicking on the link Oliver had sent and watching as it took its time setting up the best route to her.

"All right, I'm hanging up in case Ember calls. I'll update you when I have her with me." I ended the phone call before Oliver could respond.

Once I hit the first straight way, I pushed the pedal to the floor.

I wasn't sure how long I'd been driving when my phone rang. There was no music playing because I wanted to be sure I didn't miss any calls, and my phone's ringer was all the way up, scaring the shit out of me.

Grabbing it, I picked up after the first ring.

"Are you safe? I got your text and had Oliver send me your location. Don't ask, that's a later problem. I'm not far from where it says you are," I said in a rush.

Ember's sob came in crackled over the phone, but there was no doubting what I'd heard, followed by a wracking cough.

I tried to press the gas pedal harder, but I was already maxing out my speed and a turn was coming up.

"Fuck, Ember," I gasped. "I'm almost there. I swear to fucking Lucifer."

"Don't hang up." Her pleading and sobbing broke something in me.

"I'm not hanging up. I'm right here." There was nothing around for miles, but my GPS said I was coming up to her location. "Fuck fuck fuck. I'm two minutes away."

I hadn't passed any other cars while driving the last stretch taking me to Ember's location, so whoever brought her out there must have gone the opposite direction. Turning off the road, I drove for another quarter of a mile until I saw her and my heart nearly stopped.

Leaving the car running, I put it in park and threw open my door. "Ember!"

With the amount of blood soaked into the ground next to her and her closed eyes, for a brief horrific moment, I thought she was dead.

Skidding to a stop beside her, I crouched down and checked her pulse first. It was faint, but she was still alive. Relief was quickly replaced with rage at whomever had done this to her. Enzo wouldn't dirty his hands like that, but he'd pay for it either way. I'd make sure of it.

I stripped my shirt off and used it to cover Ember's wound. She groaned and I took that as a good sign, at least she was still semi-conscious.

"Stay with me, Ember," I said, gently lifting her from the ground.

She whimpered. One of her wings was definitely broken. I got her into the backseat of the car. Opening the glove box, I dug around until I found a bottle of pills. It looked like the same pills Enzo had been dealing. I figured it was better than nothing and gave one to Ember, hoping it would at least dull the pain she must be experiencing.

In Hell, we didn't have hospitals. There were demons you could go to or have come to your house to help you while using spells from grimoires, and as luck would have it, one of those kinds of demons raised me. But they were in Southside territory, which meant Ember had to make it long enough for us to get there.

"Hold on, Ember," I couldn't help saying, even though she wouldn't hear me.

When I pulled up outside my usual spot for when I got in a scrape, all the lights were off inside the house. The couple who lived there, Nico and Marge, were older and tended to sleep at night rather than during the day. But they'd been in the business of taking care of others for longer than I'd been alive. They'd taken me in when my parents dumped me on their doorstep at ten years old for a vacation that turned into a two-year road trip.

I ran up the steps to their door and pounded on it.

"Nico!" I called. "It's Jayce!" Then I ran back to the car and carefully lifted Ember's limp body. I couldn't bring myself to check her pulse again. There was nothing more I could do for her but pray to Lucifer that Nico and Marge could save her.

"Jayce?" Marge stood in the doorway, blinking in the glow of the porch light she'd turned on. Without hesitation, she moved aside and said, "Bring her in."

They had a table in the room to the left of the front door that I laid Ember on.

Marge put a hand on my shoulder. "Honey, you're shaking," she said, her voice soothing and kind, as always.

Nico came into the room and got to work. He wasn't much for talking, but he knew how to get a job done. Peeling my shirt from Ember's shoulder, he tutted.

"She's lost too much blood," he muttered to himself. "And yet."

Marge ushered me from the room. "Nico will take care of her, don't you worry." She shut the door behind us and walked me into the living room, giving me a light push to sit on the couch. "I don't think I've ever seen you so shaken up before. Who is that girl in there?"

I lifted my gaze from the floor to look at Marge. Her chin-length brown hair was perfectly straight, as always, and her clothing without a single wrinkle. Almost like she hadn't been in bed after all.

"She's my—" My what? She wasn't my girlfriend, because we hadn't had that conversation yet. "My partner. Ember. We were working on an important task for Dominic, and it went awry."

"Oh, honey," she drawled, sitting beside me and taking my hands in hers. "She's more to you than that. But I know you like to keep your personal life to yourself, so I won't pry."

"That's not true, I just haven't had anything or anyone I've cared to tell you about." It wasn't exactly a lie.

"Mm. Well, you rest, I'm going to help Nico." She patted my hands and stood, leaving me alone in the living room.

All I could think about was how badly I wanted to rip Enzo limb from limb. I kept trying to come up with some way I could do it without getting myself killed in the process, but nothing was coming to mind. He was too high up in the food chain, Jericho would demand payment for taking someone like Enzo out, and Lucifer would deliver me straight to Jericho's doorstep.

Picking up my phone, I called Dominic. He needed to know what had happened.

"How did it go?" he asked when he answered.

I bit my knuckle, trying to calm myself before I responded. "Fuck, Dom." My voice shook and I cleared my throat to try and stop that.

"What the fuck happened, Jayce." His tone changed from casual to lethal.

"It's Ember—"

"Is she okay? Tell me she's okay. Where are you? I'm coming to you."

I'd never heard Dominic panic before, even when his own parents had been killed.

"Fucking talk to me, Jayce. Is. She. Okay?" His tone sharpened with each word.

"I'm at Nico and Marge's and they're taking care of her. I think she'll be okay, but fucking Enzo ..." I trailed off, unable to form words with the rage building.

"Enzo hurt her? I'll fucking gut him. Tell me where he is," Dominic demanded.

"Shit, Dom. I was calling so you could talk *me* off the ledge. Enzo is considered high rank, so we have to be smart about this." Somehow, I had become the reasonable one.

"Fuck, I know you're right. We have to be smart about this," Dominic huffed, repeating my words.

"Are you going to tell me who she really is to you? I've never heard you so riled up over anyone before." A part of me was terrified he'd admit he loved her or something. Then I'd be the asshole who'd overstepped on my best friend's girl.

Dominic let out a long breath followed by a minute of silence. I didn't try to fill the silence, because I needed the truth from him.

"Ember isn't just a friend," he admitted.

Fuck, he does *fucking love her.*

"She's my sister," he finished.

"I fucking knew— Wait what?" I almost dropped the phone. "You don't have a sister."

He laughed dryly. "My parents kept her hidden so no one could use her as a pawn against them. I've been keeping up with that to keep her safe all this time. But she talked me into letting her join the family business, which was clearly a colossal mistake."

Oh my fucking god. Ember was his sister. This was almost worse than what I'd expected. If he found out what had happened between her and Enzo, and then her and me ...

I dug my hand into my hair and leaned back into the couch. *Fuuuck.*

"You still there?" Dominic asked.

"Yeah. Just processing." *And planning my funeral.* "Are you coming here?"

"Not yet. I trust Nico and Marge to take care of her. I have a few things I need to take care of. Keep me updated with any changes, or if I should ..." He stopped and I could have sworn there was a waver in his voice. "Just keep me updated."

"I will," I promised. "Don't do anything stupid."

"Yeah, you either."

The phone went silent, and I put it down.

A muffled scream came from the room Ember was in, and it took everything in me not to go to her. I had to trust Nico and Marge, and I did, more than anyone. Besides, screaming meant she was *alive.*

Laying down on the couch, I closed my eyes, figuring I wouldn't be able to fall asleep.

Somehow, a couple of hours passed, and Marge shook me awake. "She's asking for you."

My heart leapt into my throat, and I nodded, hopping off the couch and following Marge. She handed me a T-shirt, and I pulled it on.

Ember had been moved from the table in their makeshift ER, into the spare bedroom that used to be mine whenever I stayed there.

"She's been in and out. We gave her a lot of drugs. But she's alive, so thank Lucifer for that," Marge said.

"Lucifer had nothing to do with it," Nico grumbled as he stepped out of the room to join us in the hall. "She should have died. But *something* kept her alive."

All I could think of was the pill I'd given her in the car, but I didn't tell them that. It was a hunch anyway.

The room was dark with the curtains drawn. A tiny bit of daylight came in around the edges of the curtains, enough to see Ember lying in the twin-sized bed, her pink skin more grayish than normal, and dark circles under her eyes. Her wing that had been broken was wrapped and splayed out to the side.

"Jayce," she croaked my name, and I went to her, my fear of Dominic momentarily forgotten.

I knelt at her bedside and ran a hand over her forehead, smoothing away some of the hair that had stuck there. Her eyes were closed, but her breathing was much stronger than it had been when we'd arrived.

"I'm here," I said quietly, not wanting to wake her if she'd fallen back asleep.

"You found me," she said, smiling weakly as she opened her eyes. "I thought I was going to die."

"I thought you were too. You scared me." I took her hand that lay between us and kissed it.

She drew in a shuddering breath, and I worried she might be in pain. Tears rimmed her eyes.

"I told them everything. I had to save you ..." she said through the tears. "I ruined our mission, I'm so sorry."

I stood and leaned over so I could look into her eyes, and she would understand how serious I was. "You didn't ruin anything, Ember, and you have no reason to be sorry. Whatever you told them, they let me leave through the front gate and that let me get to you in time to save you. So, don't be sorry."

She nodded and closed her eyes. "I'm so tired." Her brow furrowed.

"Go to sleep, I'll be right here."

Chapter 18

Ember

When I woke, I was in a bed that wasn't my own. There was enough light creeping into the room around the curtains so I could see, and I didn't recognize anything. My right wing was wrapped and splayed out to my side.

Panic set it, but then I saw Jayce sitting beside the bed, asleep. I tried to sit up, but pain lanced through my shoulder, and I gasped, dropping back down.

The movement startled Jayce, and he turned to look at me.

"You're awake," he said. "How do you feel?"

I adjusted to sit up and winced. "Well, I'm not dead. So, a win is a win."

"What happened, Ember?" he asked.

It took me a few seconds for the memories of the night before to come back to me, but when they did, it was like a tidal wave. Every blow and kick, and then the knife ...

"I accidentally drank that drink I had, and I was trying to find a place to lay low for a few minutes when I overheard Enzo talking with some of his people," I said. "I'm not sure why exactly, but they were talking about stealing demons' power for Jericho, I think. I thought Jericho was already one of the most powerful demons in Hell."

"He is." Jayce ground his jaw as his brow furrowed. "But a demon's power can fade over time, and I have no idea how old Jericho is."

"Horns and wings are the only parts of a demon that can be taken for power, right?" I asked. Even if it weren't against the newer demon codes enforced by the higher ranks, my smaller wings marked me as someone without enough power to make them worth stealing, but I was grateful anyway.

"Right." He dragged the word out. Standing, he paced the room. "If we can find a way to prove this, Lucifer might step in. A demon trying to horde power like that can't be something he would approve of. It would mean killing multiple upper rank demons."

"Can we talk about this later? My head is pounding," I said, putting my hand to my temple and rubbing it.

Jayce stopped his pacing. "Yeah. I'll go get you something for it." He was out of the room before I could say anything to stop him. All I really wanted was to feel him next to me, so I'd know this was real. I may not be dead, but I was still convinced I was on the brink, back out in the middle of nowhere, waiting for someone to show up and save me and this was all a hallucination.

I closed my eyes, leaning my head back against the wall. The coolness of it helped with my headache.

When Jayce came back, he handed me two pills and a glass of water, then retreated to the center of the room. "That will help," he said.

I didn't argue and took the pills. "When can I leave here?"

"Whenever you feel comfortable leaving."

"Why are you so far away?" I asked. "Sit with me, please." My bottom lip wobbled, and embarrassment flooded me. *Please.* That had been our safe word. Using it now seemed wrong. I never would have before.

Jayce closed the distance between us and sat on the edge of the bed. "Anything you want," he said. "Tell me what you need from me, and I'll do it."

"Kiss me?" I hadn't meant for it to come out as a question, but he complied.

Leaning in, he pressed his lips to mine, softly, as if he might break me. I cupped his face in my hands, holding him there, our foreheads pressed together as we shared breath.

His phone buzzed and he sighed.

"Dominic is on his way," he said.

I blinked in surprise. "Does he know everything?" I asked.

"He knows what happened to you, and he's going to take you to ..." He hesitated. "To his house, to make sure you're safe until you fully recover." He pulled away and I knew our moment had ended. Dominic would arrive any minute, and he couldn't find us like that. But we had more important things to talk about anyway, like what I'd revealed to Enzo.

"Did Dominic tell you anything else?" I asked.

Before he could answer, Marge called from the front room, "Dominic is here!"

"Send him in," Jayce called back. "I'll give you two a minute alone," he said to me.

Dominic strolled into the room as if his sister hadn't almost died the night before, and I wanted to slap him for it. But I knew it was all an act. He always had to look the part of a leader, no matter what.

Jayce left the room and shut the door to give Dominic and I privacy. Once we were alone, Dominic's mask fell, and he was kneeling at the side of my bed as Jayce had done.

"I'm okay, Dom, really," I said, laughing.

"You almost died Em! What the hell were you thinking?" His gaze searched my face as if he'd find answers there.

"I was thinking Enzo had information we needed, so I would get it. And I did." I was probably a bit smugger than I should be.

He cocked his head and sat on the edge of my bed, so we were eye level. I told him everything Enzo had said, and he had the same realization as Jayce. That if we could prove it, Lucifer might step in and take care of the problem for us.

"There is one more thing you need to know," I said, bracing myself for his anger. "I told Enzo you have a sister."

"You what?" Dominic asked far too calmly.

"He doesn't know it's me; he still thinks my name is Mazie. But I needed to give him a reason not to kill Jayce, so I told him Jayce was dating your sister, Ember, but he knew nothing about the family business. He was only helping me as a favor, because I'm close with Ember."

"So, he thinks you're dead, but Ember is alive. That's not confusing at all." He groaned and ran a hand down his face.

"And that means you won't be safe at the mansion until he's taken care of."

I hadn't thought of that part, but since Enzo was definitely interested in using Dominic's sister to get to Dominic, then the mansion was the last place I should be.

"But if I can find someone to pose as you, we could get inside Jericho's mansion." Dominic grinned. "This could work to our advantage. I need time to plan."

"I'm sure I can stay with Mazie or Penny," I suggested.

Dominic shook his head. "No. I need them. You'll stay with Jayce. His apartment is more secure than Mazie's or Penny's anyway."

Okay, so he definitely doesn't know about Jayce and I, I thought. This would be interesting.

"As long as you're comfortable with that," Dominic added.

"I mean, I'm fine with it, but you should check with Jayce. It's his apartment, *he* may not be comfortable with it," I pointed out.

"Hm." Dominic went to the door and opened it. "Jayce."

It took a few seconds, but Jayce met him in the hall. "Are you taking her home?" he asked.

"Not exactly. I have an idea that requires Ember to not be in the mansion. You're the only one I trust to keep her safe, despite how last night ended. Can she stay with you for a few days?" Dominic asked, adding, "Until I work out my plan."

Jayce did a good job of keeping a straight face from what I could see.

"She can't stay with Mazie or Penny?" Jayce asked.

I scrunched my nose. Why was he trying to pawn me off on someone else? Did he not *want* to spend time with me? Or was there something else?

"I'm going to be using them for my plan, hopefully. And neither of their apartments has as much security as yours," Dominic argued.

"You do remember that Ember *broke* into my apartment? Right?" Jayce was really trying his best to convince my brother without saying an outright 'no.'

"That's only because Penny was with her. Will you let her stay with you or not? Because if not, I'll need to find someone else, maybe Oliver—"

"She can stay with me," Jayce said.

Dominic clapped once. "Perfect. I'll bring the two of you there now and get started on my side of things."

"I have to deal with that car." Jayce hooked his thumb over his shoulder, pointing to the front of the house.

"You mean the one you stole from Enzo's party? Yeah, I've already got someone dealing with it and retrieving yours. The fact that you didn't notice it was gone is concerning. You've been a little distracted lately, don't let it happen again."

"Stop being a bully, Dom," I chimed in. "Come help me so we can get going."

"Jayce, help Ember. I'm going to thank Marge and Nico and let them know we're leaving." Dominic patted Jayce's shoulder as he squeezed by him down the hall.

Jayce didn't move for a second, watching Dominic walk away. Then he woodenly stepped into the room and approached me almost *cautiously*.

"What is going on with you?" I asked quietly so Dominic wouldn't overhear.

"I'm sorry if I'm a little uncomfortable that your *brother* is here," he whispered back.

I jolted. *Brother.* That made his actions make so much more sense. Dominic must have told him the truth.

"Him being my brother doesn't change anything. We were keeping this a secret before, and we can continue to do so, at least until this whole Enzo thing is dealt with," I said.

Jayce shook his head. "He's your brother, Ember. This changes *everything.*"

I sucked in a sharp breath. "We can talk about this later. Just help me get to the car, okay?"

"Fine."

"Fine," I repeated. "Stand there, I can get up myself." Moving the blankets off me, I swung my legs over the side of the bed and shifted forward. The movement left me breathless, but I kept going. Reaching out, I used Jayce's arm to pull myself to my feet and had him stand on my left side, opposite to where I'd been stabbed. I left my wing outstretched, scared to pull it in and tear what had been repaired.

Latching onto Jayce's arm for support, I slowly started walking outside. Thankfully, nothing below the waist was hurting, but I was exhausted from all the healing.

"Thanks again, Marge. I'll be sending some new supplies your way," Dominic said, coming toward us from the back of the house.

"Thank you!" I called.

Marge waved to us. "Come back anytime."

Once we were in Dominic's car, me in the back seat so I could keep my wing out, and Jayce in the front, an awkward silence descended on us. I wasn't sure if Dominic would pick up on it, but it was obvious to me.

I decided I'd be the one to break it. "So, you told Jayce the truth," I said.

"I figured he'd proved himself after saving you last night, even if you should have never wound up in that position in the first place." Dominic glanced in the rearview mirror.

"And I hadn't proved myself before? I've only known you for over twenty years and have always been loyal to you," Jayce muttered.

"Ember was our family's best kept secret, I couldn't go around telling people she existed after we'd worked so hard to keep her safe all these years," Dominic said.

The way he'd worded it seemed almost as if it had been easier to keep the secret rather than reveal it, and that was why he'd continued with hiding me away. Like if I'd never stepped up and practically forced my way into the family business, he would have been happy to keep me a secret forever.

I didn't want to talk about me anymore, so I turned my face to the window and watched the houses and businesses pass by instead.

Dominic dropped us off at the front of Jayce's apartment building and promised he'd call to check in. He'd send Maurice to drop off a bag of clothes for me.

I settled in on the couch while Jayce ordered a grocery delivery and went to take a shower. I had to wait twenty-four hours to shower, because the salve Nico had put on my shoulder and wing needed time to fully heal my wounds. Marge and Nico had gotten most of the blood and dirt off me while they'd tended to me, but they hadn't gotten all of it.

By the time Jayce finished cleaning himself and the kitchen up, the groceries arrived, and he started making us dinner. I swore he was stalling so we wouldn't have to talk.

"Is this how it's going to be from now on?" I asked, turning on the couch so I could see him. "Ignoring each other because you're afraid of being near me now that you know I'm Dominic's sister?"

"I'm not afraid of being near you," he countered.

"Then come over here," I taunted him.

He wouldn't even look at me. "I'm making dinner," he said.

I scoffed. "Coward."

Jayce strolled over from the kitchen area, stopping in front of where I sat on the couch. Leaning down, he placed one hand behind me on the back cushion to brace himself.

"Say that again," he said with a smirk.

My insides twisted and my toes curled beneath the blanket covering me.

I opened my mouth to repeat my afront, but a doorbell rang, indicating someone wanted to come up to Jayce's apartment.

"Saved by the bell," he said, pushing himself away from the couch and went back to the kitchen area, looking at the monitor that showed who was trying to come up. "Maurice is sending up your things."

I peered over my shoulder as the elevator *dinged,* and it opened to reveal a duffle bag. Jayce picked it up and brought it to me.

"Now that I have this, I'm going to try taking a bath." It was better than nothing.

"Don't push yourself too hard," Jayce warned.

"I'll be fine. Do you want me to wear a bathing suit in case you have to come in and rescue me?" I teased, batting my eyelashes at him.

"Just go." He shook his head and returned to preparing dinner. It wasn't lost on me that he'd told me he didn't cook, and he was cooking for me.

I was able to walk into Jayce's bathroom where the shower and bath were by myself, Jayce had to carry the duffle bag for me and dropped it inside before quickly retreating.

Shutting the bathroom door, I breathed a sigh of relief. I stripped off the clothes Marge had loaned me and turned on the bath. When I lowered myself into the water, it soothed my aching muscles. I kept my shoulders and wings above the water, but I was at least able to wash the rest of myself.

When I finished, I had to give myself a few minutes to catch my breath. After spending the day in bed and on the couch, my body wasn't used to moving so much again.

Closing my eyes, I let myself relax. My hands dropped to my sides, brushing my ribs, and I hissed as I accidentally hit one of my bruises.

I flashed back to lying in the dirt, bleeding out, and terror filled me. Opening my eyes, I forced myself back into the present. *It's okay. I'm alive.*

I climbed out of the tub and drained it. When I opened the duffle bag, I laughed. It seemed like whoever had packed it had reached into the top drawers of my bureau and grabbed a handful from each. Which meant I only had sleepwear and tops. They hadn't thought of grabbing anything from any of the lower drawers.

It wasn't like I'd be going anywhere other than Jayce's living room, so I could make do.

I put on one of my oversized T-shirts and headed back to the kitchen and living area.

"Yeah, I'll get right on that," Jayce said. He was facing away from the stove, and the veggies were sizzling. "Why don't you find someone else to go with you?"

"You know I could never cheat on you like that!" Oliver's voice came through the phone loud and clear. Jayce had his phone on speaker. "Even though you have no problem doing it to me." He sniffled.

"Will you give it a rest? You know I'm way out of your league."

I couldn't help laughing, and Jayce turned around, his eyes widening when he saw me.

"Sorry, I didn't mean to eavesdrop," I said, walking over to the bar and sitting at the counter.

"What are you wearing?" he asked.

"What is it?" Oliver chimed in. "Ember, tell me it's—" Jayce ended the call.

"It's called a T-shirt, Jayce. In fact ..." I pointed to him. "You're also wearing one."

"But you chose to forgo pants?" Turning back to the stove, he turned off the heat and moved the pan of sliced zucchini to another burner. There was already a cooked rotisserie chicken picked and ready.

"An oversight by whoever packed my to go bag. I think there was some lingerie in there if you'd rather I put that on," I offered.

"Mm. Let's just eat." He put the chicken and zucchini onto a plate, setting it on the counter in front of me.

"I thought you said you didn't cook," I said, picking up my fork and spearing one of the zucchini pieces.

"I don't, but you needed food, and the grocery store did most of the work." He filled his own plate and sat on the opposite end of the bar. "The chicken came cooked, and the zucchini was frozen. Bon appetit."

"Well, I appreciate it, regardless."

We ate in silence. I hadn't realized how hungry I was and had Jayce get me seconds. Taking the bath had taken most of my energy.

"Now you should rest. That salve works faster if you're sleeping," Jayce said while he cleaned up.

"I would say that's weird, but I don't have a lot of experience with salve's made using grimoires." There was also a good chance Jayce wanted a break from me.

"You can sleep in my bed, I'll take the couch," he offered.

"Your bed is big enough for the both of us. I promise I won't try anything." I winked.

"Funny. But I'm not sleeping with Dominic's sister." He turned and put his hand up to stop my comment that was ready at the tip of my tongue. "And I didn't mean it like that."

"I seem to remember you promising to make me beg," I said stepping closer to Jayce and licking my lips. "But I guess you're all talk."

His Adam's apple bobbed, and I knew exactly the effect I was having on him. But he turned on his heel and walked to the couch.

"Goodnight, Ember," he said pointedly, not looking at me again.

"Goodnight, Jayce." My amusement was clear in my tone. I'd find a way to convince him Dominic wasn't to be feared.

I dreamt I was back in the middle of the deserted area, bleeding out on the ground as Georgia and Jules laughed at me. I kept trying to cry out for help, but all that came out was gargles as I choked on my own blood.

No, no, no. I won't die here, I screamed that thought over and over in my mind.

A shadow hovered over me, and my body convulsed.

"Ember, wake up. I'm here, Ember." Jayce's voice came from the shadow.

I blinked and when my eyes opened, the light was on in the corner of the room and Jayce was sitting beside me on the bed. Throwing my arms around him, I ignored the pain in my shoulder and held on tight.

"Is this real? Am I alive?" I asked, fighting back tears.

He rubbed my back, careful to avoid my healing wing.

"This is real. I've got you," he murmured.

"Don't leave me alone." I tucked my face into the crook of his neck, breathing in deeply to try and ground myself in the present. He smelled like his soap I'd used earlier. It was eucalyptus and cedar oil scented.

"Anything you want," he said. It was the same thing he'd said to me at Nico and Marge's, before Dominic had arrived and made things weird.

"I can't go back to sleep. I won't go back there." I loosened my hold on Jayce but didn't let go.

"What do you want to do?" he asked.

"Can we play a game?" I pulled back, dropping my hands into my lap.

Jayce took one of my hands in his and said, "I don't have any games, other than some decks of cards."

"That's fine. Will you teach me the card games you play with Dom and Oliver?" I asked.

"Wait here." He left and came back with a deck of cards.

He attempted to teach me High Low Jack, but after almost half an hour of trying to understand the rules, I gave up.

"Let's play something I already know," I suggested, taking the deck and shuffling it. "Have you ever played crazy eights?" I asked, smirking.

"No."

"It's like Uno, but with a regular deck of cards. Eights are wilds, hence the name. And instead of putting down the same colors, you put down the same suits on top of each other, or the same number, like Uno," I explained. "It's easy."

"Hm. Sounds easy enough," Jayce said.

While we played, we talked about random things, like our favorite foods, and our favorite restaurants and shops.

"It's only because of Mazie and Penny that I got to go to any of these places," I commented, putting an ace on top of the one Jayce had laid down.

"Do they know you're Dominic's sister?" Jayce asked.

"Yep. Dominic hired them originally to be my bodyguards. But we've become real friends," I explained.

"And no one else knows?" His disbelief was to be expected.

I shook my head. "Other than Maurice and Serena, no one else."

"That's crazy. I mean, for Dominic to keep you a secret for so long, it almost seems unreal," he said.

"When no one knows you exist, they don't exactly *look* for signs or ask questions that would lead to the revelation,"

I pointed out. "I use the servant's entrance at the mansion, so if anyone was watching me come and go, they'd think I worked as a maid or something."

Jayce's eyes widened. "I saw you that night, all those weeks ago. You were the one in the dining room."

"Guilty. I was so scared you would tell Dom you saw me." I laughed. "So, thanks, I guess, for not ratting me out."

"I thought I was going crazy," Jayce said. "I started gaslighting myself into thinking your maid Serena had purple eyes, even though I knew she didn't."

"I'd just come in from the club and got too cocky that I wouldn't be seen." But maybe I was subconsciously hoping I *would* be seen so I could stop living my life in secret.

"It must have been hard, always staying out of sight when you were in the mansion."

I shrugged. "It was my life. My parents hid me away, and so did Dom. I was used to it. But I liked to watch all the crew when they arrived and left the mansion." I toyed with the cards in my hand, thinking about those times. "I'd make up stories for everyone, and nicknames."

"Oh yeah?" Jayce put down his cards, watching me instead. "Did I get a nickname?"

One of my cards had a bent corner and I flipped it back and forth, making it worse. "I don't want to tell you. It will only boost your ego."

"Now you *have* to tell me," he teased, laughing. "I promise I won't let it go to my head."

"I didn't actually come up with yours, Mazie did. So, keep that in mind." I paused, puffing out my cheeks, and told him, "Mr. Sexy."

He opened his mouth like he was going to respond and then shook his head. "What was Oliver's nickname?" he asked.

"Don't tell him this, but he didn't get one," I said, putting a card down and continuing our game.

"Oh, I am definitely telling him." He laughed. "Weren't you worried someone would see you watching them?"

My smile slipped and I dropped my gaze to the comforter. "Someone did, once."

His brows furrowed. "But you said no one else knew about you."

"They don't anymore. I'm sure you remember Grant." I kept playing the game because I needed to focus on something other than imaginings of how Grant was killed.

Sucking in a sharp breath, Jayce glanced at the ceiling. "Fuck. Yeah. All right." He rubbed a hand along his jaw. "Dom told us he was killed by Eastsiders."

"That's what Maurice told me, too. I only found out recently what really happened. Mazie and Penny knew all along." Tears brimmed my eyes, but I wiped them away, taking a deep breath. "But enough of reliving that tragic time. I've been allowed to leave the house since Penny and Mazie came along, so at least I had that."

Picking up a card, Jayce leaned forward and said, "I don't envy you. Even though my parents were hardly ever around, at least I got to go out and live my life. I'm sorry you had to be cooped up all these years."

"It wasn't all bad. Once Dominic hired Mazie and Penny, they would take me out to clubs, though they didn't let me dance with anyone but them. And we'd do brunches, and sleepovers." I smiled thinking about those memories.

"They let you dance with *me,*" he pointed out. "That night at The Mausoleum."

"The night you stole from me?" I asked, pushing his arm playfully. "Yeah. They were distracted. Mazie was dancing in a cage, and Penny was ... Well, I still don't know where she was. But I guess it all worked out in the end."

"You call almost dying working out?" He shook his head, laughing softly.

"I call Dominic finally letting me join the family business and making friends with you and Oliver working out. I've never felt as free as the nights I was working with you." Before Jayce could say anything sappy out of pity, I threw down my last card and said, "Crazy eights. I win."

After three more rounds of me whooping Jayce's ass, we called it quits on the cards and turned on the TV in the room. In my opinion, it was far too big for a bedroom.

Jayce settled onto the right side of the bed, not getting under the covers. I didn't comment on it, since he seemed so set on keeping things between us non-sexual. Which was fine in my current state. My shoulder needed to heal, but that wouldn't take long with the salve working its literal magic.

I didn't pay much attention to whatever show was on the TV and before long, I drifted off, only to find myself right back where Jules left me.

Chapter 19

Jayce

Ember had fallen asleep, and I was conflicted whether I should wake her or not. On the one hand, she needed to rest to heal, but on the other, I couldn't stand to know she might be reliving her near death experience.

Before I could decide, her brow furrowed, and she mumbled something I couldn't make out. I didn't wait, I leaned over and took her hand, lightly squeezing it.

"Ember, I'm right here," I said.

Her eyelids fluttered and she opened her eyes, her brow smoothing. She didn't panic like she had the last time I woke her, which was promising.

"This is real," she said.

I nodded even though it hadn't been a question. She squeezed my hand, and her eyes closed.

My heart ached to be so helpless in the situation.

Somehow, though, she slept and didn't seem troubled. At some point, I fell asleep, and when I woke up, it was past midday. Ember still held my hand loosely, but she slept soundly.

I didn't dare leave her alone, because I promised her I wouldn't. It was getting near impossible to consider not being with her, despite the very real threat of Dominic killing me if he found out. It was more than that, though, I didn't want to ruin *her* relationship with her brother either.

But if she kept walking around my apartment in nothing but a T-shirt, my restraint wouldn't get me too far.

"Jayce?"

My gaze snapped to her. If she kept saying my name like that, I may not make it through the *day*.

"I'm here," I said, running my knuckle up her arm. "Are you hungry? I had bacon and eggs delivered with my grocery order."

"That sounds great!" She perked up. "Should I trust you to make it, or do you need my help?"

"Are you up for it?" I asked.

She rolled her shoulder, wincing. "I'm feeling much better, only a little pain left. And I can wash off the salve today, so that means it should be okay to use my arm, right?"

"Sometimes Nico needs to reapply it if it didn't heal well enough. I'll take a look at it after you wash it off. Nico taught me a bit about the process when I lived with them." Nico taught me a lot of things, and I wished I could remember more of them. I'd been too distracted having fun with my friends when I'd been staying with them.

"You lived with them?" Ember asked.

"Yeah, for two years, and I stayed with them often whenever my parents were busy or out of town," I explained.

226

"Now I wish I'd needled Marge for more information while we were there," she teased.

"And she would gladly give it to you, so we will be avoiding them for the foreseeable future." Not that Marge really had anything that interesting to tell.

"Unless I need a new salve applied," Ember said, smirking. "I won't miss another opportunity to learn all of your embarrassing childhood stories."

If I were to reciprocate, Dominic would be the one who I would go to for the embarrassing Ember stories. And that snapped me back to focusing on keeping Ember at arm's length.

I got up and headed for the kitchen.

"I'll start making breakfast. You take your time getting out of bed and ..."

She hopped out of bed, teetering and catching herself. "Oof." She gripped her side. "I forgot about the bruised ribs."

I couldn't help laughing a little. "I tried to tell you to take it slow."

"I'll take it under consideration for next time," she said, sounding annoyed.

In the kitchen, I put a pan on the stove and grabbed the bacon and eggs from the fridge.

"Where's your butter, or pepper?" Ember asked, coming behind the bar to the stove. "You can't make eggs without *some* kind of ..." She trailed off, opening the fridge and coming back to stand beside me.

"Butter in the pan, I assume?" I took the butter from her and grabbed a knife.

"Where are your baking sheets?" she asked, turning in a circle.

I pointed to the bottom cabinet to our left. When she bent over to retrieve a baking sheet, her T-shirt rode up and I had to force myself to look away before her full ass was revealed.

When she stood beside me again, she reached in front of me, grazing the front of my jeans to reach the oven temperature.

Sucking in a breath, I stepped back. "You can handle this for a few minutes, right? I've been wearing this since yesterday, so I'm gonna go change." I angled myself away from her so she wouldn't see the obvious hard-on she was giving me.

"Yeah. I'll yell if I need anything." She smirked as if she knew exactly what she was doing to me.

While I changed into a fresh pair of jeans and button down, I imagined myself being murdered by Dominic to help kill the mood.

Get it together, I chided myself.

As if Dominic had sensed me thinking about him, a text came in on my phone.

Dom: *How's Ember doing?*

> **Me:** *Better. Still a little*
> *sore but healing well*

Dom: *Good. Keep me updated*
I'll call later

A part of me wondered if Dominic knew about Ember and I and this was all a test. But Dominic wouldn't waste time with tests. He'd jump straight to disembowelment if he knew the truth.

After breakfast, I offered to clean up while Ember showered and washed off the salve.

As I finished drying the dishes, Ember cleared her throat.

"So how do you want to do this?" she asked.

Turning, I choked on my own spit when I saw Ember standing in the doorway to my bedroom in nothing but a towel.

"You said you wanted to look at my shoulder," she reminded me.

"Right, yeah. Let me take a look." Walking toward her, I kept my eyes on her wound.

Ember tilted her head to the side and brushed her hair out of the way. "It looks okay to me," she said. "And I can move my wing again." She flexed her wings before folding them both against her back.

I brushed my thumb beneath the wound on her shoulder. "It looks much better." The skin was a little bruised and puckered, but otherwise it looked good.

"So, I should put some clothes on then," she said, but she didn't move away.

I inhaled and that was a mistake. She'd used my soap, and she smelled like *me*. An unusual possessiveness overcame me, and I suddenly wanted her to only ever smell like that.

"You should put on some clothes," I agreed, moving my gaze from her shoulder to her face.

She was biting her bottom lip, like she often did, and without thinking, I gripped her chin with my thumb and her lip popped out from between her teeth.

I dropped my hand and backed away, turning on my heel. "I'm going down to the lobby to grab some more ..." I trailed off, not exactly sure what I was trying to say, I just needed to get out of the apartment for a few minutes.

"Oh, okay," she murmured.

The elevator doors closed, and I slumped against the back wall. In the lobby, I called Oliver. If anyone could distract me from my Ember problem, it was him.

"Why the hell are you talking to me right now when Dominic gave you the holy grail of living arrangements? I thought you two were getting hot and heavy?" Oliver asked. So much for him distracting me.

"Don't fucking say that, Oliver," I groaned. I couldn't tell him the truth about Ember being Dominic's sister, but I had a feeling even if I did, he'd be on team Ember.

"Well, if you need me to come over and run interference, I'll gladly do so. I miss you and Emmy."

"Don't call her that." I rubbed my hand down my face.

"We made an agreement, she can call me Olly, and I can call her Emmy. Take it up with her if you have a problem with it," he said defensively.

"Have you heard from Dominic? I'm wondering how his plotting is going." I turned the subject away from Ember.

"Nothing. But he called a meeting with a select few of his lieutenants and runners, which I happen to be a part of. I'm assuming since you're on babysitting duty, you won't be attending?" he asked.

"He didn't tell me about it, so you would be correct. Fill me in after," I said.

"No way! This is the first time *I've* been in the loop on something you aren't! I'm making this high last as long as possible." He sounded way too excited.

"Oh, fuck you. I've gotta go." After a second, I added, "Be here in an hour."

"Yes, sir. Love you, too!"

I sat in the lobby, avoiding Ember for a few more minutes before heading back to the elevator.

Chapter 20

Ember

I'd dressed in a lace trimmed nightgown that was barely longer than the oversized T I'd worn the day before and then borrowed a T-shirt from Jayce's bureau. I'd only had one, and the top of the nightgown was far too revealing for casual wear. I tied the shirt at the side, making the nightgown look more like a skirt.

Jayce still wasn't back when I finished dressing, so I texted my group chat with Mazie and Penny to see if they wanted to facetime. They both said they were busy, but they would call when they could. Jayce was taking his sweet time doing whatever he needed to do in the lobby. I knew it was an excuse to get out of the apartment.

It wasn't that I didn't understand Jayce's aversion to pissing off Dominic, but it did sting a little that maybe he didn't think I was *worth* the risk. We'd only known each other for a few weeks, so I shouldn't really care as much as I did. But I liked Jayce. A lot. And being around him without being *with* him was ... Difficult.

Maybe when I talked to Dominic next, I could convince him to let me go home. I could stay out of sight; it wasn't like I hadn't been doing it my whole life.

Wandering to the kitchen area, I put away the last of the dishes Jayce had left out to dry.

The elevator ding announced his return, and I pretended to be busy cleaning a spot on the island counter. I didn't want him to think I'd been waiting around for him to come back.

"You don't have to do that," Jayce said.

Turning toward him, I dropped the dish towel onto the counter. "I don't mind. It gives me something to do." I leaned back against the counter and crossed my arms over my chest.

Jayce walked toward me, pausing and cocking his head to the side as he glanced down at what I wore. "Is that ... Is that my shirt?"

"Oh." I unfolded my arms and looked down. "Yeah. It was either this or a crop top, so I figured you wouldn't mind."

"Yeah, it's fine." He shook his head. "It looks better on you than it ever did on me."

A tension formed between us, and I wasn't sure what to do, so I grabbed the towel I'd been using and started wiping the counter again.

Jayce sighed. "I said you don't need to do that." He came up behind me and put his left hand over mine, stopping me from cleaning.

Slowly, I released the towel, but Jayce's hand remained over mine, and he didn't move away. I could feel his body heat from how close he stood to me. The tension seemed to buzz between us.

I leaned back slightly, and my back touched his chest. His hand tightened on mine for a second.

"Ember," he murmured, and it sounded a little like a warning. If he wanted to move away, though, he was the one with the power to do so. It wasn't like I was holding him in place.

Pulling my hand out from under his, I turned to him. "What is this?" I asked. "Because two minutes ago you were avoiding me."

His eyes shuttered closed, and he sucked in a breath.

I continued. "I know you're worried about how Dominic will react—"

Jayce opened his eyes and the hand that wasn't half-caging me against the counter cupped my cheek. "Fuck Dominic. I want you, Ember."

A thrill ran through me, and I couldn't help but smile. "Oh, really? What are you going to do about that?" My heart was racing.

He smirked. "What would you like me to do?"

"Kiss me." It came out as a whisper, and he was quick to react, doing exactly as I requested.

Our kiss started slow and soft and became more frenzied. I dug my hands into his hair, and he gripped my waist, pulling me against him, while pressing me back against the counter.

Jayce's hands drifted down, and he lifted me onto the counter, stepping between my legs. The skirt of my nightgown bunched up, almost baring me entirely.

I draped my arms over Jayce's shoulders and leaned my head back as his lips trailed down my neck to my collarbone. His hands moved up my thighs, raising goosebumps in their wake.

"What now, Ember?" he asked, lifting his gaze to meet mine.

"Touch me," I breathed.

"Where?" His thumb stroked my thigh.

Gasping, I said, "Everywhere."

He chuckled and moved one of his hands to my inner thigh, slowly dragging it up until he grazed my center where I was already wet for him, his brows rising in surprise.

"You aren't wearing underwear," he stated.

"Before you go on thinking I did that for you, it's really because whoever packed my bag didn't pay attention to what they were packing and I have none."

"Lucky me." He grazed his thumb over my clit, and I moaned in anticipation, my toes curling. Capturing my lips with his own, he swallowed my following moan as he drove two fingers inside me, curling them against my inner walls.

I clenched my legs around his waist and tried to pull him even closer. I wanted to feel him with every inch of my exposed skin. Tugging on the hem of his shirt, I pulled it up and he broke off our kiss, removing his fingers from inside me. I gasped at the sudden emptiness.

He tugged off his shirt and tossed it somewhere. I reciprocated, taking off my shirt, which was technically his, and dropped it beside the counter.

His thumb skimmed over my almost healed wound on my shoulder, and I sucked in a breath. There was no pain, but it was a reminder of how close I'd come to death.

To distract myself, I traced a line down Jayce's torso with my pinky, past the snake tattooed there, to a series of what appeared to be tally marks above his hip.

"What's this?" I asked.

"Oliver and I started keeping track of our hits, trying to see who could collect the most notches," he explained, brushing a finger over the marks. "I'm winning."

As morbid as it was, it made me laugh. "Normal people would keep track with a pen and paper."

"Mm." He gripped my thighs, pulling me to the edge of the counter so my core was pressed against his hard length. "Are you starting to have second thoughts, Ember?"

I reached between us and stroked him through his pants. "Never," I said.

A hiss escaped him. I kissed him and I did it again.

One of his hands trailed up my side to my breast and he stroked his thumb over my nipple. Once, twice, three times, before pinching it through the fabric of the nightgown. I arched into him. His other hand returned to my pussy, playing lazily around my clit, before he pumped two fingers inside me.

"Fuck," I moaned, letting my head fall back.

"You're perfect, Ember," Jayce murmured, moving his fingers in and out, curling them every so often at just the right time, until I was about to climax, and he removed them entirely.

"Jayce," I whimpered. "Fuck me." Unable to wait anymore, I started undoing his belt for him.

"Anything you want," he said, finishing what I started and dropping his pants, along with his underwear, and kicking them aside.

I stared at him openly. It wasn't like I didn't know *exactly* how big he was from when I'd sucked his dick in the car, but it looked bigger out in the open. Licking my lips, I put my hands on his hips and tugged him closer. The tip of his cock nudged at my entrance, but he didn't press into me.

"Are you sure this is what you want?" he asked.

I gripped the edge of my nightgown and practically ripped it off. "I'm sure, Jayce. I want you."

He bent his head to mine and kissed me, easing his cock inside me. The gentleness was a change to how fast we'd been moving before. I winced as I stretched to accommodate him but sighed in relief once he was fully seated inside me. The pain was minimal, and it felt *amazing*.

"Are you okay?" Jayce asked, his hand cupping my cheek.

"Mmhm." My thighs were trembling as he pulled out and pumped back inside, a little quicker that time. "Yes," I sighed.

I'd used plenty of different vibrators, but nothing compared to the feel of Jayce inside me, especially as he picked up the pace.

I leaned back on the counter, propping myself on my elbows, as Jayce gripped my hips to hold me in place. Using one hand, I played with my nipple, groaning in delight.

"Oh fuck, Ember, you look so good," Jayce said, leaning down to wrap an arm around me and pulling me up so he could suck my other nipple into his mouth. The added sensation brought me closer to the edge, my pussy clenching around his cock.

His fingers found my clit, teasing it, and pleasure rippled through me. I gasped and moaned simultaneously, and Jayce spilled inside me. Thankfully we had no need to worry about birth control. Demons couldn't bear children until they'd been blessed by Lucifer. Or cursed, as some people claimed.

In the aftermath, I lay flat on the counter, panting, with my wings splayed out beneath me, and Jayce leaning over me. His hands were braced on either side of me, the cords of his muscles turning me on all over again.

"You should really let me clean up this counter now," I said, giggling. "Unless ..."

"Unless?" Jayce quirked a brow. He was still inside me, and it was a sensation I hadn't known would feel so good until that moment.

"Unless you were planning on a round two." I smirked, trailing a finger up his arm.

He straightened, pulling himself out of me and leaving me feeling as if something was missing. I thought he would turn me down.

Instead, he held out a hand to me, helping me off the counter, and said, "Only if round two can be in the shower. I may have invited Oliver to come over." He glanced at the clock and cringed. "He'll be here in fifteen minutes."

"Why would you do that?" I deflated.

He rubbed the back of his neck. "I thought I'd need someone to run interference, and from what just happened, I'd say I was right."

I scrunched my nose. "I don't think fifteen minutes will be enough time."

"You don't believe I can make you come again in less than fifteen minutes?" he asked, stepping closer and licking his bottom lip. "Want to bet?"

The heat pooling between my legs told me he would win that bet, but I'd happily lose.

Nodding, I bit my lower lip.

Scooping me into his arms, Jayce carried me toward the bathroom.

"Let me know if anything hurts," he said, his gaze drifting to my wound.

"I'm okay," I assured him. "No pain."

It turned out fifteen minutes was plenty of time for Jayce, and he won the bet twice over.

Of course, that meant we were getting out of the shower when Oliver showed up, yelling, "The cock blocker has arrived!" A few seconds later, he must have seen the clothes we'd left in the kitchen, because he followed up with, "Jason Milicent Orion, you couldn't last *one hour?!*"

Jayce had me pinned between him and the bathroom vanity, my arms up around his neck, and his hard length pressed against my stomach.

"Jason Milicent?" I asked.

His lips moved up the side of my neck. "It's just Jayce and I don't have a middle name. Oliver is full of shit."

Jayce didn't seem phased at all, which made me more relaxed, but I was a *little* worried Oliver might tell Dominic.

"Shouldn't we go out there?" I asked, putting my hand over the snake tattoo on Jayce's sternum.

"Maybe he'll take the hint and leave," he said, lifting me onto the vanity.

I wrapped my legs around him and kissed him.

"I'll be out here whenever you two finish." Oliver's voice was right outside the bathroom door. "Unless you'd like a third."

"Not today, Olly," I called.

"That implies it will happen another day!"

"Get the fuck out of my room, Oliver," Jayce snapped. "We'll be out in a second."

"I'm going, I'm going."

I didn't unwrap my legs from Jayce as he started to pull away. The thought of Oliver in the room next to us increased my arousal significantly.

"Oliver will know what's happening," Jayce said as if reading my thoughts.

I bit my bottom lip and fluttered my lashes at him, reaching between us and aligning his cock with my slick entrance. "Fuck me hard, Jayce."

With a single thrust, he was inserted fully, and he had to stop me from slamming my back against the mirror. I moaned in delight. He was careful of my wings.

Pulling me back to the edge of the vanity, Jayce removed himself from me. "Off the counter," he commanded. I was quick to follow his orders. "Bend over and put your hands on the shower bench." Again, I did as I was told and braced myself.

Jayce's hands caressed my hips before his fingers dug in and he slammed his cock into me, picking up the pace and moving me with him. I came faster than I had in the shower, and he finished shortly after.

He spun me around, kissing me roughly. "As soon as Oliver leaves—"

"Dominic!" Oliver's voice came through the door all the way from the living room.

Panicking, I stepped away from Jayce and grabbed a towel, wrapping it around myself, as if that would help anything.

"Oh, no. Jayce was showing Ember how to use the shower," Oliver said.

"Fucking hell," Jayce groaned, grabbing his own towel. "Stay in here. Turn on the shower. I'll do damage control."

I nodded and turned back to the shower, turning it on.

Jayce stepped out of the bathroom, shutting the door softly behind him.

Chapter 21

Jayce

I crept to my dresser, grabbing pants and a shirt, and pulled them on as quickly as I could manage.

"Why are you here?" Dominic asked Oliver. I'd been hoping Oliver was bluffing trying to get us out of the bathroom, but that was *clearly* Dominic.

"Moral support," Oliver said. "Jayce said Ember needed some cheering up, and I figured I could help."

I ran my hands through my hair and stepped out of my bedroom. It had never been an issue not having a door to my bedroom, but after today, I was installing one.

"Hey, Dom. I thought you would be calling, not stopping by," I said.

Oliver was in the kitchen area, leaning against the island. Dominic was still between the kitchen area and entryway. He wouldn't have seen the clothes on the floor yet.

"I come here at least once a week for cards, so it wouldn't seem out of the ordinary for anyone watching me," he explained.

"Right," I drawled. My gaze darted to my shirt by the couch. "Ember's washing off the salve, and then we were going to play cards with Oliver, if you want to join."

"Sure. I can't stay too long, but I could play a round." He strolled over to the couch and paused beside my shirt.

"I slept on the couch last night, sorry. If I'd known you were coming, I would have cleaned up," I lied, grabbing it and tossing it into my room.

Oliver joined Dominic on the couch, so I headed for the kitchen area, finding the pile of clothes Oliver had kicked to the side of the island so Dominic wouldn't see them. I'd have to thank him for covering for Ember and me later.

I took the pile to my bedroom while Oliver distracted Dominic with conversation. Ember popped her head out of the bathroom door and waved me over.

"Is everything good? Can I come out now?" she asked, glancing toward the bedroom doorway.

"All good," I said.

"Can I borrow some sweatpants or something? All I have is ... Well, you know." She waved her hand toward the duffle bag.

I handed her a pair of sweatpants and a T-shirt, then returned to the living room. Oliver had already poured himself and Dominic some whiskey and had the cards ready to play.

Sitting in the armchair to the side of the coffee table. I was trying not to seem too tense, or awkward, or else Dominic might start asking questions I wasn't ready to answer.

"How's Ember? Is she adjusting okay?" Dominic asked, keeping his voice low so Ember wouldn't overhear.

"I'm fine, Dom," Ember said, coming out of my bedroom in my clothes. Something about seeing her in my clothes was so fucking hot, and that's what got us into this whole mess in the first place.

"What are you wearing?" Dominic asked.

She'd rolled the waistband of the sweatpants over a few times so they wouldn't drag, but they were still clearly too big for her. She'd tied up the shirt like a belly shirt, the bottoms of her wings sticking out the back.

"*Someone* sucks at packing clothes and filled my duffle bag with nothing but random tops and a few night gowns. So, Jayce lent me some of his stuff." She came over and pushed Dominic's shoulder playfully.

"I knew I shouldn't have had Maurice pack your bag for you. But I've been so busy dealing with your whole mess ..." Dominic trailed off. "Oh well. As long as you're comfortable wearing Jayce's clothes. I think bringing another bag here would be a red flag."

"Yeah, it's fine," Ember said, taking a seat on the other side of Oliver on the couch.

Dominic shuffled the cards, dealing them to everyone but Ember. "Em, you play with Oliver for the first round so you can learn," he said.

She scooted closer to Oliver, and he put his arm around her, handing her the cards. It took all my restraint not to walk over and rip his arm off her. I tried to focus on my cards, but Oliver kept whispering in Ember's ear, making her giggle.

Dominic didn't seem to notice, or at least he didn't say anything.

Every time Ember played a card Oliver praised her, and she leaned back against him, grinning. My hands were shaking with rage, but I had to bite it down and take it.

"I didn't realize you and Oliver were so close," Dominic commented, eyeing Ember.

She patted Oliver's knee. "You're the one who set me up with self-defense training with him. He's easy to be friends with. You should know that well enough."

"Thank you! I will take that compliment and live off the high of it for the rest of the day," Oliver joked. "And after what you went through, our classes are even more necessary, so I expect you back once you're all healed up."

Dominic leaned back, resting his elbow on the arm of the couch. "She'll be back; that's for sure. And Mazie and Penny will be accompanying her."

"Do you not trust me?" Ember asked, frowning.

Shaking his head, Dominic said, "I trust you, but I want to make sure they're brushing up on their skills. I don't know what they do in their spare time, but I want to make sure they're ready to defend you if the time comes."

"He sure cares about you, Emmy," Oliver said. "Why don't you worry about *me* like that, Dom?"

I twisted my mouth trying to hide my smirk. Oliver still had no idea Ember was Dominic's sister. He'd be pissed once he learned I'd known longer than him.

"As much as I care about your well-being Oliver, for some reason there's a part of me that will always be a little more worried about Ember. She doesn't have your skills yet." Dominic grinned and laid his hand down. "I've got to get back to the mansion, but I'll check in later."

Ember hugged Dominic goodbye, and Oliver insisted on getting a hug as well. I watched it all, fighting the need to roll my eyes.

Once Dominic was gone, I turned on Oliver. "What the hell was that?"

Ember sat back on the couch, curling her legs up under her, and she wore a smirk as if she was enjoying the show.

Oliver scoffed. "I was throwing him off your scent, obviously. And it worked! He didn't suspect a thing."

That reminded me Oliver had made sure Dominic didn't see our clothes in the kitchen, so I *did* owe him.

Cooling down, I unclenched my jaw and rolled my shoulders. "Thank you."

Oliver put his hand to his chest and gasped. "A real thank you? Damn, I never thought I'd see the day. I think I'll bask in this moment for a while." He closed his eyes and lifted his chin.

"All right, I can't deal with you anymore. Get out." I pointed at the door when Oliver opened his eyes.

"That's pretty rude, honestly. But fine. I'll leave you two to return to your extracurricular activities." Slapping his hands on his knees, he stood and headed for the door. "Remember, if you're ever needing a little something, or someone, extra, call me. I'd literally kill myself if I found out you chose someone else as your third."

Ember laughed. "I've got your number, Olly," she said.

Oliver stopped mid stride, and pure elation brightened his face. "Oh my god, Ember, do not tease me like that. I'm being so serious."

"Goodbye, Oliver," I said.

The elevator dinged and he got in it, thankfully. I was worried I'd have to forcefully remove him with Ember getting his hopes up like that.

"You know he's never going to give up on us now," I said, moving from the chair to the couch, opposite Ember.

Crawling toward me, she settled between my legs with her back against my chest. I wrapped my arms around her.

"Maybe I'm interested in his offer," she said.

"Well don't let him know until you're absolutely certain. His heart can't handle it." I'd never truly considered taking Oliver up on any of his propositions, but for some reason, picturing Ember between the two of us changed things.

"I can tell you're thinking about it, too," Ember murmured, turning her face to me, smirking and shimmying in my lap.

"Are you sure you want to play this game?" I asked, trailing my fingers down her arm.

"Absolutely." She turned in my lap fully to face me and I noticed the dark circles beneath her eyes. I'd almost forgotten she'd nearly died less than forty-eight hours ago.

"Well, as much as it kills me to say this, you're still healing, and you need to rest." I wanted to kick myself for saying it, but the thought of Ember in pain was worse than a little discomfort on my end.

She knelt in front of me, pouting, and I almost wanted to give in, but my priority was to help her heal.

"We can watch a movie and maybe tomorrow we'll do something a little more ... Physical."

"Fine." Ember sighed and turned around, settling against me again.

I put on a movie and Ember fell asleep halfway through. It wasn't long before she started twitching in my arms, and mumbling. Then came the screaming. I gently shook her awake.

"Ember, it's okay. You're okay."

She settled again and fell back asleep.

Reaching over to the coffee table, careful not to jostle Ember, I grabbed my phone and texted Dominic.

> **Me:** *Ember's having nightmares*
> *about the other night*
> *Do you know anything that*
> *helps her with that kind of thing?*

It took a few minutes before he responded.

> **Dom:** *She used to have nightmares*
> *after our parents died*
> *The only thing that helped was having*
> *her sleep in my room*
> *After a while of not waking up alone*
> *she started to do better*
> *She was seven then, but if you*
> *could sleep in the same*
> *room as her it might help*

> **Me:** *Okay thanks. I'll try that*

> **Dom:** *I'm not saying to sleep*
> *in the same bed. I'll kill you*

I knew he wasn't joking, and I couldn't bring myself to respond. Instead, I sent a thumbs up.

Once the movie ended, I carried Ember to bed and guilt prickled at me as I laid down beside her. As much as I dreaded telling Dominic the truth about Ember and me, it would have to be sooner rather than later. Lying to Dominic was the last thing I thought I'd ever be doing, and it didn't sit right with me.

The next day was the meeting Dominic had yet to tell me anything about. All I cared about was being able to tear Enzo apart for what he had done to Ember.

Ember slept until almost five p.m. I kept getting up to do little things, like go to the bathroom, or grab a snack, but I didn't want to be away too long in case she had a nightmare. But she seemed okay ever since the one on the couch.

After Ember woke up, we ate breakfast and Dominic called to check in. Ember put her phone on speaker while we talked to him on opposite ends of the couch. It was like we had silently agreed he'd know if we were touching.

"How did you sleep? Did you have any more nightmares?" he asked.

Ember glared at me. "You told him?"

I put my hands up in surrender. "It seemed like something he might know how to help with. So yeah, I told him."

Dominic laughed. "It's okay, Em. I used to help you with your nightmares after our parents died. Remember?"

She pursed her lips. "Yeah." I could tell she was holding something back.

"And they eventually went away. So, I'm sure these ones will too. I have to go, but call me if you need anything else, okay?"

"Okay," Ember said.

When Dominic hung up, Ember wouldn't look at me.

"I'm really sorry if you didn't want him to know," I said. "But I hate seeing you suffering and I figured it wouldn't hurt to ask him if he knew how to help, since he knows you best."

"Dom doesn't know nearly as much as he thinks," she said quietly. "I lied to him when I told him I stopped having those nightmares."

"Oh." I let out a huff.

She twisted her hands in her lap. "Yeah. So whatever *advice* he gave you will be useless."

"Can I ask when the nightmares actually stopped?"

She trilled her lips. "Never, I guess. Up until these new nightmares, they weren't as frequent, but I still had them," she paused, seeming to consider something, and then continued. "And it wasn't our parents being killed that gave me the nightmares. It was watching Dominic kill those two runners from Eastside. I told Dominic the nightmares stopped because I didn't want him to know they featured him. I didn't want him to know I had nightmares about *him* killing me the way he'd killed them."

Even with all the demons I'd killed since becoming an enforcer, I'd never had nightmares, so I had no idea how to help Ember. But I wanted to.

"Come here," I said, holding a hand toward her. She bit her lip and moved closer, sitting in my lap and draping her arm over my shoulders, while her legs stretched out on the couch. She played with the hem of my T-shirt she wore, avoiding my gaze.

I took her hand and held it, so she'd stop fidgeting. "Tell me about your nightmares. Both of them," I said softly. At some point in time, Marge had told me talking about your problems could help you overcome them, so I figured it might work for nightmares, too.

"Well, as Dom probably told you when our parents were killed, Lucifer brought the two demons responsible to our house for Dom to kill in retaliation." Her grip tightened on my hand. "Dom told me to wait in my room and not come out until he said it was safe, but I didn't listen. I watched everything that happened from upstairs."

"Dominic was seventeen when your parents were killed, right?" I asked, doing the math in my head. "That would mean you were seven." *Shit.* Even for a demon, seeing that kind of thing when you were young could mess you up. Especially a demon as sheltered as Ember had been.

"Yeah. And at first, the nightmares were reliving that moment, but then they started to morph. Sometimes I'd switch places with those two Eastsiders, and other times, it was like Dominic had been taken over by something, and he sought me out to kill me." Her voice trembled. "I know Dom would *never* hurt me, and I didn't want him to think I was afraid of him, so I told him the nightmares stopped."

"*Are* you afraid of him?" I asked.

"Only in the wake of the nightmares. Once the emotions of them fade, it's like I come back to my senses. Like I said, I know he wouldn't hurt me." She took her hand from mine and traced the lines on my palm.

"Maybe you *should* tell him about that nightmare. It might help you to have his reassurances that he'd never hurt you. And, for what it's worth, I'll never let anyone lay so much as a finger on you." I brushed my thumb over the top of her hand. "You'll always be safe with me."

Ember smiled, and I wanted to burn the memory into my brain to have that image with me always. She was so beautiful when she smiled.

"And once Oliver teaches me some more self-defense, I'll be able to kick anyone's ass who tries to come for *you,*" she teased.

"I look forward to seeing that. Now, tell me about your more recent nightmare."

Her smile disappeared. "You know about that one. I'm back in the middle of nowhere, slowly bleeding out after Georgia and Jules leave me to die. But in my nightmare, you never come." Her voice cracked, and tears rimmed her eyes.

My chest ached knowing there was nothing I could do to soothe her fear.

I wrapped my right arm around her and held her close. "I will *always* find you," I said. "If I have to find a dream walker and come into your nightmares to save you there, too, I will." I didn't know any dream walking demons personally, but for Ember, I'd use every contact I had to find one.

Chuckling, she said, "I don't think that's necessary, but I appreciate it." She kissed my cheek. "Can we do something a little more fun now?" Her hand moved from my shoulder to my hair, playing with it.

"What did you have in mind?" I asked, smirking.

She kissed me slowly, and I savored the taste of her.

Readjusting, she straddled me and removed her shirt, letting her wings unfold behind her.

"Your turn," she said, plucking at the hem of my shirt. She leaned back so I could pull it over my head.

"Happy?" I asked, cocking an eyebrow.

"Mmhm." She ran her hands down my chest to my abs.

A faint *click* had me flipping Ember onto the couch and grabbing her shirt, covering her with it as I rolled off the couch and ...

Fucking hell. My glock was still in the bedroom.

I stood slowly as two men pointing their own glocks at me approached. Someone slunk in behind them, using the other two to conceal themself.

"Put that on, Ember." I spoke low and raised my hands. She scrambled to do as I'd said.

"What an interesting development. Enzo will be extremely interested to learn *she's* still alive." The demon on the right, a purple demon with long, black hair pointed his gun to where Ember was still concealed by the couch. He looked vaguely familiar, probably from Enzo's party. "Though we were told you were dating Dominic's sister." He pointed his gun at me.

They haven't figured out the truth about Ember's identity. At least we had that going for us.

"No one ever said anything about him being faithful," the other one said.

Ember came to stand beside me, and I pushed her behind me. She gasped and squeezed my forearm as Penny stepped out from behind the two men.

Penny rolled her eyes. "Enough of your yapping, Josh. Let's get this over with."

The purple demon, who I assumed was Josh, smirked. He and the other gun toting demon continued their advance.

"Are you here to kill us?" Ember asked, her voice soft and sure, which was surprising considering she'd just learned her best friend had betrayed her.

"Jericho wants you both alive," Penny said. "After that, it's up to him what happens."

Josh stepped up to me first, pressing the barrel of his gun against my temple. "If either of you try anything, I don't care what Jericho said, the other one will die." He jerked his head to the other demon, a gray demon with white hair. "Take the girl, Kal."

Ember went quietly, most likely still in shock over Penny. I already had the wheels in my mind churning, considering all the different scenarios that might play out and how I would get Ember home safely.

Even though it killed me to do nothing, the safest plan I had was to let them take us to Jericho and then find a way to escape when neither Ember nor I had a gun pointed at us. I was prepared to do whatever it took to make sure she got out of this alive, but I couldn't do that if Josh killed me.

"We'll cooperate, but if you hurt her, I swear to Lucifer and whatever God there may be, I will end your miserable life." I'd promised Ember she'd always be safe with me, and I'd already fucked that up royally.

"Come on, boys, let's not keep Jericho waiting," Penny said, turning on her heel and striding to the stairway entrance they'd used to get in.

I'd changed my passcode after Ember had broken in, but somehow, Penny must have figured it out again. I would kill her, too, as soon as I got the chance.

Chapter 22

Ember

As hurtful as it was to see Penny step out from behind Kal and Josh, it also made sense. It was like something clicked into place when I saw her, and realization washed over me. She'd been acting strange for weeks, and now I understood why. It didn't stop me from wanting to strangle her, though.

What I really wanted to know was when it had all begun. Had she always worked for Jericho? Was our entire friendship a lie, or was this new? Did she suddenly decide she hated me so much she'd gladly hand me over to my brother's biggest rival? That last one would hurt the most.

But she hadn't told Josh or Kal I was Dominic's sister. They still thought I was Mazie. So, I had no idea what to think.

Getting down the stairs took some time, but when we reached the alley, a blacked-out SUV was waiting for us. Penny got into the driver's seat, while I was forced into the way back with Kal, and Jayce sat in the middle row with Josh. Jayce turned so he could see me, but his gaze was pinned on Kal, watching his every move.

For some reason, this wasn't as terrifying as my nightmare. Maybe it was because I had Jayce with me, or maybe it hadn't hit me yet that we'd been kidnapped. I also had my phone in my pocket and knowing Oliver would probably be checking our location at some point comforted me.

The car ride was tense and silent, and felt way longer than it probably was. Jericho's mansion was much like mine and Dominic's, but smaller than Enzo's, which was surprising. We pulled up to a wrought iron gate and it opened almost immediately, like they'd been waiting for us.

Charred looking tree-like formations lined Jericho's driveway, mimicking some kind of foliage that couldn't grow in Hell.

Inside the foyer of Jericho's mansion was dark and moody. The walls were maroon with gold framed artwork. There was a grand staircase straight ahead as we entered, with an elegant stair runner meeting us at the front door.

I could almost forget I had a pistol shoved into my back as I walked, if Kal would stop ramming it against me any time he wanted me to take a step.

In the center of the room was a glass bowl atop a white pedestal filled with the purple pills Enzo had been dealing. It seemed odd, but then again, the only drug lord I'd met was my brother. Dominic could be the odd one.

"Welcome." A deep, booming voice echoed through the room and an older demon stepped into the room from a door on our left. He had green skin, dark green hair, and large horns that pointed toward the ceiling. "What an honor to welcome members of my greatest adversary's crew into my humble abode."

"Your invitation was nearly impossible to decline," I said, unamused.

Kal wrapped an arm around my chest from behind, pulling me roughly against him and pressing the pistol against my temple. "Do not speak in such a way to our lord," he hissed in my ear.

A small commotion beside me caught my attention, but Kal held me in place. The sound of a gun cocking was unmistakable, and my body stiffened.

"I warned you not to hurt her," Jayce said, the malice in his voice sending a thrill through me.

Jericho tutted. "Now, is that any way to treat my men in my own home? Lower your weapons, the both of you."

The power Jericho emanated made me understand how he had remained the leader of the Westside for so long. I couldn't imagine why he would be stealing other demons' power when he was so powerful all on his own.

Kal released me and backed away. I turned and Jayce backed away as well, putting the pistol he'd taken from Josh on the floor. With the power Jericho possessed, a gun would only inconvenience him, not kill him.

"That's better." Jericho nodded. "The two of you." He pointed to me and Jayce. "Will come with me. Kal, take care of that." He waved a hand toward Josh, and I spared a glance at where he'd fallen. His head was at an angle it should not be capable of. Jayce had killed him.

Jericho turned back into the room he had come from, expecting us to follow.

Placing a hand at my back, Jayce lowered his head and murmured in my ear, "I'll do whatever it takes to get you out of here, but if you're hurt, take one of the pills. They're what saved you the last time."

I furrowed my brow and shook my head, but Jayce had already passed me, grabbing a handful of the pills and waving me after Jericho. When he caught up to me, he dropped some of the pills into the pocket of his sweatpants I still wore.

"Don't question it, I'll explain once I've gotten you out of here," he said.

I took his hand, and we walked through the door, following Jericho.

Inside the oversized study, there were horns and wings mounted on the excessively tall walls. I tried to conceal how horrified I was by the sight.

"Why are we here? Why not kill us?" Jayce asked.

Jericho walked to his desk, stopping in front of it and leaning back against it, crossing his legs in front of him.

"I truly only wanted the girl. Though, I was expecting Dominic's sister and not a demon who is supposed to be dead." He cocked his head to the side. "But now that you're here, and I know you're not as far removed from all of this as we were told, I may have a use for you."

Penny had been the one to say Jericho wanted us both alive. Maybe I could still trust her after all. I wouldn't get my hopes up, though.

Jayce moved so he was between me and Jericho. "You do realize that if you had taken a high rank demon like Dominic's sister to kill her, Lucifer would be bearing down on your doorstep to even the score," he said. I knew he was bluffing because I wasn't considered a high rank, but hopefully Jericho didn't know that.

"Mm," Jericho mused. "You lack foresight, but I should expect that of an *enforcer*. I swear all of you are exactly alike. All brawn and no critical thinking skills." He'd figured out Jayce's role somehow. Probably from the way Jayce had easily taken out one of his men. "What Dominic failed to realize is that by hiding his sister away all these years, he showed me how much he truly cares for her."

This was all my fault. If I'd never pressured Dominic into letting me work for him, *none* of this would be happening. I'd set this whole thing into motion.

Looking at Jayce, I couldn't regret my decision. If I'd stayed hidden, Jayce and I would never have gotten together, and that was worth anything that came next.

"Dominic won't come for *me*, if that's what you're thinking," I said, lifting my chin and feigning confidence. "He'll know this is all a trap, and he won't walk into it."

Jericho laughed. "Oh, I know he won't come for you. We're killing time here. You really think I'd put all my eggs in one basket, hoping Ember would be at Jayce's apartment? And yes, I know his name isn't Brock."

It probably wasn't hard for him to figure out that information, but it was concerning because it meant if he could find that out, he might be able to realize the truth about my identity.

Smirking, I said, "We should have known better than to try and fool you, Jericho. Though, it was all too easy to fool Enzo. Where is he, anyway?" I made a show of looking around as if he'd come out from behind the curtains, or through the door.

Jericho twisted his mouth in consideration. It made me wonder what was going through his mind.

The doors opened behind me and multiple sets of footsteps entered. I didn't dare turn, but Jayce did, and he scowled. Grabbing my hand, he pulled me around, positioning me behind him, my back to Jericho.

Enzo strolled in, an easy grin on his face as his gaze passed over Jayce and found me. He licked his lips and stopped a foot away from us. Three other men entered behind him and stopped on either side of us.

"I must say, as furious as I was with your scheme, a small part of me is thrilled to see you alive and well." Closing the distance, Enzo held up his hand as if he was going to cup my cheek, but Jayce's free hand lashed out and gripped his wrist, stopping him.

"Do *not* touch her," Jayce growled.

I inhaled sharply, and my stomach flipped.

"You seem to forget who is in control here," Enzo drawled. Jayce released his wrist. "Give me permission to kill him." Enzo's gaze flicked to Jericho.

"No," I gasped, turning to Jericho. "You said you had a use for him."

Jericho's eyebrows rose and he nodded to the men Enzo had come in with. Two of them grabbed Jayce and the other took hold of me, tearing us away from one another.

A scream ripped out of me. "No! Please don't hurt him! I'll do anything, I'll ..." The words were on the tip of my tongue. The admission. But Jayce gave me a look that silenced me.

"Before you kill me, at least let me prove something," Jayce said, not bothering to fight against the two demons holding him in place.

"What are you talking about?" Jericho asked, his lip curling.

He nodded his head toward me. "Your drugs are what saved her life. Let me take them before you kill me, and at least you can find out how well they work," Jayce suggested.

"That's the stupidest thing I've ever heard," Enzo muttered, rolling his eyes.

"But what's the harm in it? If I'm right, you get to kill me twice. If I'm wrong ..." Jayce shrugged, far too cavalier as he spoke of his own death.

"You can't," I said, but no one was listening to me.

Enzo looked at Jericho, waiting on his command.

"Go ahead," Jericho said.

I struggled against the demon holding me back. I'd never wished more that I'd inherited my mother's power. With that, I'd easily be able to break free.

"You can't kill him," I gasped. "Like you said, he's Dominic's enforcer. He's considered an upper rank as a level four." As much as I wanted to remain confident, my voice wavered and sounded pathetic, even to my own ears.

Jericho laughed. "Lucifer makes exceptions when it comes to fours. Jayce came into my sector, stole one of my men's cars, and attempted to intervene in my business."

"After *you* started selling in Southside!" I yelled.

Lifting his hands, Jericho frowned. "Prove it." He paused. "I, on the other hand, have video evidence of Jayce's actions."

No, no, no. This was not supposed to happen. Dominic was supposed to have a plan to deal with Jericho, what the hell was he doing? My heart was racing, and I wouldn't be surprised if I passed out.

Enzo pulled a purple pill from a pouch in his pocket and popped it in Jayce's mouth. "I really hope you're right about this, because killing you twice would be so ... Satisfying."

Jayce's throat bobbed as he swallowed.

"Give it a minute, and then pull the trigger," Jericho directed.

Enzo circled Jayce and the men who held him. He came back to me and stood beside me, facing Jayce.

"Should I make *you* do it?" he whispered, so no one else would hear. "As punishment for your betrayal."

Fear coursed through me, and I leaned away from Enzo, but his man held me in place.

"Have you ever killed someone before, Mazie?" he sneered. "It's exhilarating. I'm sure Jayce understands that."

"All right, Enzo, enough. Shoot him so we can move on with our lives," Jericho drawled.

"You'll learn soon enough," Enzo said, raising his pistol and taking aim.

I held my breath as I waited for him to pull the trigger, unable to take my eyes from Jayce. He watched me, nodding once as the gun fired and the two men holding him released him, so he fell to the ground, blood blooming from the center of his chest.

"No!" The word tore out of me, and I jolted forward before the demon holding me regained control, pulling me back.

Enzo tutted. "Shame. I was really hoping to get the chance to kill him again."

Jerking my head to face Jericho, I lowered my voice and put as much venom behind my words as possible. "I will *kill* you for this." Tears streamed down my face, but I paid them no mind. My grief would only be a distraction, and I needed to make sure I followed through on my word.

I couldn't bring myself to look at Jayce, his stillness triggering me. There was a chance, no matter how small, that he'd come back to me, but I couldn't wait around for that.

The door opened and closed behind me as Enzo left to meet the demons who were bringing in Dominic's 'sister.' At least I still had that ace up my sleeve.

"Take her to the spare room and lock her in. I won't need her for what comes next," Jericho instructed the demon holding me.

Panic coursed through me. I didn't want to leave Jayce behind, and I didn't want to miss Dominic when he came. Although maybe it was better if he didn't know I was there. Then I wouldn't interfere with his plan, whatever it was.

I didn't struggle as the demon holding my arms behind my back steered me out a side door of the office and down a short hall to a small closet-like room, with nothing in it. The door slammed behind him when he left, and the lock clicked into place.

Chapter 23

Dominic

Mazie had been taken by Jericho's men, as planned. One of my men who was better at spell work than I was, used his grimoire to put a spell on Mazie that would allow anything she saw or heard to be transcribed in a journal until the spell was deactivated. Then, when she got Jericho to talk about stealing other demon's power and killing upper ranks, we could have physical evidence to show Lucifer.

I'd already received a call from one of Jericho's men saying they had my 'sister' and if I wanted her to stay alive, I'd be at Jericho's mansion within two hours. So, I was taking my time, giving Mazie a real chance at getting Jericho to confess. Nyle was waiting with the journal, ready to take it to Lucifer as soon as anything incriminating came up. But there was no guarantee Lucifer would react right away.

My phone vibrated in my cupholder, and I glanced down to see Oliver's name pop up.

I furrowed my brow. He didn't usually call me. We were close friends, but not as close as he or I was with Jayce.

"This is Dominic," I answered.

"Yeah, I know. I called *you,*" he responded sarcastically as usual. "For some reason I had this nagging sense to check my locations app and Jayce and Ember aren't in the apartment anymore."

Warning bells sounded in my brain before Oliver continued.

"It looks like they're in Westside territory, and if I had to guess, it's Jericho's place," he said.

"Fuck," I hissed. "Thanks for letting me know. I'm already on my way there."

"Me too."

"Stay out of this one, Oliver," I commanded. "This plan is hanging on by a thread, I don't need any more complications."

"I'll stay away, unless I hear otherwise, but I want to be close enough to be of use. I know they're your friends, but they're my friends too." He sounded more serious than I'd ever heard him.

"Fine. I don't have time for this. I'll text you if I need you. Goodbye." I hung up and pressed the gas pedal to the floor. I couldn't put off my arrival anymore. If Jericho still believed Ember and Mazie to be opposites, that meant Ember wasn't a necessary piece of Jericho's plan, whatever it was. He could dispose of her at any time, if he hadn't already.

At the very least, I could plan accordingly. So long as Ember was still alive, Jericho would most likely try to use her against me, even if he didn't realize she was my *real* sister yet.

I needed to know what was happening inside before I went in.

Picking my phone back up, I called Nyle.

"Nothing yet," he said when he answered.

"Tell me what's happening," I commanded.

"Mazie arrived at the coordinates of Jericho's mansion. There's a handful of other demons, all listed by name here," he paused. "Six of them currently. Jericho has mentioned using your sister to get to you, but not what he's planning on doing, and nothing about any past killings."

"Okay." I breathed out slowly, trying to calm myself. It would do no one any good if I went into this without a clear head.

"He hasn't really given Mazie any opportunities to talk and steer the conversation that way, either," Nyle said.

"Let me know immediately if that changes. I'm about fifteen minutes out from Jericho's, so after that, no contact until you hear from me." Lucifer forbid they took my phone when I entered the mansion and figured out our plan before we could get the evidence we needed. This would all be for nothing.

The next fifteen minutes, I heard nothing from Nyle. I texted him as I approached the mansion, letting him know not to contact me.

The wrought iron gate at the end of Jericho's driveway opened for me as soon as I pulled up, and when I reached the mansion, there were four demons waiting for me.

I could overpower them easily, but I needed to figure out the situation inside first. If I reacted without thinking, Ember or Mazie could be the casualties. They were my priority. Though I didn't want Jayce caught in the crossfire either, as my enforcer, he was prepared to die for me.

The four demons accompanied me into the foyer. I scanned my surroundings and took stock of everything. The wall behind me was filled with weapons on display. Jericho stood at the foot of the grand staircase, a bowl of purple pills on a pedestal in front of him. Mazie was seated beside Enzo and a demon I didn't recognize on the stairs, her hands tied behind her back. The demons at my back rounded out the six that Nyle had mentioned.

Ember and Jayce were not in the foyer. I cursed inwardly but kept my face neutral.

"Now what? Are you going to kill me so you can take my power?" I asked. If Mazie hadn't been able to get him to talk, maybe I could. The demons behind me moved forward, I assumed to rejoin Jericho.

Jericho smirked. "Not exactly."

I gasped as one of the demons punched my side, a pinching sensation alerting me to the needle they'd plunged in. Lashing out, I caught the demon who'd done it by the collar of their shirt and flung them across the room. They crumpled to the floor.

My energy sapped from me, and I fell to my knees.

Jericho strode forward, crouching in front of me and resting his forearms on his thighs as he cocked his head to the side. "I'll be keeping *you* alive, unlike your parents. And your sister," he pointed back at Mazie, who cried out as Enzo yanked her to her feet and shoved her forward. "Will be my insurance so you don't go squealing to Lucifer."

My mind raced even as my thoughts became hazy.

"Eastsiders killed my parents," I forced out. It was hard to even talk.

"Because that's what I wanted you to think," Jericho said. "Do you really think two random demons from the Eastside would be powerful enough to take down two upper-ranks? Are you truly that *stupid?*" He stood and spat on the floor in front of me. "Maybe I'll show you your mother and father's wings that I have hanging in my office, above where your enforcer's body is growing colder by the second."

No. Jayce.

"So," I huffed, unable to say more than one word at a time. "It. Was. You." I needed to make sure Mazie heard it too. If nothing else, this evidence would damn Jericho.

"Yes, Dominic. It was me. I killed your parents. And now, I'm going to take your wings and force you to live with the knowledge, with no way to redeem them or yourself because if you do, I'll kill your sister, too." His eyes lit up with excitement.

"I'm not his sister!" Mazie blurted. "So, you have no leverage to keep him from going to Lucifer. And his men know he's here, so you can't kill him."

She doesn't know Ember's here, I realized. Otherwise she would have remained quiet.

Jericho whirled toward her. "You're lying to save yourself," he growled.

"His sister is still out there. Do you really think he'd let you take me so easily if I were truly Ember?" Mazie said. I wished I could yell at her to stop talking, but then I'd give away Ember's true identity.

My eyelids drooped as the drug made it harder to fight off the drowsiness.

Enzo appeared thoughtful as he held onto Mazie's arm, keeping her from getting to me, and I saw it the moment it all clicked into place for him.

"The other one," he said. "*Mazie.* She's the one who originally told us about the sister. She's the one we found with the enforcer. Who else would Dominic trust with his sister's life?"

"Bring her here, I need to know." Irritation leaked into Jericho's voice. His perfectly crafted exterior was cracking.

If I could smile, I would, but even that felt like too much at the moment. I hadn't felt so helpless since the first time Ember had a nightmare, and I realized there were some things I couldn't save her from.

Time must have passed without me realizing because Ember was being brought into the room, and then she was beside me. It was getting harder to keep myself conscious. At some point, I remembered seeing weapons on the wall behind us, and a half-assed plan formulated in my drug-addled mind.

I waited until Jericho was engaged with Mazie, and I slumped toward Ember.

"Ember," I gasped, trying to stay quiet.

She turned her head to look down at me, so I knew she at least heard me.

"Sword. On. Wall." I used as little words as possible, because each one was a true effort to get out. "Take. My. Power."

Her brow furrowed.

"Cut. Off. My. Wings."

Chapter 24

Ember

Cut off my wings. I couldn't do that. Demons weren't like angels. If their wings were severed, they'd never grow back. Most of their power would return to them slowly, but they'd never be the same.

I couldn't condemn Dominic to a life without his wings. But did I really have an alternative?

"I lied. I *am* his sister," Mazie said, obviously trying to confuse them and keep Jericho distracted.

If I did this, I had to do it before Jericho's attention returned to me. Enzo was watching Mazie and Jericho, and the demon beside me who had brought me into the entry way seemed indifferent to it all. I took one step back, and no one said anything, so I took another.

The sword was within reach, but once I grabbed it, I'd have seconds to act. As a third level demon I'd have the power to sever Dominic's wings, but it would take everything in me to do it with one strike. I had to be ready, and I had to be precise. I didn't even think about what would happen if the sword was too dull. I had to imagine any weapon Jericho would hang on his walls would be prepped to kill.

I took a deep breath, not at all prepared for what I was about to do and lunged for the sword. Grabbing the hilt, I slid the sword from its display. Jericho, Enzo, and the demon who had been closest to me all moved toward me, but they were too late.

Swinging the sword, I closed the distance between myself and Dominic, bringing it down and severing his wings from his back. Dominic's agonized scream split the air, and blood spurted from the wound, spraying us both.

Time seemed to slow. I thought I heard Jericho yelling, but everything was muted. Power surged through me and made me feel stronger than I'd thought possible.

Keeping hold of the sword now coated in Dominic's blood, I swung for the demon who'd been on my left, shoving the sword through his chest. He dropped and I pulled the sword free with ease.

"You will pay for this," Jericho said, visibly shaking from his anger. I'd taken the power he'd so desperately wanted for himself.

"I was about to say the same thing," I said. With my new strength, came incredible speed as well. It was like my body wanted to move and use as much of the power as it could.

Enzo had moved away from Jericho, so I made a note to go after him next, but Jericho seemed too frozen by his own anger and shock to escape.

I held the sword to his throat, and he gripped either side of the sword, blood flowing from where it cut into his hand. He struggled, attempting to keep me at bay, but his power was no match for Dominic's.

"Lucifer will kill you if you kill me," Jericho said through gritted teeth.

I grinned. "And I'll die happy knowing you no longer exist to strip any other demons of their power."

Overpowering Jericho, I pulled the sword back and swung again, removing his head from his shoulders in one swift motion.

I went to Mazie next, freeing her from the rope that tied her hands behind her back. She threw her arms around me.

"You did it Emmy," she breathed.

Adrenaline coursed through me, and it was a struggle to stay still while she hugged me. As if we both remembered Dominic at the same time, we turned, and she ran to him.

I had to deal with Enzo.

"What a show you've put on," Enzo drawled. He'd stopped in front of the doors to Jericho's office. The memory of Jayce lying in a pool of his own blood on the other side propelled me forward.

Before I could reach Enzo, the doors behind him opened, and Jayce stumbled out. He held one of the horns that had been hanging on Jericho's wall and when Enzo turned to him, he shoved it through Enzo's chest.

"I told you I'd kill you for what you'd done," Jayce snarled.

Enzo dropped to the floor, clawing at the demon horn protruding from him, but the blood was flowing out too fast, and his heart had most likely been pierced.

I flung myself at Jayce, wrapping my arms around him. He was far too pale for my liking, and unsteady. I pulled back and put his arm over my shoulders so I could help keep him on his feet.

"You're alive," I murmured. "The pill worked."

"You all need to get out of here before the rest of Jericho's men come back." Penny's voice sparked a new anger in me. She'd come down the stairs and stood at the halfway point, looking unsure.

"Give me one reason why I shouldn't kill you right now," I snapped. If I wasn't the only thing keeping Jayce on his feet, I'd already be at her throat with the sword.

Penny dipped her head, and she almost appeared *shameful.* I rolled my eyes. It was probably all an act.

"I truly am sorry about this, Ember. I never pretended to be your friend. It was always real for me, and I promise I'll explain everything later. But right now, you need to leave," she insisted.

"She's right, Ember," Mazie said, though I caught the disdainful look she'd been giving Penny. "We need to get out of here before more demons arrive." She helped Dominic to the door.

I nodded, not sparing Penny another glance, and followed Mazie. It was much easier with my new strength to help Jayce. Before, I probably would have been struggling to get him out the door, but now I only moved slowly so I wouldn't worsen his injuries. Just because he was alive, it didn't mean he was out of the woods. He and Dominic would both need medical attention from Nico as soon as possible.

We made it to Dominic's car, and Mazie wrapped Dominic with a blanket from the trunk. The pill Jayce had taken had almost stopped his bleeding, but there was no telling what damage had been done internally.

I pulled a pill from my pocket, making Dominic swallow it. If it had saved Jayce's life, it could help Dominic too.

Dominic and Jayce were both propped in the backseat of the car, while Mazie drove and I sat in the passenger seat. Neither of us had much experience with driving, but she'd at least done it before.

"We need to go to Marge and Nico's house. They're close to the border of Southside territory," I said. We were a little more North in Westside than the time when Jayce and I had attended Enzo's party.

"Got it. Do you know where, exactly?" Mazie asked.

I bit my lip and shook my head. "Not really. I was unconscious when Jayce took me there. I kind of remember what it's near, though. Head toward King Dumplings. I think I can get us there from that point."

Miraculously, we made it to Marge and Nico's without too many wrong turns. They had to bring a second table into their workroom and made Mazie and I wait in the living room while they worked. We both cleaned up a bit, but Dominic's blood stained my hands.

About ten minutes after we arrived, Oliver showed up at the door.

"How did you ..." I started to ask, but then I shook my head. *His location app.* "Never mind. Come sit with me and Mazie. Jayce and Dominic are in with Marge and Nico."

"But they're both alive?" he asked, following me into the living room.

I nodded. "I think so."

"Tell me everything," Oliver demanded.

I told him how Jayce and I had been taken from the apartment, and everything that happened at the mansion.

He was shaking by the end of it.

"I'm glad you killed them, or else I'd have to." He shook his head. "I knew I shouldn't have let Dominic convince me to stay away."

"There was nothing more you could have done. By the time Dom arrived, Jayce was already down, and Jericho was the most powerful there besides me after I took Dom's wings." Talking about it made me want to throw up. In the moment, adrenaline had taken over and helped me do what needed to be done. Now, the blood staining my hands reminded me of the drastic measure I'd taken.

Dominic's wings would *never* grow back. And while I had his power, it would slowly seep away, not mine to keep. It might last me a few years, or decades, but I'd never be as strong as I was in the moment I'd killed Jericho.

What I'd done was the only way we were getting out of that mansion alive, but there was a chance Lucifer would retaliate against me for killing a high rank demon, no matter what Jericho's intentions were.

A phone buzzed on the table.

"It's Dominic's," Mazie said, reaching for it. "Want me to answer it?"

"Yes, please," I said, not ready to deal with anything in the outside world yet.

"Dominic's phone, this is Mazie." She paused, nodding slowly. "Okay. Thank you," she said before hanging up.

"That was fast," I said.

"It was Nyle. He was able to get all the information to Lucifer, including the fact that we killed Jericho, and we'll know soon what will happen next." Her nose and brows scrunched.

"*We* didn't kill Jericho, *I* did," I said. "If anyone has to face some sort of punishment for that, it should be me."

She shook her head vigorously and reached across the couch to take my hand. "No. If we go down for this, we all go down together."

My resolve finally broke and I dissolved into sobs. Mazie pulled me to her side and hugged me close.

"I'll get an update on the boys," Oliver said, giving us a minute alone.

I wasn't sure how long I cried for, or when I laid down in Mazie's lap. At some point, it all ceased to matter, as she stroked my hair and we waited for it all to be over.

When Oliver returned, he said nothing. The silence was becoming too loud for me to bear, so I decided to take a walk. Mazie accompanied me.

The sky was bright, and it was too hot, but I didn't mind it. Being out in the daytime, while most demons were asleep, was actually kind of pleasant. If I didn't think about the two demons I cared about most in Hell being near death.

"Have you heard anything from Penny?" I couldn't help asking Mazie. As much as I hated Penny for helping Jericho's men, I couldn't shake the need for an explanation. She'd said she never pretended to be my friend, but what kind of friend was she if she was hiding that she'd been working for Jericho?

Sighing, Mazie shook her head. "No. I don't think we will until things calm down on the Westside. They just lost their leader, so until they elect a new one, it will be utter chaos over there."

"Did you ever suspect she was working for Jericho?" I asked.

Mazie shook her head. "Never. She fooled us all. Me, you, and your brother."

At least I wasn't the only one who had been duped. If she'd been able to convince Dominic she was trustworthy enough to know about me, then she must have been a master at deception. It made me feel slightly better.

"If Penny does come back around, will you be there with me? I don't think I can face her alone," I asked, biting my lip.

"Of course." Mazie took my hand and squeezed it. "I don't think Dominic would ever let you be alone with her again anyway. Jayce wouldn't either, for that matter."

"Mm." The mention of them made me want to turn back to check on them.

Mazie nudged me with her elbow. "A lot has changed since I last saw you."

I linked my arm with hers, leaning my head on her shoulder. "What do you mean?"

"With Jayce." She smiled. "You seem like you really like him, and him you. I'm happy for you."

My phone vibrated in my pocket, and I whipped it out. Oliver's name popped up.

"What's happening?" I blurted when I answered it.

"Jayce is stable, and Dominic is awake," he said.

Tears of relief streamed down my cheeks. "We'll head back. Thank you, Oliver." I hung up and turned to Mazie. "They're going to be fine. But Dom is awake so we should get back. I want to see him."

We turned back to the house, quickening our pace.

Chapter 25

Jayce

I think I did die, briefly. The shot missed my heart, or else I would have been done for. The stupid purple pill Jericho had been producing couldn't work miracles. It slowed bleeding and boosted our natural regenerative abilities. At least, that's what I would guess. I gave a few to Nico so he could figure it out for himself and maybe recreate the effect to use in his own work.

It had been two days since the whole mess, and I'd finally been able to leave Nico and Marge's and return to my apartment. Dominic had left the day before, with Mazie and Ember accompanying him.

I'd convinced Ember to leave me behind. She'd been insisting on staying with me, but Dominic would need her more. I could understand her reluctance to leave, seeing as not even a week prior the roles had been reversed. But I would heal and be back to normal soon enough, while Dominic would never be the same. His power would come back, to an extent, but his wings would never grow back. He'd need Ember by his side to navigate that.

And we'd still yet to tell him about us. It almost seemed like it would be a slap in the face after everything that had happened. Like, *oh by the way Dom, you trusted me with your sister, and I fell in love with her while you were busy trying to save her and wound up losing your wings and power. Are you okay with that?*

We'd find a way to tell him. Soon.

To my surprise, Dominic called a meeting the next night. It was Thursday and would normally be a meeting for only his lieutenants, but he was calling in *everyone*. Even some of the lower ranks.

Ember texted the afternoon before the meeting.

Ember: *Can you come a little early for the meeting? I think it's time we tell Dom the truth*

                                    Me: *Of course. Be there soon*

I wasn't sure why Ember thought it was the best time to talk with Dominic, but I wasn't going to pressure her to keep this secret any longer. Selfishly, I was a little relived Dominic no longer had his full power, or else he could kill me far too easily. At least now he'd have to work for it.

Slipping my leather cut on over my hoodie, I steeled myself for whatever would come next.

When I got on my Harley, it felt like it had been weeks instead of a few days since I'd last rode it. I had to drive my car more often than I'd like, to keep a low profile, but now that most of the Westside crew knew who I was, it didn't matter.

Dominic would probably have to find someone to replace me as an enforcer, but I couldn't bring myself to care.

The hot wind whipped past me as I rode. It never cooled down in Hell and I never got used to it. But when I rode my bike, it was almost bearable.

Pulling up outside of Dominic's mansion, it was strange to think Ember had always been there. Every time I'd gone to a meeting or to talk with Dominic, Ember had been right upstairs, and I'd never suspected anything.

This time, she met me at the door. Seeing her lifted a weight off me and it took all my willpower not to pull her into my arms and kiss her. But Dominic might be around. Suddenly I couldn't wait to tell him the truth.

That didn't stop Ember, though, she wrapped her arms around me, and I did the same on instinct.

"You're here," she huffed. "It's been weird sleeping alone."

We talked on the phone before bed the two days we'd been apart, but it didn't replace having her beside me. I'd been struggling to sleep since my near death and the only thing that helped me relax was her.

"Come on. Dom is waiting in the meeting room." Turning from me, she took my hand, and we walked side by side through the foyer.

It was a bit of a shock to see Dominic without his wings. I'd seen him after Nico had healed him, but I wasn't used to it. I couldn't imagine what it was like for him.

The other thing I noticed immediately was he wasn't wearing a suit or even a button up shirt like he normally would have. For the first time since he'd taken over for his parents, he was wearing blue jeans and a zip-up athletic jacket.

He leaned back in his chair, his elbows resting on the arms of it and his hands steepled in front of him. "I told Ember I'd hear you both out, but I lied," he said when we entered the room. "I already know what you want to tell me. It became obvious the second Ember asked if we could all talk. Now I feel so stupid for not seeing it. And as much as I want to kill you for hiding this from me, Jayce," he pinned his gaze on me, "I'm reminded I probably wouldn't win that fight right now."

"You have every right to be upset with me, and I wouldn't stop you if you wanted to get a few good punches in," I offered.

"Don't be stupid," Ember snapped. "The both of you are acting as if I don't have a say in my own life, and I'm sick of it." She released my hand. "You can be upset we lied to you, Dom, but you have no reason to be upset over the fact that we've chosen to get together. It doesn't change that Jayce is your best friend, and I'm your sister."

Dominic's jaw clenched and he wrapped his knuckles on the table. "Leave us, Ember," he commanded.

"No. Whatever you have to say, I should hear it," she argued.

Shaking his head, Dominic said, "I'm not going to kill him, I promise. Leave us, *now.*"

She looked at me and I nodded. "Don't worry about me. Go."

"Fine," she said, lifting her chin. "I'm going to my room. You two can talk your shit out." She turned and left.

I took a seat at the end of the table, farthest from Dominic. He was staring at his cut on the wall.

"We've been friends for almost twenty years," he said, not taking his gaze from that wall. "I trusted you with my life, and more importantly, with Ember. There is quite literally *nothing* in this world or the next that I care about more than her."

I cleared my throat and said, "For what it's worth, I do love her, and I'd never hurt her."

"You lied to me." He blinked slowly, turning to look at me. "You say you'd never hurt Ember, and yet since she met you, she's nearly died *twice.*"

I did my best to remain calm under his cold stare. He'd never looked at me that way before, and fear clawed its way up my spine.

"If she even comes close to getting hurt again while you're together, I *will* kill you, Jayce," he said. "Remember that."

"That's fair." I dipped my head to him.

"You love her?" he asked.

"I do."

Dominic jerked his head in a nod. "Tell *her* that." He stood and leaned on the table. "You can stick around until the meeting. Let Ember know I want her there this time. Take a right at the top of the stairs, and her room is the last door at the end of the hall."

"All right." I didn't know what else to say.

I waited a few minutes after Dominic left before heading to Ember's room. I'd never been upstairs in the mansion before, which maybe should have been suspicious, but I assumed Dominic was more private than the rest of us. Which made sense since he was the boss.

The last door at the end of the hall was shut, so I knocked softly, not wanting to make a racket in the too-quiet house. I couldn't imagine what it must have been like growing up there, especially after their parents died. Only two people in such a large space, it seemed ... Haunted. I could understand a little better why nightmares plagued Ember.

"Come in," Ember called.

I opened the door and leaned against the doorway, taking in the sight of Ember sitting at the end of her bed and the rest of the room.

"Your bedroom is almost larger than my whole apartment," I teased.

Scoffing, she said, "Not even close. How did it go with Dom after I left?"

"I'm standing here, aren't I?" I sighed.

"Mm. You can come *into* my room, you know." She smirked.

I took a step and closed the door behind me. "Dominic wants you to be at the meeting," I said, still not moving closer to Ember. For some reason, I was nervous. After everything we'd been through and done together, I couldn't understand why I was nervous *now*.

Tell her that. Dominic's words came back to me, followed by my own. *I do love her.* I'd never said as much to Ember. It seemed too soon. But maybe Dominic was right, maybe I *should* tell her. After both of us nearly dying, it felt more pressing.

"Something's bothering you," Ember said, cocking her head. "Tell me what's wrong."

One foot in front of the other. *What is wrong with me?* I could kill a demon without batting an eye, but the thought of telling Ember I loved her and the possibility of her shutting me down was nauseating.

Before I knew it, I was standing in front of her, and she wrapped her legs around mine.

"Nothing's wrong," I clarified. "But there is something I need to tell you."

She took my hand and laced her fingers through mine. "You're starting to worry me."

"I love you, Ember." The words came out so much easier than I'd thought they would, and the nerves faded away. I cupped her cheek in my free hand.

She smiled at me, which I assumed was a good sign. I hadn't scared her away, yet. Pulling me down to sit beside her, she straddled me and gripped my face in her hands before kissing me.

She paused and asked, "Does that mean you want me to be your girlfriend?"

I kissed her, trailing my hands up her back and said, "If you want that too."

"Only if you take me for another ride on your bike," she said, playing with my hair at the back of my neck.

"Are you using me for my bike?" I teased.

"Well, that. And I love you too."

I couldn't help but smile.

There was a knock on the door.

"The crew is arriving," Dominic said through the door.

I kissed Ember before lifting her and setting her on her feet. "Let's go see what this is all about," I said.

Chapter 26

Dominic

Ember and Jayce sat to my right, Oliver beside Jayce, and all my lieutenants to my left. I tugged at the collar of the stupid athletic jacket I wore. I don't know what made me reach for it instead of my usual suit jacket, but something felt wrong about going about everything as usual.

If I closed my eyes, I could almost feel my wings, like they were haunting me. And maybe it was for that reason I couldn't don one of the suit jackets that had holes in the back specifically for my wings. The jacket I wore was from before my wings grew in and it had no slits. It fit a little snuggly since I hadn't worn it in almost fifteen years.

"Thank you all for being here tonight," I said once everyone was settled. "I'm sure you've all heard by now what transpired, but I wanted to set some things straight."

I glanced at Ember, thinking about what it was like not knowing whether she was alive or dead for the second time in less than a week. And now she was becoming further entrenched in my world just by being at the table.

"First, I'd like to introduce my sister Ember to everyone. As I'm sure you may have heard, I kept her hidden from everyone the entire time I've been the boss here, and my parents did so before that. But she is joining us now, and I expect you all to welcome her as you have any other new recruit." I paused to scan the faces in the room. There were a few who looked surprised, but most everyone must have already heard the truth through the grapevine.

"Next, as you can see for yourself, I no longer have my wings. My power will return to me in time, so I don't want anyone worrying about that. In the meantime, Nyle and Jayce will be taking over as the leaders of our crew."

Murmurs arose. *As I expected.* I hadn't told anyone, not even Nyle or Jayce, that I'd be stepping aside temporarily. It was something I'd decided at the last minute. I'd reconsidered after learning of Jayce's betrayal, but he was still more qualified for the job than anyone else.

I raised a hand to quiet the room. "Jayce is too well known to continue being an enforcer, so I'll leave it to him and Nyle to choose his replacement. When I return from my leave, Jayce will become a lieutenant, replacing Jeffrey who has been wanting to retire for some time." I had at least consulted Jeffrey before making *that* decision.

Everyone in the room knew better than to try and contradict any of my decisions or speak before I asked for input.

"Westside will be scrambling for a while, so we shouldn't have to worry about them selling in our territory anymore. But as always, keep an eye out. Otherwise, it's business as usual." I leaned back in my chair. "You are dismissed."

No one moved for a few seconds, most likely surprised by how short the meeting had been and all the information I'd dumped on them. But I couldn't handle sitting there in front of them any longer. I needed to get as far from Southside as possible, as soon as possible. Which was why I was leaving at daybreak to visit the human world for a while.

"Are you sure you want me taking over with Nyle? And then for Jeffrey ..." Jayce brought me back from my thoughts of escape.

"I wouldn't have said it if I didn't think you could handle it. But of course, you can always say no." It was hard to look at Jayce, so I kept my gaze on the exiting demons.

"I'll do my best to live up to your expectations," he said. "Thanks, Dom."

I left the room and headed to the kitchen. Maurice was there making bread. He glanced at me but kept kneading the dough.

"Rough meeting?" he asked.

I leaned against the island in the middle of the kitchen, watching him. He'd worked in the mansion as long as I'd been alive, and probably long before that.

"Have you ever known another demon who lost their power?" I asked. If anyone in my immediate circle would be helpful in this area, it would be Maurice.

He paused his kneading and turned, leaning back against the counter and crossing his arms.

"A long time ago, when it was much more common for demons to steal other demons' power, I knew a few people who it happened to," he said. "A close friend of mine lost her horns to a greedy demon hoping to stockpile power, much like Jericho was attempting to do. She spent a long time grieving the loss of

287

her horns, even after she regained most of her power," Maurice said.

I rolled my shoulders, half expecting my wings to unfurl from my back.

"But she didn't have as large of a support system as you do. You have your crew, Ember, Jayce, and Mazie—"

My head snapped up. "What?"

Maurice turned back to his dough, but I didn't miss the sly smile. "Sorry, I misspoke. Mazie is Ember's friend, not yours."

My heart pounded in my chest, and I pushed away from the counter. "I'm leaving in the morning. Please take good care of Ember while I'm gone."

"Of course, sir."

I strode out of the kitchen unable to shake the realization that maybe Maurice saw more in the mansion than I'd thought.

Chapter 27

Ember

Lucifer finally sent word of his decision after Dominic left for Earth. I had no idea why Dominic would ever want to go there, but I hoped it would help him come to terms with losing his wings.

"As was proven, Jericho had been stealing higher-rank demons' power for many years under the radar. And since he was the demon truly responsible for the deaths of your parents, Marcus and Wendy Russo, I will overlook his death," Oliver read the letter aloud to Jayce and I. "You're in the clear."

He set the letter down on the bar and took a sip of his beer. Jayce had talked me into going out with him and Oliver to Fever Dream to celebrate the letter after I'd spent the past few nights sulking.

"Tomorrow's your first meeting as the boss. How's that feel?" Oliver asked Jayce.

Jayce shrugged. "Nyle's mostly handling everything. I'm focusing on choosing my replacement."

"Any prospects? I feel like I should get a say since they'll be my new best friend." Oliver smirked.

Shaking his head, Jayce laughed and said, "No one yet. But I'll be sure to let you know."

My phone vibrated in my pocket, so I pulled it out. I gasped when I saw a text from Penny.

Penny: *Can we meet at Mazie's?*

"What is it?" Jayce asked, his brow furrowing.

"Penny wants to meet at Mazie's." I grabbed my purse from the bar and stood. "Can you drop me off?"

"Absolutely not. If Dominic knew she was around, he'd send me or Oliver after her," he said. Oliver perked up as if that sounded like a great time to him.

I glared at Oliver. "You're not killing her," I said and returned my focus back to Jayce. "Dominic's not here, so it's your call to make. Just let me talk to her. I *need* to know the truth."

His jaw clenched and he shook his head, but he gave in. "I'll bring you there, but I'm not leaving you alone with her."

"Mazie will be with me," I protested. It wasn't that I didn't want Jayce there, but this felt like something Mazie and I should do ourselves.

"We can argue about it when we get there. Come on." Jayce put his arm around me and waved to Oliver. "See you later, Olly."

We'd taken Jayce's bike, so thankfully we couldn't argue on the *way* to Mazie's. Not that there was much to argue about. These were my friends I had to figure things out with, not his.

But it was hard to stay annoyed with Jayce while my arms were wrapped around him and my thighs pressed against him on the back of his bike.

When we pulled up outside Mazie's apartment, I hopped off the bike and blocked Jayce from doing the same.

"Stay here at least," I said. "I promise, if she tries anything, I'll call you." We'd set up my phone to call Jayce, instead of taking a screenshot, if I held down the power and volume up button. There'd been too many emergencies lately, so we were taking as many precautions as we could.

"Fine," he grumbled. I kissed him before turning and heading inside. Mazie buzzed me in, and I took the stairs instead of the elevator. I needed a few seconds to collect my thoughts, and it wasn't like Jayce's apartment building with way too many fucking floors.

When I reached Mazie's door, she was waiting outside.

"Why are you out here?" I asked.

"I didn't want to be alone with her in there." She shuddered. "It's weird."

"Well, let's get this over with."

Mazie nodded and opened her door, revealing Penny waiting for us on the couch. She gave us a weak smile.

"I'm glad you came," she said.

"I'm only here because you owe us an explanation, at the very least," I said.

Mazie and I sat at the bar, keeping our distance from Penny.

"You're right." She sighed. "Well, the first thing you should know is that Jericho was my father."

My gut twisted and I scowled. "Of course he was."

"But in blood only. He never gave two shits about me. He had been siring children for years in hopes that some of them would present with a power he could take for himself. So, I guess I'm lucky that, even though I have horns, my power wasn't enough for him to want to steal."

"You're not going to win us back by making us feel sorry for you," Mazie said. "We all have sob stories."

I glanced at Mazie and realized I didn't know much about her past before we met. I'd make it a point to ask her about that someday.

Penny sighed and said, "I know that. I don't expect either of you to forgive me, but I want you to know all of this. In the beginning, when Dominic hired me, I *was* doing it in hopes of exploiting my friendship with Ember. I wanted to get information I could give to Jericho and make him finally *see* me. But once I met you Ember, I knew I couldn't do that."

"Because of my winning personality?" I couldn't help saying.

Penny laughed. "Essentially. I *truly* became friends with you, Em, and I never wanted to hurt you. Same with Mazie. But I couldn't walk away from Jericho's crew, or else I'd make him suspicious, and he might look into me, and then find you. It was better to keep on as usual and stay under his radar."

I scoffed. "So, you were *protecting* me by continuing to betray me? Was that also your intent when you were helping Jericho's men break into Jayce's apartment to kidnap me?"

"I knew they'd find a way in, with or without me, so I figured I could at least keep from them hurting you or Jayce," she said.

Which she had, so I at least had to give her credit there, no matter how minimal.

"Are you still working for Westside?" Mazie asked.

"No," Penny said, sitting up straighter. "I did what I could to try and steer them away from seeking revenge for Jericho's death, and then I left. I can't say whether they'll listen to me, but I can promise I'm never going back there."

"Okay." I wasn't sure what else to say. I wasn't ready to forgive Penny or trust her again, and I was pretty sure Mazie felt the same way.

"I'll give you both some time. I'll understand if you never want to see me again, but I'll keep hoping someday you might be able to forgive me." Penny left Mazie and I alone to process.

"Do you think she's telling the truth? Or do you think she's still working for Westside?" Mazie asked.

"If she were lying, why wouldn't she have told Jericho about me a long time ago? He could have used me as leverage then, instead of waiting all these years," I pointed out. Penny may have betrayed us by working for Jericho, but she'd never told him about Dominic's biggest weakness, which had to count for something.

"You're not wrong. Maybe someday I can forgive her. But not tonight," Mazie said. "Do you want some ice cream?"

I nodded eagerly. Ice cream fixed almost anything. Mazie got us big bowls, and I texted Jayce, letting him know he could come up, or go back out with Oliver. He chose to go back out with Oliver with a promise to pick me up on his way home.

"It's kind of crazy how much has changed for us so quickly," I said, taking my bowl of ice cream from Mazie.

She settled onto the couch beside me. "And it seems like it's going to keep changing."

I leaned into her, comforted by the knowledge that at least no matter what happened next, we'd be going through it together.

About the Author

H. M. Huntress is a self-published author and content creator. She has been writing stories since grade school and is driven by the desire to share her writing with the world while encouraging others to do the same. All her books are currently available on Amazon. If you want to connect with her on social media, find her at the handle below!

TikTok & Instagram: @authorhmhuntress

I'd love if you left a review for *A Demon's Deception* on Amazon, Goodreads, or social media!

Scan here for updates on future projects and events!

A Demon's Deception

Check out my other books!

The Forbidden Waves Series:
Forbidden Waves
Ruthless Tides

Beneath Venomous Sails

The Underworld Duet:
A Demon's Deception

The Broken Angel Series:
Broken Angel
Condemned Angel
Forsaken Angel

The Unbound Series:
Unbound
Disgraced
Awakened
Ruined

Standalones:
Haunting Memories